Brendan Prairie

✳

DAN O'BRIEN

SCRIBNER

SCRIBNER
1230 Avenue of the Americas
New York, NY 10020

Scribner and design are trademarks of Simon & Schuster Inc.

Set in Adobe Goudy Old Style

Designed by Ellen Sasahara

Manufactured in the United States of America

1 3 5 7 9 10 8 6 4 2

Library of Congress Cataloging-in-Publication Data

O'Brien, Dan
Brendan Prairie: a novel/by Dan O'Brien.
p.   cm.
I. Title.
PS3565.B665B74   1996
813'.54—dc20   95-54166
CIP

ISBN 0–684–80368–2

For my mother,
Inez O'Brien Senn,
who talked me out of law school

Acknowledgments

I WOULD LIKE to acknowledge the support of friends
Marjorie Braman, Bill Harlan, and Michael Siegel. They read
early drafts and, hopefully, pointed me in the right direction.
I received support from many people but this book owes its
existence to Gail Hochman, superagent, Mark Gompertz,
supereditor, and Kris O'Brien, superspouse.

1

A LIGHT GREEN Chevrolet snaked along Highway 85 in the heart of the Black Hills. The car was from the United States Fish and Wildlife Service motor pool in Denver, Colorado, and the driver was Special Agent Margaret Adamson. It was a September morning and Margaret was on her way to the six-hundred-acre meadow where Mountain Air Estates would soon be constructed. The day before she'd done a ground inspection of the site with Andy Arnold. He was the local representative of the Arizona–based development company that owned the property. He was a promoter and obviously beguiled by his wealthy associates, but he seemed all right to Margaret. They'd driven around the perimeter of what, on the map, was called Brendan Prairie. With pride, Andy Arnold had pointed out where the condominiums would be in relation to the sewage disposal plant, how the roads would spoke out into cul-de-sacs for maximum privacy, where the two-hundred-room hotel would stand.

After the overview, Margaret set out on foot to have a closer look at what she had seen from Andy Arnold's Bronco. Andy was not dressed for a hike but he came along anyway. He was an energetic man and Margaret admired his moxie. He stayed right with her all afternoon and answered every question Margaret put to him. There was a line of yellow earth-moving machines along the north boundary of the property, motionless as dinosaurs in a museum. Margaret didn't ask what they were doing there before the Fish and Wildlife Service had given the project an official go ahead. There was no sense making Andy squirm. He was doing his best at a job he felt was his big chance. When Margaret's okay came, he would be ready to start at the earliest possible moment. He was a believer in the project, sure that it was a good thing for everyone and he was afraid Margaret would find some bureaucratic reason to stop it. There had already been the usual series of delays.

Like many people, Andy didn't have a good understanding of Margaret's job. She was there to make sure Mountain Air Estates had complied with the environmental regulations that had been established for projects like this. She was there to protect the taxpayer's interest. Most of the work had been done at her desk in Denver. This was just an on-site inspection before the final permits were granted. Margaret had followed this proposal for nearly a year and knew the minute the state of South Dakota issued a permit for Mountain Air to pump a million gallons of water from the creek in the next drainage, to make the golf course a reality, the rest was academic. A permit like that would alter the entire ecosystem of the creek and Margaret was glad she had had no part in signing off on that one. Andy Arnold and his friends must have lots of influence to pull off such a coup.

In a way, Margaret was glad her part in the permit process was cut and dried. At the end of the day, leaning against the hood of the Bronco, she'd told Andy what she had known she would have to say, that she would sign off on the environmental compliance and recommend that no further impediments be put in the way of Mountain Air Estates. There were beads of sweat on Andy's face that wetted his black hair where it had fallen against his temples during the hike. He stared at her incredulously. He was having trouble believing that he was going to get to go ahead with his project, that his fight with the bureaucracy was over. "You'll tell them that at the public meeting tonight?"

Margaret nodded. "That's what I'm here for," she said.

Slowly Andy's face formed a smile. It broadened and confirmed to Margaret that he was a handsome man. He tapped the hood of the Bronco. "I'll be damned," he said. "That will make it quite a meeting." He tapped the Bronco hood again, then reached out and tapped Margaret's shoulder in a similar way. "Going to be quite a meeting."

Now Margaret gripped the steering wheel of the Chevrolet

doubly tight. There was something about driving an automobile that freed her mind. Sometimes, driving on a lonely highway, she saw the future clearly. Sometimes the rhythm of the road made the past come alive. Andy had been right. It had been quite a meeting. It had been good for Andy Arnold and he had been visibly elated. He had even asked her out for a drink afterward. And she would have considered it if her part in the meeting had not turned unexpectantly repugnant.

She took her foot off the accelerator and felt for the brake. The turn to Mountain Air Estates was coming up. She still had some details to take care of, checking with other agencies, a few forms to fill out, that sort of thing. It might take a couple more days. Then she'd be going back to her desk in Denver. She had hoped there would be time to see her old friend Bill Malone. She let the car drift and tried to keep the image of Bill out of her consciousness. She turned onto the gravel road and winced as the first stones hit the undercarriage of the Chevrolet.

When she found out she would be going to the Black Hills her heart had jumped. Mention of the Black Hills always brought Bill Malone to mind and even though she had not seen him for many years, he still had a certain power over her. She had wanted to see him and planned to call after her work was finished. She had dreamed that they might get together and talk over old times, might spend some time together in a setting that would not dredge up the wrong memories from the past. Instead she found herself listening to Bill rebut Andy Arnold's contention that without the new jobs Mountain Air promised the community would die.

The sincerity in his voice touched her. It was passion she remembered, but coming now from an older, wiser man. He had become thinner, too. The light hazel eyes were the same, the dark brown hair still longish and slightly disheveled. But the strength of the shoulders was gone. He did not seem as tall as he once had. The elements he loved had wrinkled his face in the best way, but when he walked to the microphone, he limped badly. At the meeting she closed her eyes and listened to him explain that it is stability that creates community, that sudden change and accelerated growth always leaves a community poorer in the end. She heard the same man speaking who had once stirred her more than any other. She had closed her eyes not so much because the sound of his voice took her back, but because she knew that the battle her old friend was waging was already lost, and that she would be the one to deal the final blow.

Now, in the car on her way to the Mountain Air Estates, she briefly closed her eyes again. Bill had no idea that she was at the meeting until she stood up to deliver her poison message. What a reunion it had been. The thought of it made her want to keep her eyes closed. But driving blind was too scary and when she opened her eyes there was a sheriff's car close in her rearview mirror. She jerked her Chevrolet to the side out of instinct, sure he intended to stop her for reckless driving. But he pulled around and sped up the road leaving her in his plume of dust. A feeling of dread came over Margaret. She believed she had a sixth sense, a way to detect trouble, and something in the way the sheriff's car passed her stirred and frightened her. What could be the hurry? There was only Brendan Prairie at the end of the road.

She pushed the accelerator down and followed the sheriff around the last curve before the country opened into grassland. At the other side of the prairie the line of mustard-colored earth movers stood motionless where they had been the day before. Now there were men standing around the machines. The sheriff's car wound its way through parked pickup trucks and cars. One of the vehicles was Andy Arnold's Bronco and when Margaret was close enough she saw that Andy stood in front of the first machine, a huge, scarred front-end loader with the word CATERPILLAR written in raised black letters on the side above the engine. But there were other words written on the side of the loader and on other machines in the line. FUCK OFF, GO HOME, spewed angrily from spray cans. Andy Arnold stood looking at the vandalism with one hand on the hip of his Dockers. The other hand hung loose and from the fingers dangled a bright yellow hard hat. A half dozen men dressed in work clothes and wearing battered hats like Andy's stood watching as the sheriff swung out of his car, straightened slowly, and pulled his hat on as if it too was a hard hat and he was going to work. Margaret recognized him the instant he stood up. She had seen him leaning against a side wall at the public meeting the night before. He was a man in his middle sixties but he approached Andy with a fatigue that seemed older.

Margaret pulled up beside a dented pickup. The front left fender was primer gray. She got out and walked to where she could lean against the fender. That was close enough to hear what the sheriff and Andy were saying.

"They do any real damage, Andy?"

Andy Arnold pointed with his chin. The sheriff's watery eyes followed Andy's gaze to the smashed windshield of the giant loader. It was plain to see that the sheriff wanted this to be easy and understandable. "Probably kids again," he said. "Just raising hell."

"Kids, my foot. Kids don't write things like that," Andy pointed again with his chin, this time at neatly printed words on the side of the loader bucket. SAVE A TREE, SHOOT A DEVELOPER. "This is the third time this site's been vandalized, Sheriff. I don't think this was kids out for a good time. Whoever did this is crazy, vicious, and dangerous." Andy turned away from the old sheriff who looked as if he was searching for something to say that would smooth the situation. He came up with nothing and stood looking at the ground as Andy waved one of the workers over. After the wave, Andy's eyes caught Margaret's and he tried a smile. But Andy couldn't pretend he was happy. He looked away from Margaret and waved again to the workman even though he was already coming.

"Let's get this show on the road, Bass." Andy said. "We're not going to let a little bit of paint slow us for one second."

Bass was young but cool and confident. He was clearly the foremen of the crew. He pushed his hard hat back on his head before he spoke. "They could have done some damage to the engines, poured sugar in the tanks or something."

"Well, let's see if they start," Arnold said. "This project has overcome a lot more than a cup of sugar. Let's get 'em rolling."

"We should really give them a good going over," Bass said.

Arnold moved a step closer. "We're not going to let them win this. That's what they're after. Delay. I won't allow it. Now let's start moving dirt."

Bass looked at Andy and thought for a moment. He looked up to the loader, then back to Andy. He began nodding his head, then pulled his hard hat down tight. "You got it," he said. He gave Andy a tiny nod and took the two long strides to the ladder that led up the side of the loader.

Andy clamped his own hard hat on. By the time he had moved down the gradual slope to the front of the loader the machine had roared to life. Black smoke chugged from the diesel stack and Bass raised the bucket off the ground where it had rested, anchoring the twenty-ton machine to the earth. The noise of the engine filled the meadow and bounced off the forest edge. It was deafening. Even from fifty feet away Margaret could hear nothing. The earth vibrated through the soles of her shoes.

Andy moved toward a small knoll and waved for Bass to come ahead. He pointed to the grassy mound and Margaret could see that the grass was little bluestem. The seed heads were ten inches long and swayed in a breeze that Margaret had not noticed. She could not hear over the engine noise but she could read Andy's lips. "Start here." It was then, in the increased rubble of power, that Margaret felt again that something was wrong.

But she didn't know what it was until the loader began to roll down the hill toward where Andy stood smiling out at the meadow with his back to the machine. She could see only the side of Andy's face. When she looked to the loader she could see the side of Bass's face, too. Both men grinned at the prospects of the job ahead. But when the loader began to pick up speed Bass's smiled flagged. By the time the loader had doubled it's pace, Bass's face had gone gray. Margaret saw him pump the brakes but the loader didn't slow.

Everyone saw what was happening. Everyone but Andy Arnold who stood looking out over the project he had worked so hard to see begun. He was still smiling, probably imagining the pristine meadow with homes, a tennis court, a hotel. Margaret's scream was lost in the engine roar and Bass's attempt to stop the careening machine by dropping the bucket only made its impact with Andy Arnold more tragic.

For Margaret it all happened in slow motion, muted by the roar of the diesel engine. The front lip of the bucket hit Andy in the center of the back and he folded backward. The upper part of his body flattened into the bucket. Margaret watched long enough to see Andy's Dockered legs and new work boots dragging limply for a few yards under the bucket. But she turned away when she saw that the loader bucket, driven on by the weight of the machine, would be stopped only when it came in contact with the first mound of earth Andy had wanted moved.

2

BY LATE September most of the songbirds were gone. The fence lines had been vacant of lark buntings for a month, the redwing blackbirds were no longer clattering in the cattails, and only a few robins flitted in the buffaloberry bushes at the bottoms of the draws. The accipiters—the shortwinged hawks—had gone with the songbirds. Now was the time of year that Bill Malone loved. It was Indian summer, the time of passage peregrine falcons, when the swing of seasons on the Northern Plains seems to slow and gives the inhabitants a chance to relish the abundance produced by summer.

The landscape Bill moved through was soft, both in color and texture. It was a picture painted in luxuriant shades of tan and yellow, the grasses stretched to full height and dried there, every clump fit for a centerpiece on a civilized dining room table. He moved slowly through what was a huge garden in his eyes for two reasons; first, he wanted to savor this time on the prairie and second, he was crippled. It was an old injury. His right knee did not bend the way it once did, and he had to hold that foot out to the side and swing it over the roughness of the earth. Descending was most difficult. He led with the good leg and twisted his back as he sidled down even the slightest incline. This maneuver wrenched his hips, and after an hour everything began to hurt. But he walked anyway because he knew it was vital to him. The distance he walked was only a tiny fraction of what he used to cover but he tried not to let that bother him. He was sure that if he ever stopped walking, even for a few days, he'd never start again, and that would be the end of him.

So he walked four or five times a week—around the campus

where he taught biology—if the weather was poor, and in more remote places whenever it was possible. His area of choice was the open grasslands in the interior of the Black Hills. He preferred to walk the drainages where oak and aspen grew. Brendan Prairie was his favorite. The elevation of the prairie was nearly six thousand feet so the buttes thirty miles to the north were visible, and that long view made it very special. He'd found it first when he was a boy and rediscovered it when he'd returned to the Black Hills, when he'd needed solitude most. But these days he stayed away from the high meadows. Today he walked the open prairie northeast of Spearfish. He would rather have gone to Brendan Prairie but he was afraid he might find signs of development. Just thinking of it wrenched his heart.

A wrenched heart. The idea of it made him smile. Maybe it was just heartburn. He'd gotten drunk after the public meeting the night before, and he had been suffering since he'd awakened that morning. In fact, it had been nearly ten o'clock when he'd finally rolled to a sitting position on Cooney Jenkins's couch. He was not really used to that kind of drinking. From time to time it had been a problem but he had always been able to function. This morning he'd barely managed to get to school to teach his class, and the institution walls had been overly close. The lacy autumn air was crisp and smelled of coming frost. He simply couldn't force himself to make the biology department curriculum meeting that began at four o'clock. The siren air called to him through his open classroom window and he felt an undeniable need to take it in like medicine for his hangover.

But he didn't go to Brendan Prairie because he couldn't face the country. There was a nagging feeling that he'd let everybody and everything down. He felt he had made a fool of himself at the meeting. He'd stood up and pleaded for another environmental study. But it was too late.

Seeing his old friend Margaret Adamson after so many years had stirred up layers of memory—incident and scene tumbling together. There was heat from the crowd. Faces turned to him—some intent, others bored. And at first he'd spoken reasonably. But the questions were absurd and he finally resorted to shouting like a child, calling the developers names as if that might do some good. He should have spoken to Margaret. He wanted to, had planned to, but the room began to crush in on him and he had to get away. It was a pitiful way to act and he'd begun kicking himself even as he was shaking his fist at them. He had gone on kicking himself right through the best part of the bottle of Jameson whiskey and who knew how many beers. He'd kicked himself in the bad dreams he'd had on Cooney's couch. He was kicking himself now, as he walked over the grassland that stretched north and east for seven hundred miles.

The walking helped. He needed it so much that if he missed a day or two of walking he felt his grip slipping. He had learned that his mental well-being was directly connected to those walks, to being out-of-doors. In his younger years he had been so physical that he never had to deal with any of the consequences of inactivity. It was only after the accident—over sixteen years ago now—that he was forced to confront the parts of him that were less physical. Before then he hadn't given much thought to his place in society, his responsibilities, or needs. It had taken him quite a while to consider any of that honestly. He was still working on it and the walking helped.

Usually when he walked like this his mind went blank. In fact, that was what he strived for. A little Zen. He figured it cleaned the files, let him get out of his own way. That was what he was hoping for that afternoon when he'd left his office and driven north into this quiet September. He'd hoped he could just check out, walk an hour or so, see what birds had started their grand trip, which ones had moved in from the north on their way south. It was a special time of year. A lot was happening on the grasslands. He should have been able to fold himself into late September and, when the walk was done and the afternoon spent, he should have found himself leaning against the car with the sun sifting through the evening clouds, wondering where the time had gone.

But late September wouldn't have him. His mind was not interested in the chokecherry crop or the level of water in the potholes. He was caught in the old times, and all he could think about was that first really cold spell in January when the temperature crashes, the world goes white, and Arctic gyrfalcons invade the Northern Plains.

He'd been stuck in a past January all the way from town. After he'd parked the car he'd slid his right leg from the seat and stood up. A family of sharp-tailed grouse—seven of them—had flushed not fifteen feet from the car. Ordinarily that would have been a very good sign. Next to the falcons, the sharp-tailed grouse was his favorite species. But today, as he watched their whirr-glide, whirr-glide into the distance, it only intensified those memories of January. The sharp-tailed grouse was one of the prey species that attracted gyrfalcons down from the tundra. And it was the gyrfalcons that attracted him. Gyrfalcons attracted lots of people, and the memories tried to take off from there. But Bill Malone fought them. His walk became not only a physical struggle, but a mental struggle, too.

For the first mile he pretended he didn't know why. But when the rhythm, and the air, and the warm sunlight finally began to work their magic, he admitted that he knew what had set those silver ghosts free in his mind. He admitted it was the tight, concerned face of Margaret Adamson that had opened the flood gates. He hadn't seen her for many years and by force of will he managed not to think about the life that had connected them for so long. He tried to fend off the memories, but the gyrfalcons kept pressing in on his mind. By the time he reached the confluence of two draws he was walking faster, but it seemed the old times were catching up.

It was as if something foul was afield. Only a month ago his daughter Allison had begun asking difficult questions about her mother, Ellen. Maybe it was just coincidental. Allison was twenty years old now, about the age Ellen was when Bill met her. It was probably only natural for Allison to want to know more than she had been told as a child. Still, all of it, Allison's questions, Margaret Adamson's reappearance, and now the gyrfalcons, seemed in concert. He could feel a pressure in his head that was separate from the hangover.

At the confluence he noticed a doe mule deer with her

half-grown twins. All three deer stood motionless in a buffaloberry bush not fifty yards away. If he went on he would
frighten them and so he decided it would be a good place to
turn around. He headed back up the draw toward his car, forcing himself to notice the different grasses growing in the bottom of the draw. He named them. Little bluestem on the side
hill, dropseed in draw bottom. Wheatgrass, grama, prairie sand
reed. He said the names fast, hoping to avoid the thought of
Margaret Adamson and his daughter's questions.

Bill made himself lean against the car and watch the sun set
as he had planned. His head still hurt from the night before and
his guts felt empty. The air was cooling and that felt good, but
the sunset was not spectacular. In fact, he wasn't giving it much
attention. Margaret Adamson and Allison were moving toward
each other in his mind. He could see their faces. But there was
another face, beautiful like Allison's but without Allison's piercing dark eyes. The eyes of this face were light green, the lips were
full, always glistening with Carmex. He could smell the Carmex.
He could taste it. But the face was not clear to him. Was it round
or oval? He dwelt on the smoothness of the skin and found himself assigning clichéd colors to the cheeks. It dawned on him
that he was making most of this up. He could not really remember the face. It had been too long ago. Ellen Mayhan had been
dead for a long time now, and it was parts of their daughter's face
that Bill was assigning to her. It made him shake his head. He
wished the walk had worked and thought that perhaps he should
try it again, before he started building a female body of imagined
parts.

But it was too late to walk the draw again. Darkness
stretched across the prairie and holes and hummocks were going
invisible with shadow. Bill hadn't walked the country at night
for years. No, it was time for cripples to head for town where the
ground was hard, smooth, and predictable. Maybe a walk around
the campus or the park. Maybe that would work. Even though
his head still hurt, a drink at Bell's Steak House or the Silver
Dollar sounded good. He smiled at himself. Rapid fire thoughts,
like a lunatic's.

He decided it was partly the time of year that was making him crazy. Maybe it was being outside. He should go back to town. But when he turned from the pink-skyed west to get into his car he was startled by the moon that had crept above the horizon behind his back. "Oh shit," he said. It was gigantic, round, and seemed to pulse. The landscape to the horizon was silver with new light reflecting off sage brush. "Full moon. No wonder."

Bill Malone slipped into his car and sat watching the moon. He had thought he was on the mend—about finished toying with thoughts of the past—but that moon was too strong. It transported him backward through time.

HE WAS STILL bathed in moonlight. But now it shimmered on that January snow that had been lurking just off stage all day. It was many years before, on the High Line of northern Montana, and he was a student. The semester at the University of Montana had begun but he was two hundred miles from the class-rooms in Missoula and the tiny wood-warmed house he shared with friends. This was an annual trip that he sometimes made with one of those friends, but on this particular trip he was alone. Most of the people he knew were getting close to graduation and already a separation was beginning. One of the best of those friends was Margaret Adamson. Now she was too concerned about missing school to do something so irresponsible as take a trip to the High Line. But for Bill, in those times, this trip was crucial. He'd just have to find a way to catch up. Drop a class or two if he had to. Maybe drop the whole semester. That part of his life wasn't so important. What was important was the promise of what stretched out in front of him; a thousand square miles of unpeopled prairie and dark, winter sage rolling in foot hills to mountains beyond. It was three nights after the first sub-zero front had moved down from Canada and he'd driven all day to get to this spot. The pickup, parked along the snowy gravel road behind him, ticked its heat away. It was the only thing that grounded him in the twentieth century and in a few minutes even the mechanical noise was gone. Then it was as though he had ascended into the sky. With the snow below it was impossible to tell where the stars began, which light was original and which reflected. The cold was as brittle as the surface of the Europa and the solitude complete.

Standing there with the night all around him, Bill knew she was out there. Somewhere, on a side hill of sagebrush or a cedar fence post set too far from the cottonwood bottoms for owls to haunt, stood a motionless, silver transient, for whom the cold and solitude were comfort. Somewhere within the land that Bill surveyed was a gyrfalcon freed by the downward slip of Arctic air to wander the Northern Plains.

On those nights Bill would lay curled inside his sleeping bag under the topper that covered the bed of the truck. If he slept at all it would only be from sheer exhaustion. During the night he would jerk awake, clattering with the cold and tense with excitement. He would lay awake and imagine the gyrfalcon warm and content, with one foot up, curled into the down of its flank, and its belly feathers fluffed and pushed down over the foot she stood upon. Her head would be calmly tucked behind her wing and Bill was sure she would be dreaming of ptarmigan and Arctic hares crossing open ground.

He could remember the sound of the constricting cold snapping outside the pickup and the lure pigeons cooing and shuffling in their cage beside him. But by morning the silence would be complete; the snow a stable muffling blanket over sage and freeze-dried grass, the pigeons fluffed-up quiet against the frost that had accumulated under the topper in the night. The prairie glistened when he raised the rear door of the topper. The night sky was gone, replaced by immense pale blue, and the snow sparkled as if it had absorbed the stars and was trying to hide the firmament.

Now the new sun reflected off a trillion ice crystals and every branch and leaf of sage was glazed to twice its usual thickness. He felt like a mouse in a stemware shop and turned to take in all three hundred sixty degrees. In those days Bill Malone would often emerge from his sleeping bag naked and stand on the prairie, or in the mountains, for a long time before the cold would drive him back into the truck for his clothes. And there was seldom much breakfast. Sometimes coffee boiled quickly over a camp stove, but never on this first morning of gyrfalcon trapping. He was always too excited. And besides, gyrs were used to hunting in protracted Arctic twilight. The first hour of light was always best. If he didn't find them before nine o'clock they would usually have killed and eaten and he might have to wait until the next day. Sometimes he never saw them again. Twice Bill spent a whole week on those frozen plains and came home empty-handed. On those years he contented himself with training and flying a different species of raptor.

In some ways those years with a prairie falcon or goshawk were the best. Those birds were more manageable than wild gyrs. But there was something about gyrs that he could not stay away from. He once told Margaret they were like wild, beautiful, psychotic women. "They're not for everyone," he said, "nice to dream about but not much fun in person." And even though his notions were romantic, they were true. Wild-caught gyrs were explosive and for all their size and strength, they were fragile and very difficult to keep in good health.

Of his falconer friends, Bill was the only one who really studied passage gyrs. Occasionally someone would catch one and try to train it but the attempt almost always ended in disaster. The bird would not adjust to confinement and would hurt itself. Or it would never tame down. Or it simply flew away when it was flown free. Only Bill applied himself to the task of learning about those wild, giant, light-colored falcons. And the more he learned, the more he was fascinated. Until he was finally hooked. It was one of the things he was known for and he caught a gyr almost every year until the damaged knee made it impossible to follow a half-wild falcon across an enormous sage flat as it flew down grouse in frigid February.

Finally he could fly a freshly caught gyr free in three weeks. He would catch grouse with her within a month and release her, no worse for wear, before the last snow left the high plains. It took all his time for a period of three months. He became obsessed. There were those that said he was ruining his life. But those were mostly the people who had never wakened all alone on a silent, frozen prairie and then gone looking for the life that, in winter, was nearly invisible. It was the part he loved most, the part he missed desperately.

Hunting for gyrs in January was not unlike hunting the grouse a month later. The engine would turn over slowly and it was not uncommon for Bill to twist the key with fingers crossed for luck. After five minutes the truck's heater had still only blown a six-inch hole in the windshield's frost. Bill used the time to fit a pigeon with a leather harness to which he had tied twenty-five monofilament nooses. For the first few miles the pickup would thump hard when the frozen tires returned to the flat spot that had rested on the ground all night. But by the time H-frame power lines converged with the path of the gravel road, the windshield was mostly clear and the tires were running smoothly. He laid his binoculars on the dash to warm them so the humidity from his face would not fog them into uselessness. He tried to have all this done before the sun was fully above the horizon.

Sometimes he would drive for only a few minutes, some years most of a day, before he would see the first odd bump on the cross bar of a power-line tower. Almost always it was a rough-legged hawk—another Arctic visitor, but a much lesser bird than the gyrs. There was almost no chance of mistaking a rough-legged for a gyr. Even without binoculars Bill could detect their slouched stance and sloppy feathers. If the sun was right, color became as important as silhouette. The rough-legged's muddy brown was easy to differentiate from the gyr's light-washed breast. The native prairie falcon looked most like the gyrs but was smaller, and that time of year prairie falcons were rare. Eagles looked mammoth compared to gyrs, but occasionally a light-phase, ferruginous hawk would trick Bill into slowing down and reaching for the harnessed pigeon in the shoe box beside him on the seat. But if the hawk flew, the wide, deep beat of the wing would instantly give it away as a sluggish mammal-eater.

As a rule of thumb, Bill figured he would see a hundred other raptors before he saw his first gyrfalcon. But this year he had only counted a half dozen rough-leggeds and a golden eagle before that sharp, compact silhouette appeared on the fourth tower ahead of him. The binoculars were warm from the defroster as he raised them to his eyes to be sure. There was really little doubt. He was using the binoculars because he wanted to gaze at her. She was the first gyr he had seen since he had released Blanche Dubois the spring before. He shut off the pickup so he could hold the binoculars steady, then he raised them slowly to savor the moment.

He was not disappointed. She was a gray-phase female in her immature plumage. He was always amazed when he twisted a bird a quarter mile away into crisp focus. The wild ones never look wild; it takes weeks of poorly managed captivity to make them look anything but calmly magnificent. This one, like all wild ones, looked just the way Bill wanted his birds to look the entire time they were in his care. Her feathers were puffed out but not loose and floppy like buteos. She appeared round with sable eyes that squinted at the distance, as if she could see forever. Her shoulders were broad and her wings crossed high on her back. "She's perfect," he whispered as he lowered the glasses, "body and mind." And he closed his eyes and vowed that, if he caught her, he would do everything in his power to keep her that way.

Sometimes these birds are so fresh from the Arctic, where there are no pigeons, that they don't seem to know they are red meat. Sometimes they watch for several minutes before bailing off their perch. Occasionally they land beside the pigeon and cluck at it as if to question it before reaching out and pulling it in with their talons. But this bird did not hesitate. She launched off her tower and held her wings steady for only an instant before she tilted downward and began a crisp, cracking wing beat that built in tempo as her speed doubled, then redoubled.

Through the binoculars, Bill watched her level off a foot over the snowy ground and swim through the air, deceptively, as if moving in a slow current. But the sage below was flipping past at the rate of fifty feet with each wing thrust. She hit the pigeon so hard its head flew off and arched upward in a fine spray of bright arterial blood as the gyr pitched up thirty feet, then slammed downward onto the decapitated, flopping pigeon.

Bill learned later that a noose had snagged one of the gyr's toes on that first pass, but the monofilament had snapped like cotton thread when the gyr came to its end. He sat in the car watching with the binoculars as the gyr stood, suddenly very calm, on the pigeon carcass. She reached over almost gently and crushed the exposed vertebra of the neck. When she straightened up, squinted her eyes, and loosened her feathers, Bill knew she was going to rouse. The shake began at her shoulders and shimmied down to her tail. For an instant the feathers remained fluffed—down to the tiny feathers under her chin fanning outward—then she leisurely flattened everything to crispness. Before she turned her attention to her meal every feather was exactly in its place. She began by rolling the pigeon onto its back and plucking the breast.

It was nearly five minutes before the gyr actually began to eat and all that time Bill watched for the subtle movement of one foot that would tell him that a noose had closed and the gyr was caught. She seemed to relish the meal but ate fast with an eye toward the four horizons where predators might appear. Her head bobbed down to the warm pigeon breast then back up to survey her surroundings. A few small pigeon feathers stuck to her beak and when she raised a foot to scratch them away Bill saw there was resistance. He eased the pickup into gear and crept forward. When he was within a hundred feet he stopped and slowly slid from the cab. The gyr glanced at him but was not frightened. It was very possible that she had never seen a human before and took Bill for some puny sort of bear. He was obviously too slow and clumsy to catch her if he made a rush. She went back to eating and only looked up occasionally as he moved closer.

Then Bill was fifteen feet away—a little too close to ignore—and she looked him full in the face for the first time. Her eyes took his breath away. They were miniature black holes and Bill felt himself being sucked into her consciousness. She was exquisite, each gray-brown feather rimmed in buff and bleached from constant exposure to the elements. She was one of those elements, as honest and wholesome as the rain or sunshine. He took another step and she tensed up; this was too close. Another step and she jerked the pigeon back. But Bill had secured the line attached to the harness and the harness loop was cinched tight around one toe. She was caught but didn't know it. He always tried to make this realization as painless as possible. He got as close as he could by moving gently and being careful not to threaten her with his eyes. But when she finally gave up the pigeon, turned to flee, and found she was fast, he did not hesitate. He moved in quickly and made her roll back on her tail by moving his right hand slowly above her head. Her eyes followed the hand and she simply tipped backward. Her beak was opened, but more paralyzed than threatening. With the other hand Bill reached in gently and grasped her feet firmly. Then he lowered his right hand to tuck the precious wings into her sides. By then he was on his knees in the snow, and he transferred control of everything to the left hand. He took the hood from his coverall pocket and, with a fluid motion, eased it tenderly over the falcon's head. Her beak closed and he snugged the braces with his teeth and the fingers of his right hand. After he loosened the monofilament noose, he leaned close and smelled the sweetness of her feathers.

SITTING IN his car, twenty years later, Bill Malone could recall the smell precisely. Kinnikinnick, granite, blood, and a hint of ocean spray. It was night now. The September moon was high and even though the world had cooled, the air felt warm when compared to his daydream.

He had named that bird Belknap because Fort Belknap was the first town he passed on his way home. He was a long way from Missoula, but he drove straight through and woke Margaret sometime after midnight.

She took care of Bill's apartment while he was gone. She fed the fish and the iguana for him. She made sure the plants and the pipes didn't freeze. She knew the apartment's idiosyncrasies. By then she had spent many nights there with Bill.

"You're crazy," Margaret said stumbling from the bedroom. "What the hell . . ." and her voice faded for a moment when she saw Belknap hooded and jessed on the back of a kitchen chair. "Jesus, Billy, she's gorgeous."

Billy. That's what Margaret called him in those college days. Billy Boy. And he had called her Maggie. His wildness was balanced by her seriousness. They had been good for each other and, later, worked well together for years. It was much later that they found themselves on opposite sides of a question neither of them understood. Even then, he was never sure why. He wondered if they were still on opposite sides. He could hear that she didn't want to say what she said at the hearing the night before. It was out of her hands and he didn't blame her. He wished he'd gone up to her and said hello. But he couldn't. By the time she spoke he had already lost his temper. It had been one of those sham meetings, put on to create the illusion of fairness, and he'd stormed out, pushing people from the path of his limping gait. At the thought of the way he had left the meeting, he closed his eyes, as if the heartburn and headache had returned.

3

A MESSAGE TO call Sheriff Larson at the Lawrence County Court House was waiting for Margaret Adamson when she returned from her afternoon of finishing paperwork at the United States Forest Service office. She had spent a couple terrible hours with Larson that morning after Andy Arnold was killed and hoped that would be the end of it. After the ambulance took Arnold's body away and all the witnesses were interviewed there was an awkward time when everyone hung around the parked cars. No one said much but they seemed to need to be with one another. It was eerie and after a half hour Margaret pulled herself together and got away. She didn't want to dwell on what she'd seen, so she did her best to go on with her day.

The Black Hills National Forest offices are in the town of Custer, and Margaret had forced herself to take a side trip to see Mount Rushmore. She had never seen the monument and was saddened by the thought that she might never again have the chance. The monument was huge and stark white against the dark ponderosa pine trees of the Black Hills. Had it not been for the trauma of the morning the huge sculpture might have been inspiring. But instead of inspiration she was overwhelmed by the sense that it was terribly out of place. She came away wondering what sort of men dreamed it up.

In a daze she wound her way north from the monument and had dinner at a little restaurant in Hill City called Oriana's. It was half café, half bookstore. She spent an hour perusing the books without really seeing them. She had a salad that she managed to realize was surprisingly fresh. There was a pasta dish with a delicious light cream sauce. This was her first visit to the Black Hills and despite her morning's experience, she could see that this was a unique and pleasant place. She had always suspected that it was because Bill Malone wouldn't be living there if it wasn't.

She drove slowly and stopped often, looking for birds as a way to clear her mind. On a fence post near the edge of a high meadow, there was a powder blue mountain bluebird. A flock of piñon jays crossed the road as it dipped into an oak draw, and dusky yellow-green warblers fluttered manically in the branches of a sumac bush. Margaret wasn't sure what kind of warblers they were. Bill would have known if they were Audubon's or myrtle warblers. He would have known if the shrike she saw on a telephone wire was a northern or a loggerhead. It occurred to her several times that it would have been nice to take the tour with Bill. In fact, at a gas station along the highway she stopped and screwed her courage up enough to call. But there was no answer. That disappointed her but relieved her, too. She wasn't sure what she'd say to him after all these years. He was likely angry about what she had said the night before. Certainly it roused his twenty-year-old anger with her for working for the Fish and Wildlife Service when he'd been arrested by her fellow agents.

The infraction had been a technicality, but he was still convicted. There was a fine and a suspended jail sentence. She suspected those things were minor to Bill. What hurt him, she knew, was the confiscation of the gyrfalcon he had just trapped. She found out later that he never got the bird back. They had gone their own ways by then, he with his family and she with her career that was listing toward law enforcement. They hadn't talked for a year or so, but she called when she found out what had happened. Because she worked for the agency that had busted him, she suspected Bill would not be happy. But she didn't expect the intensity of his anger. The arresting officer's name was Mathews and she asked him what happened to the falcon. She had never liked Mathews. He had come over from the FBI when they had downsized and never let anyone forget that he still had friends in powerful places. He was condescending, especially to women, and had a sickening way of smiling at Margaret. He shrugged his shoulders and said they released the falcon at the same place Bill trapped it. She thought that information would make Bill happy. But he wouldn't listen. He barely managed to hold his temper over the phone. It was a mechanical conversation, filled with exaggerated politeness. It was the last time they ever spoke.

So she'd spent most of the day driving around the hills trying not to think about what she had witnessed that morning and ended up thinking about that bad time in her life with Bill. But she couldn't help noticing the beauty of the hills. The aspen streaked golden up the hillsides of dark pines and the blue sky was puffed with pure white clouds. By the end of her day she had come to some balance. She was nearly done with her business. She would not think about Andy Arnold. She would bring her business to a close in another day and before she left she would see Bill Malone again. She made that promise as she mounted the front steps of the Franklin Hotel. But there was the note from Sheriff Larson waiting for her at the desk. It had arrived at eight o'clock, only a few minutes before, and said to please return the call.

They had given her the corner room were Calamity Jane was supposed to have once slept. There was a sign to that effect just outside the room, and Margaret came nose to nose with it as she jiggled the key in the lock and bumped her shoulder against the door. It was a very old hotel and had obviously once been a lovely place. Her room had a corner window with curved glass to match the shape of the stone on the outside. The hotel, like a lot of the town, was a little shabby. The window sill needed painting and the bedspread was threadbare.

The shabbiness, Andy Arnold had told her during their hike, was the target of the special gambling legislation that was rejuvenating Deadwood. A share of the profits would go to historic restoration. In a few years, Deadwood would again be the jewel of the West, and Arnold assured her that the economic lift from his development would only help. It sounded sad to Margaret, but she didn't say anything. She'd run into this reasoning all over the West and was mostly reconciled to it. She could see that the town needed something, but she made it clear to Arnold that she was there to assess the biological situation and the economy was not her concern. Her job was simple. She didn't have much choice.

After Bill stood up at the meeting and made his plea she wished there was something she could do to help. But there wasn't. It was a done deal and, knowing that, Bill seemed a little pitiful. She had been shocked to see that something serious and permanent had happened to his leg. He hobbled to the microphone and, to her, looked very old. Even his voice was battered. But the quality of the voice mixed well with the words he chose. He spoke eloquently about wilderness, water, and solitude. He touched on the things that were important to everyone in the room and used Brendan Prairie as a metaphor for the whole planet. But she had been to many meetings like this and knew that, when Bill was done, those in charge would thank him and go right on as if he had never spoken. The things that Bill Malone talked about the night before were not in the law, and decisions were made according to the law.

Her part was simply technical. She'd looked over the data carefully and it depressed her to come to the conclusion she had come to, but facts were facts. There was no reason to think that Mountain Air Estates would present an unreasonable threat to the environment, as there was nothing hazardous or poisonous about their plans. Of course, she knew that Bill had been right, too. The area would never be the same and in the long run the Black Hills would be impoverished because of what would happen at Mountain Air Estates and other places, as more land was developed to service the development. The same thing was happening with the legalized gambling but people only saw the short-term money. Humans pushing out other species was not considered an unreasonable threat.

Overpopulating delicate ecosystems was acceptable to the powers that be. The problem was that it had never been acceptable to Bill Malone. He had spoken for ten minutes and when he was finished the crowd was silent, an embarrassed hush. She looked at the faces and saw that some in the audience understood what Bill had said, perhaps for the first time. Their eyes were steely and their jaws were set. But the people at the head table hadn't heard. The anger in Bill's voice when they asked him to sit down destroyed the mood he had created but did not surprise her in the least.

Now she was sitting on the bed with the sheriff's note in her hand. It was almost nine o'clock. If she called anyone, it should be Bill. But maybe that could wait. What was another day? In her old capacity as special agent with law enforcement responsibilities she would have been in constant contact with the sheriff and the other enforcement people who were on Andy Arnold's case. But now she was mostly a biologist. She'd been trying to move away from police work and just now she didn't want to talk to a law dog, even if he was an old toothless one. Her shoes had already been kicked off and she had unbuttoned her blouse. The bed was going to feel good. She picked up the phone and dialed the number. It rang twice before the tired voice of Sheriff Carl Larson sighed. "Hello?"

"It's Margaret Adamson, Sheriff. I hope I'm not calling too late."

"Not at all," Larson said. He seemed to come to life, but beneath the words was still the profound weariness that Margaret had noticed that morning. "I've been just sitting here. Been waiting for your call. I'd like to talk with you."

"Sure."

"I mean I'd like to come down and talk."

"It's after nine."

Larson stammered. "I'm close. It won't take long."

"It's about Andy Arnold?"

"Yes."

"Could we do this over the phone?"

"I'd rather not. You're a cop. You understand."

"I'm up here as a biologist." She wanted Larson to know that, but she'd worked enough as a cop to understand how tough it could be. "I suppose I could meet you in the lobby."

"Give me five minutes."

Margaret hung up and lay back on the bed. She stretched and settled in just to see what it was going to feel like. She needed some sleep. She tried to jog at least four miles every morning and that meant she had to get up early. Then it struck her that Andy Arnold was dead. She'd been keeping that thought at bay most of the day. He'd seemed like a decent kind of guy. Maybe not her type, but decent. She smiled. She didn't have a type. She didn't have a man, hadn't had one for years. Margaret knew she was not beautiful. She was five feet four inches tall, powerful for a woman, maybe a little overweight. She wore her reddish brown hair short and they said she had a nice smile. She tried the smile, then she smirked. Maybe Andy was her type, now that he was dead.

CARL LARSON was sitting on a stool in front of a slot machine when Margaret came down the stairs into the lobby. There were only four other people in the room, but they were playing the machines and the room was electric with the sound of buzzers and bells. It was too bad slot machines had been moved into the lobby. Once it had been a magnificent room with tiled floors and a high metal ceiling. Now it was filled with flashing lights and crude noises designed to lure people away from their money.

Larson stood when he saw Margaret. He carried his western hat and slid his hands around the brim as he moved to meet her. His close-cropped white hair and pencil mustache made him look distinguished. He smiled but he couldn't keep the fatigue out of his expression. "Could I buy you a cup of coffee?" he said.

"It keeps me up this time of night. Maybe a hot chocolate."

They went into the hotel café and sat at the counter. A few other customers sat at the far end of the long room. They laughed but it was impossible to understand what they were saying. The waitress brought Larson a cup of coffee as soon as she saw him. Margaret ordered her hot chocolate and the waitress smiled and called her sweetheart.

Their stools were only three feet from the cash register and Larson leaned over and took a few toothpicks from a ceramic Indian who held them in his quiver. He offered one to Margaret. She shook her head and he put one in his mouth. The other toothpicks were slipped into the band of his hat. Larson made small talk until the waitress brought Margaret's hot chocolate.

"So what can I do for you?" Margaret asked.

"I just thought I'd better touch base with you. I mean it's not often that an accident like what happened this morning is witnessed by one law officer, let alone two. I thought you'd want to know it looks like an accident. Breaks failed. Andy Arnold was in the wrong place at the wrong time."

"An accident? Pure accident?" Larson was watching her. She couldn't help thinking he was judging her response. "What about the vandalism? What about sabotage?"

Larson shrugged and looked away. "It crossed our minds. But there's a history of vandalism out there. Nothing really malicious. It was just an accident. Isn't that the way you saw it?"

Margaret held her hands palm up. "It's your baby, Sheriff." She kept an eye on Larson as she sipped her hot chocolate. He stared at his cup of coffee. He wouldn't raise his eyes to meet hers.

"Your report would be consistent with ours?" Larson said, still not looking up.

"I'm not doing a report on what I saw this morning. I do very little law enforcement anymore. As little as I can get away with." She watched Larson stir his coffee, thinking. "If you're asking if I'm going to contradict what you come up with, the answer is no. It's your investigation. If you find the brakes failed then the brakes failed. I'm just a biologist."

Larson finally smiled. "We're going to check everything out, of course. But this is a quiet place, Mrs. Adamson."

"Miss," Margaret said. "Miss Adamson."

"Andy Arnold should have been more careful," Larson said. "That's the bottom line. The foreman, Bass, too. Could be some negligence on the part of the maintenance crew. We'll check into that. But it looks like an accident to us."

"Who is us?"

Larson's eyes slipped away again. "I've talked on the phone with some of the partners."

"Arnold's partners?"

"They thought it was probably an honest accident."

"They could tell that over the phone?"

"On what I've found on the preliminary investigation." He looked squarely at Margaret and she saw again how tired he was.

"This couldn't have waited until tomorrow?"

Larson shrugged and finished the last swallow of his coffee. "There's some state guys coming in tomorrow. I just wanted to be sure all my ducks were in a row."

"Okay," Margaret said. She let herself smile. "But I run in the mornings, early."

Larson's face showed genuine regret and he reached out and pulled the bill toward him. "I'm sorry," he said. "I forgot. Young people need their sleep."

"Thanks," Margaret said. "I consider that a compliment."

"I don't sleep much myself. Maybe it could have waited until tomorrow."

Margaret had been warming up to Larson and now the way the sheriff slumped on his stool, the bill limp in his hand, touched her. The waitress came and tried to give him more coffee but he held his hand over the cup.

"So, how long have you been sheriff of Lawrence County?"

Larson picked up the empty cup in both hands and blew gently into it as if the coffee was still too hot to drink. "Thirty-two years," he said.

"Long time. I'll bet things have changed a lot."

"You'd win that bet. I've seen them come and go." He studied the coffee cup then looked at Margaret and smiled. "And I'll be gone after the first of the year."

"Retirement?"

"Big time." He looked away and Margaret could see that he was thinking of what he would do.

"You got a plan?"

Larson nodded. "It's just me. I got a recreational vehicle. Figure I'll go someplace warm. Do some fishing in the ocean." He seemed to forget that she was there. "It's going to be nice." He spoke mostly to himself. "There are things about this job that are tough. They're getting tougher."

4

BILL MALONE drove his car slowly. He was no longer interested in a walk around the campus. He needed something but he wasn't sure what. Maybe a drink. The hair of the dog. He didn't need the alcohol, it was more a need of company. But, while it was true that he had friends he sometimes ran into downtown, it was also true that he had a twenty-year-old daughter who, though she was in great demand as a college senior, might need company, too. He hadn't been giving her his best and that bothered him. Still, it was difficult. She had started this asking about her mother and that was the last thing Bill wanted to talk about.

Of course Allison knew her mother had been killed in a car accident when she was still a baby. Growing up, Bill had told her that Ellen had simply lost control on a gravel mountain road in New Mexico. That was the truth, as far as it went, and until a few months ago, it had satisfied her. But when she'd come across the photograph of Ellen, looking sultry as a movie star, sitting on the top of the backseat of a Mercedes Benz convertible, she had brought it to him with a questioning look on her face.

It was a picture that he had saved but not looked at for years and when he raised his eyes from it to meet Allison's he could see that she wanted to know what really happened. Bill had only been able to say that that was the car she was killed in, and, no, the car had belonged to someone else. Even that much came hard for him and when Allison saw the hurt in his eyes she reached out and touched his arm. "It's okay, Daddy." She leaned over and kissed the top of his head. But she'd wanted more and Bill knew she had a right.

It wasn't long afterward that Andy Arnold and his out-of-state partners made public their plans to build Mountain Air Estates on Brendan Prairie. They tried to get the people of the state to allow higher gambling limits by saying the project would never work without them. They promised jobs even though unemployment was low. When the people turned them down, a miracle happened. They found a way to build the project with the existing bet limits. Bill knew that as soon as it was built they would try to blackmail the state into Las Vegas–style gambling by threatening to shut down. They would talk about the great loss of jobs.

Those were bad times and while Mountain Air was playing its game, Allison was extracting parts of her family's story from him. She learned some things but there was a great deal more. She knew there was and he knew one day he'd have to tell her everything. He dreaded it, not for her because she was tough like her mom, but for himself.

Bill was thinking about all this when he pulled up in front of Bell's Steak House. Bell's was more of a restaurant than a bar and it wasn't his favorite place. For one thing, the lounge was sometimes used as a storage room for the kitchen. Lots of times there were boxes of napkins or canned fruit stacked on the corner tables and that made him feel like he was drinking in a warehouse. He didn't like the decorating either. Someone had decided the lounge needed a waterfall. A façade of rock covered one wall and the masons had created a pool at the bottom of the fake cliff. An electric pump had been thrown in the pool and plugged, dangerously it seemed to Bill, into the wall socket where the water it circulated to the top splashed down over everything. But, worse than the electrical danger, was the poorly stuffed mountain lion that crouched on a rock shelf halfway between the pool and the source of the waterfall. It didn't look at all like a mountain lion. Its right hind foot was bent into a contortion no lion could tolerate, and the shape of its head was distorted. The neck was thin and much too long. Of course, someone had mounted the cat with its face in a hideous snarl. It reminded Bill of a cartoon character. Every time he came into the bar, he half expected to be sold a roll of pink attic insulation.

Sitting in the car he wondered why he even wanted to go into a place like this. He knew the reason was that Bell's was on his way home and he fully intended to be heading home soon. He knew he was vulnerable and tonight he was trying to plan ahead.

The first thing Bill saw when he entered Bell's was the damned mountain lion perched on the electric waterfall. It was more ridiculous than he had remembered. The cat was snarling its cartoon snarl and Bill rolled his eyes. Perhaps the cat was afraid it was going to fall into the pool and get electrocuted. On his way to find a barstool, Bill averted his eyes.

There was a little activity on the steak house side of the building but no one near the bar. Bill took one of three stools and watched the waitresses moving back and forth on the dining side. The place was very dead. He only wanted a drink. Of course, it would be nice to have a bartender. He swiveled in his seat and looked around. The boxes from the kitchen were there as usual. Could it be that the bar was closed for some reason?

But then there was a young man asking Bill what he wanted to drink. He was wondering again if he wanted to be in this place at all but he responded to the young man by ordering a whiskey and soda.

The drink had been in front of Bill for only a minute and he had tasted it and knew that it was a good strong one, when he felt a fresh rush of air as the outside door opened. Bill turned to see a woman walk into the lounge. She was young and pretty and stood in the entry looking around. There wasn't much to see, just Bill and those boxes from the kitchen, but she came in and walked up to the bar and took a stool. She smiled and Bill said hello. He took her in briefly, seeing that she was dressed richly in tan slacks and a tweedy coat. She did not look like she was from Spearfish and he turned his attention back to his glass.

"It's a beautiful evening," the woman said.

Bill nodded. "Very nice," he said. "September around here is known for nice evenings."

"It's so funny. I'm from Chicago. I had it in mind that South Dakota was bitter cold."

"It can be," Bill said. He liked her Chicago accent and could feel his curiosity rising.

She ordered white wine. Bill wanted to say no to a second drink but he didn't. "My name is Anne and I'm here trying to sell the college an all-weather athletic track." She answered unspoken questions like a mind reader.

"I think they have one, Anne."

She shook her head and laughed. "Not a good one," she said and opened her eyes wide, tilting her head to show how she was going to sell this new track idea. Bill wondered if Bob Flannagan, the athletic director, would be able to resist.

When the drinks came, Bill thought about buying hers. He had a stack of bills on the bar but he didn't move. He'd seen something in her smile that he wasn't sure he wanted to encourage. He wasn't really surprised when the woman pushed a twenty toward the bartender and said she'd get both drinks.

Bill drank faster. He smiled and talked with Anne, found out her last name was Casey and that she had been married briefly but was now separated. He was vague in his answers to her questions and could feel the whiskey warming his insides. After a few minutes Anne stood up and put her hand on his arm. "Can you direct me to the little girl's room?" She leaned close and he could smell her perfume.

He pointed. "Other side of the bar. Clear to the back."

"Thanks. I shall return."

Bill nodded and watched her walk. She was taller than he had thought. Her legs were long and her body trim. Athlete, Bill thought. He watched her move until she was out of sight, then he looked down at his drink. One swallow left. He downed it and looked at his watch. It was still early but time to make a decision. He told himself he should go home. But Allison might not be home. She might be out for several more hours. What the hell, he thought. He ordered another whiskey soda and a glass of white wine.

The drinks arrived just as Anne returned. "Thanks," she said as she raised the glass. "You folks are friendly out here."

Bill raised his glass. "Thank you," he said. "You're not bad yourself, for a city girl."

Later, she smiled and said something that seemed odd to Bill.

"I love this bar." She turned to the waterfalls. "Look at that," she said. "A fountain right in a bar."

"You can't win them all."

"I think it's nice," Anne said. "You've got a lot of nice things here in the Black Hills. There's been a lot of development since I was last here."

"How long ago was that?"

Anne laughed. "Maybe ten years."

"Yeah, things have changed in the last ten years. Mostly for the worst."

"There's been a lot of good, too. A lot of good development."

"All developers should be shot," Bill said. He said it evenly and let his eyes rest on Anne. Her smile never cracked. They had nearly finished their fourth drink.

"Well," Anne said, "I still love the tiger." She nodded toward the ledge near the top of the waterfall.

"It's a lion," Bill said.

"No."

"I admit, it's hard to tell. But that's what it was when it was alive." He took a long pull on his drink and twisted around to look at the cat. "Poor sorry son of a bitch," he said.

"What?" Anne was giggling at the face he was making.

"It's sick." Now Bill was talking almost to himself. "It's like stuffing a person and putting them on the wall."

"I guess I don't like mounted animals either."

"See that neck? Imagine your dead grandmother with a fifty-five-inch chest." Anne laughed at that but when she looked at Bill she saw that he was not joking. His eyes had narrowed. "Complete disrespect," he said. "I hate it. And that two-bit waterfall. It's a parody. It's dangerous."

Anne tried to laugh again but Bill was paying no attention to her now. The bartender had come from somewhere in the back and stood watching Bill.

"It's supposed to be a touch of nature," Anne said.

Bill took a sip of his drink. He could feel an unreasonable anger swelling inside himself. He wasn't drunk but he was using the alcohol for an excuse. He could have stopped himself right

there, but he didn't want to. "Well," he said, "it offends me."
He took the swizzle stick out of his drink and tossed it into the
water.

"Hey!" It was the bartender. "Don't throw trash in the pool."

Bill looked at him hard. The bartender's skin was too void of
wrinkles. A kid shouldn't talk to him that way. He felt things
slipping and, though something in him didn't want that to happen, something else did. So he let it out. "Fuck you, kid, the
whole damn thing's trash." He wadded up his napkin and tossed
it in, too.

They stared at each other for an instant and when the bartender said nothing, Bill stood up and went toward the rock
wall. As he went, he picked up a bar stool. He stopped with the
lion at eye level and the water tumbling down and splashing at
his feet.

The bartender got there just as the head came off the lion
and the first leg came off the stool. Bill got in two more good
swings with the chair and sparks were popping all up and down
the wall when he was finally pulled away. His stiff leg hurt his
mobility but he wrestled the bartender to a standstill and they
stood in the middle of the barroom panting at each other. The
waitresses from the restaurant were gathered around but not too
close. Anne was gone.

"You're crazy," the bartender said with a voice full of emotion. His face was red and it was hard to understand him. He was
finished. He had turned out to be just the kid he looked like.

Bill started to say something but decided against it. He wasn't
really mad at the bartender. Instead of speaking he took a few deep
breaths and stood up straight. When he headed for the door the
bartender repeated himself. "You're crazy." He moved like he
might take a hold of Bill again but a stone look stopped him.
"I'm calling the cops," he said as Bill stepped through the door.

He pushed out into the September night and was overcome
with remorse. He didn't really know what had happened to him.
That damned lion had been up there forever and he'd always

resisted the temptation. The mistake was stopping in the first place. Where was Anne? No. Go home. He should go home.

But now he wasn't ready to go home. He cruised past his turnoff and on downtown where he pulled into a parking place in front of the Silver Dollar Bar. This was his bar. He should have gone here in the first place. Just walking through the doors made him feel better.

There were only a few other patrons. Two were on stools at the bar. A couple embroiled in deep discussion sat in a corner booth. The light was poor, mostly from the bank of video lottery machines along the north wall. A woman in sweat clothes played one of the machines. The light and the sound made Bill hesitate. Above the machines was a sign: Please Don't Shoot the Video Lottery Players—They're Doing Their Best. The sign was the handiwork of Rob Martin. Rob owned the place and was a friend of Bill's. He waved as soon as he recognized Bill standing at the door.

Bill came to the bar and took one of the open stools. "How's it going, Rob?"

"Little slow." They looked around as if to verify this. Their eyes stopped at the woman playing the video machine.

"I see you're collecting a little stupidity tax," Bill said. "But you're right. Quiet."

Rob nodded. "It'll get better. It's the beginning of the semester and the kids still got some cash from Daddy. I figure things will liven up a little later. And how about you? How's the bird-man of Spearfish?" Bill shrugged and Rob went right on. "That reminds me. Did Cooney Jenkins get a hold of you?"

"Haven't seen him since last night late," Bill said. "I slept on his couch but he was gone when I got up. Give me a whiskey soda."

"Coming up." Rob mixed the drink but didn't stop talking. "He come in here a couple hours ago with a bird in a box. Said it hit his window and was hurt."

Bill winced. This happened to him all the time. People knew he taught biology—and ornithology when there were enough students interested—so they assumed he could fix hurt birds. It was a grisly task. Birds did not heal well. He ended up euthanizing ninety-five percent of them. "That so?"

"Yeah. He said he was going to try you at home. He didn't show up over there?"

"Maybe. I haven't been there yet."

The front door swung open and a half dozen students breezed in and stood briefly in the light from the video machines. They were joking. It felt good to have noise in the background. Bill sipped his whiskey slowly as the students found a booth. He stirred the ice cubes with his finger and thought about nothing.

"Did you hear about the accident up at Mountain Air?" It was Rob. He spoke as he poured a pitcher of beer.

"No," Bill said.

"A big loader got away. Somebody got run over. Killed him." Rob grabbed five glasses with one hand and a pitcher with the other. The jukebox started up and, as Rob passed, Bill shrugged. He wasn't sure how to respond to Rob's news. He stared at his drink and listened to the bar getting busy.

There was no more time for Rob to talk. Time passed and Bill raised a finger when he needed another drink. Rob made the drinks between trays of beers for the students who were steadily filling the place. At ten-thirty a waitress came on duty but still Rob was too busy to talk. He kept Bill's glass full and marked the drinks on his tab. By eleven-thirty Bill was feeling as lonely as he had felt walking on the prairie.

He swiveled on his stool and leaned back against the bar with his drink cradled in his hands. Now the place was half full. The booths were all occupied and several video machines were blinking and whistling as they swallowed coins. Bill recognized a few locals and people from the university but almost everyone was a student. Some he had had in class and when they saw him they waved or shouted a greeting. But no one approached him.

Bill glanced over the group in the very last booth; four young women and a boy, all younger than Allison. Beside them, at a table, two more women sat leaning toward each other in a conspiratorial way. Bill's eyes passed over them then snapped back.

The sun-bleached hair of one of the women touched something in Bill's memory. He stared at the hair for a moment trying to sort the feeling of déjà vu from the present. No. It was nothing. He spun on his stool and held up his glass toward Rob. "Last one," Bill said.

But when the drink came he was still thinking about the sun-streaked hair. He had always had a weakness for outdoor women. He sipped on the drink and recalled women from the summers he had worked for the Park Service. Margaret had graduated with an MA in biology by then and was working her way up the federal wildlife ladder. For a time she administered the peregrine falcon recovery program in the national parks of the Rocky Mountains. Bill was still a few years from a BA owing to his habit of taking time off. He was also perpetually broke and in search of summer employment. When Margaret called and mentioned the word *job*, she got Bill's attention.

"You can't believe how screwed up the Park Service is," Margaret told him over the phone. "It's like an unwritten rule that you aren't allowed to go out in the field. I think they're afraid you'll show them up by actually doing something."

"Are you offering me a job where I have to stay inside."

"No. That only applies to permanent people like myself. Temporaries do all the real work." Margaret hesitated, wanting to get this part just right. "We'd really have to cheat a little to make everyone happy."

"How do you mean, cheat?"

"Well, what I need you to do is check up on all the sites where peregrines are being released in national parks, from Colorado to Montana. They get released as babies and are fed for a couple months by attendants camped out in the parks. A lot can go wrong. I need someone who knows about birds, can talk to people, think on his feet, doesn't need to stay in motels or take time off, and doesn't mind driving seven hundred miles after walking to the top of a mountain and back."

"For minimum wage, right? Where's the cheating come in?"

"Your job description would be filing clerk."

"You wouldn't ask me to file things, would you?"

"No. I don't plan on even seeing you." She paused. "Well, it would be nice if you'd stop by occasionally."

Bill laughed. "You can't keep me away."

"The door is always open."

"And these attendants," Bill said. "They camp out in pairs all summer?"

"You're getting it. College students. Lots of them working their first wildlife jobs."

Bill had been on the fringe of it his whole time at Missoula, but when he took the job Margaret offered he found himself in the center of the subculture of temporary workers that tries its best to take care of America's wildlife. In the seven years he worked part-time for the Park Service he saw plenty of sun-streaked heads, women's and men's, and lots of strong, tanned legs growing out of hiking boots and disappearing into Patagonia shorts. He was good back then; strong and lean himself, doing something important. In those days there was lots of everything a young man needed. There was the challenge of the job, the comradery, the freedom, the physical nature of the work, and the gyrfalcons in the winter. He couldn't help thinking that those were the very best years of his life and he wondered how things had changed so drastically.

When he got that far into thinking about his past, his mind resisted. If he wasn't careful he would end this kind of reminiscence by concentrating on the pictures flashing briefly through his foggy consciousness. First the landscapes that the birds had drawn him to—the mountains of the Rockies, the sandy, hard-scrabble desert of Utah, rolling Arctic tundra. Then faces. He'd see Margaret at her desk in Salt Lake. Then Jamie Eaton dressed in full Orvis gear sitting in his convertible with a huge, handsome smile. Occasionally he would see Ellen with tiny ringlets of sun streaked auburn hair moistened by perspiration and clinging to her cheek near the corner of her eye. But tonight he didn't want to study those faces, so he forced himself to stop this thinking and move.

He left the last swallow of his drink in the glass on the bar.

Suddenly the need for fresh air overcame him and he waved a hasty good-bye to Rob. He lurched toward the door too fast, and people looked at him and got out of his way. But no one seemed to really care about this older crippled man. He stopped at the door and surveyed the crowd once more. He was looking for the girl with the sun-streaked hair but couldn't pick her out. She had faded into the din of the barroom where a faint blue haze of cigarette smoke was rising.

As THE door shut behind him he sucked at the cool evening air. He reached out to touch the corner of the building and looked up to see a few stars outshining the streetlights. God, he thought, it is a beautiful night. The car was only a few yards away and he breathed deeply as he covered those last few steps. Once in the driver's seat he had an urge to just sit, but he couldn't. Now he wanted to be home, wanted very badly to see Allison, and he knew he needed to keep moving.

But he ran the stoplight on the corner of Fifth and Main and a police car pulled out of nowhere and switched on its light. Bill popped the heels of both hands against the steering wheel and swore. How dumb can you be?

Both cars pulled to the side of the street and Bill watched closely as the policeman got out and ambled forward. It was Jim Berry and Bill clicked his tongue. He knew Jim Berry. He was in for a bad time.

"Billy, Billy, Billy," Berry said. "You got to take it a little easier." His face was stern. It was a small town and Berry was one of those policemen who watched too much television.

Berry pointed his flashlight into Bill's face then around the interior of the car. "We been having a little party?"

Bill looked up at him, trying to show he was sorry. He was. Berry nodded his head almost imperceptibly. "Been drinking," he said.

"A little," Bill said. Berry let him sit there and think about it. A small pickup moved past them and pulled over in front of Bill's car. It was Cooney Jenkins's old Datsun with the beat-up fiberglass topper. Bill smiled to himself. Cooney was out cruising again. When did he sleep?

"You didn't start this party at Bell's Steak House did you?" Berry was speaking close to Bill's ear now. "Maybe a little lion taming to get the evening rolling?"

Bill didn't answer. Cooney had gotten out of his pickup and was coming their way. He wore his usual ragged clothes and his gray beard glowed with an aura, backlit by the headlights of on-coming cars. "Howdy, Jim," Cooney said. "Looks like you got a bad one." He came to a halt, looked past Berry to Bill and raised his eyebrows as if he was surprised. The raised eyebrows were a habit of Cooney's, one of the things that made it possible to for-get that he was retarded in some ways.

Berry mumbled a hello. It was impossible to be gruff with Cooney. "Yeah," Berry said, "got an APB on a Tarzan look-alike, harassing big cats."

"Must be a mistake, officer," Cooney was smiling an awkward grin. "This hombre specializes in birds. In fact, he's got a hurt one waiting for him at his house. I was looking for him to come do some vet work." Bill knew this was partly B.S. But Cooney could be irresistible when he talked slow and earnestly, so Bill stayed rigid and let him work. "Maybe I should take him home so he can have a look. Poor little guy hit my window. He's pretty banged up."

There was a moment of silence, but even before Berry spoke Bill felt the officer's resolve slipping away. Berry shook his head in mild disgust. "Yeah, okay. Get him out of here. But this car stays. He can pick it up in the morning."

Cooney smiled through his scruffy beard. "Thank you, offi-cer. It really is an errand of mercy."

It took a couple minutes for Cooney to clear enough junk off the passenger's seat so Bill could get in. Berry stood beside Cooney and glared at his windshield. "Hey," Berry said, "clean this windshield off first. You couldn't see fifteen feet in front of you through this."

Cooney squinted at the glass as if he had just noticed it was dirty. "It is a little buggy, isn't it?"

Berry nodded, not amused. What an asshole, Bill thought,

but he kept himself from saying it out loud. "Hand me a rag, please," Cooney said. Bill dug into the trash at his feet and came up with something. He handed it out the window to Cooney and when the cloth came into the light, they both saw it was an old, torn cavalry officer's jacket. It had been Cooney's favorite for years. Bill remembered when he'd worn it everyday, along with a World War II aviator's cap. The old jacket stopped there between them and they looked at each other. Cooney shrugged and took the jacket.

Berry watched over him as he scraped some of the bugs off the windshield. Bill looked back down at the trash on the floor in front of him. There were old engine parts, soda cans, a mountain of fast food containers, and a half dozen library books.

Then Cooney slid back into the driver's seat. They were moving when Bill pulled another book from under himself. He held it up as they passed under the first streetlight. *The Joy of Succulents.*

"Great book," Cooney said. "I'd lend it to you but it took me a while to read and now it's a month overdue." Bill couldn't help smiling. He knew Cooney was telling the truth. He had watched him reading. It was painful, one word at a time, the battered dictionary never more than a few feet way.

Cooney drove carefully with the headlights of the police car shining hard on the back of their heads. They turned onto Dartmouth Street and Berry followed until they turned into Bill's driveway. Bill and Cooney sat silently as the police car passed behind them. After the car was gone everything was completely quiet. There were only a few lights burning on his entire street. One was in Bill's own kitchen.

"Thanks," Bill said.

"Not a problem," Cooney said. He had already put the pickup into reverse. Bill started to say more but Cooney gently stopped him. "See you tomorrow night for dinner."

As Bill walked to his house he saw Allison's pickup truck was in the garage and that made him feel better. She was nearly grown, but still he worried. The light being on in the kitchen felt warm and inviting but he wasn't sure he wanted to face her.

He took in more of the substantial September air as he walked along the side of the house toward the back door. It was a simple house; boxy, split-level, with a deck and mortgage. It was painted an off-white and was so middle American that sometimes Bill could not believe that he actually lived there. The yard was just a patch of tame grass that he had to mow in the summertime. Nothing really lived there except a few thrushes in the honeysuckle he had planted. In winter a band of English sparrows, a couple of juncos, and the occasional crossbill hung around the feeder, but they roosted somewhere else. He had built the deck himself and he was proud of it. But now, as he mounted the steps, he noticed again that the forty-five degree angles in the corners were not perfect. The little gaps that were left after the wood dried and shrunk were sometimes all he saw when he looked at the deck. But it was hell for stout, he thought, and he bounced a few times on the top step to prove it.

Allison was still up. She sat in her red housecoat at the kitchen table, almost as if she was waiting for him. But she never really waited up. Bugs, her ancient tomcat, was curled in her lap. She was reading an economics textbook and smiled when he came into the kitchen. Bill noticed that the book was open to the middle. She was a long way into it for the beginning of the semester. He touched her shoulder and she looked up. "Doing a little late-night training?" she asked.

Bill shrugged. "Can't expect to get into shape if you don't work out." He slumped in the chair opposite her and they sat smiling quietly at each other for a moment. He held her stare but was afraid she was going to ask where he had been the night before. She had been at the public meeting and knew about him making a fool of himself. She knew that construction began that morning at Mountain Air Estates. But she didn't ask where he'd been the night before and Bill felt relief and a pinprick of disappointment. Maybe she hadn't even missed him.

"I'm feeling a little like an old drunk," he finally said.

"What do you mean? You're not a drunk." She smiled and he tried to smile back. "Come on, Daddy. We both have a big day tomorrow."

Bill nodded and they rose. Bugs flowed silently from Allison's lap as she stood up. They all moved toward the hallway but when they got to the kitchen door, Allison stopped. "Oh, I forgot. Cooney brought over a hurt bird. It's in that box." She pointed to a small cardboard box in the quietest corner of the kitchen. She had received hurt birds before and knew to keep them cool, quiet, and in a dark place. "He says it's a merlin. It flew into his window. Knocked itself goofy."

"Yeah, I heard about it." Bill said. "Probably broke its neck, probably cold as a mackerel on the bottom of that box." He stared at the box from across the room and Allison stared at him. "I'll have a look in the morning."

"Don't you want to look at it now? Don't you think you should?"

Bill shook his head. "No. We should go to bed. Morning's soon enough."

He switched off the light and Allison followed him down the hall toward the bedrooms. When they came to her room she reached up on her tiptoes and kissed his cheek. He turned his head, embarrassed about his alcohol breath and was aware that her lips came into contact with a stubbly cheek. After she kissed him she looked into his eyes. "I love you, Daddy." Her voice was untypically plaintive. "More than anything."

He nodded. "I love you, too." But he had some trouble meeting her dark eyes.

5

ONCE IN her room, Allison felt exhausted but was not sure she could sleep. She let her housecoat drop to the floor at the edge of the bed and slipped naked between the sheets as she always did. But tonight her skin against the clean sheets did not feel sexy. It made her feel creepy and she got out of bed and found a pair of pajamas in her dresser drawer. Still she couldn't sleep. Her door was open a crack and she could hear her father running water in the bathroom. He was brushing his teeth and she smiled. He was so fastidious about some things. She was sure he had flossed first, and for some reason the innocence of her father flossing his teeth made her cry.

But she was too tired to cry hard. This was the second night she had not slept but the fatigue acted like a pot of coffee. She lay on her side and stared at the wall of her bedroom. She was not religious but she closed her eyes and prayed the prayer she'd been repeating for nearly a year now. There was no clear notion of God in her mind but she asked that her father be allowed to be happy. "He deserves it," she said. He was a very good man who had been unlucky. He was not good at coping with change. He was sentimental, not really a fighter. She thought it would be easier for him if he was, but it wasn't his fault. That came in your genes. She must have gotten her fight from her mother.

In a year she would be gone. If not a job, graduate school. She wondered what would happen when he was alone. He hadn't been alone since he was young. She had an envelope full of old pictures and knew he had been very different. There were shots of a young, strong man wearing a climbing helmet and harness with his weight against a rope. He was smiling and backing off a cliff. A picture of baby falcons in a wicker backpack and one of her father with a great silver falcon on his fist. That was the picture that said the most. The bright smile was as different from the gray face that had settled on him since the announcement of Brendan Prairie's fate as an expression could be. It was that old look that she longed to put back on his face.

But there had been other pictures in that envelope. The ones of her mother. She had looked so confident. She was tall and strong like Allison, with lighter hair and a set to the jaw that Allison was just beginning to notice in herself. It seemed to Allison that her mother had been prettier, though the resemblance shocked her.

It must have been quite a life. All the people looked so healthy and happy. The women were beautiful and the men handsome. There was a man with thick black hair. His eyes were large, with long lashes. His smile was breathtaking. On the back of the picture, in a looping hand that she knew was her mother's, was written the name Jamie Eaton.

She found those pictures a couple years before, tucked away in a faded candy box in the storage shed where her father kept a mountain of old out-of-date gear. He almost never opened the shed, and she found the box only by chance.

It was the morning after the night her father had failed to come home for the first time. To her knowledge she had never spent a night alone in the house. He had always been there when she went to bed and when she woke up in the morning. But that morning—it was a Saturday in the spring of her first year of college—there was no coffee perking when she woke up, no sound of running water in the shower. When she called into his bedroom there was no answer and that frightened her. The bed was made, it had not been slept in, and the house was empty. There was only a chill slipping down the hallway and immediately she feared the worst. She thought of squealing crashes on midnight highways, shattering windshields, and deafening impacts.

After she had checked the house thoroughly, she went back to her room, and in a conscious attempt to stay calm, forced herself to dress slowly. She tried to tell herself that her father might have found a woman. It had always been a fantasy of Allison's that her father would find a girlfriend and bring her home. When she was younger, she had wanted a mother for herself, but as she grew older and began to understand what men and women could give each other, she began to want a woman for her father. It was another thing he deserved. But her father had never stayed out all night with a woman. As far as she knew, he had not had a date since her mother died.

She had come into the kitchen resolved to call the police. By then there was no question in her mind that he was injured or dead. As she reached for the telephone, she thought she was prepared to hear it from the authorities. But her hand froze inches from the receiver. Through the back window she saw the door to the storage shed was open. It was always kept shut and locked and she thought, My God, we've been robbed, too. That tragedy made some kind of sense until she saw the large, bright, orange bundle in the yard.

Then her brain began trying to put the pieces together. She walked to the window to look closely into the backyard. Her fingertips touched the glass gently. What in the world?

But then the orange bundle moved and she saw a scramble of brown hair. It was a person in a sleeping bag, but still her mind was not ready to recognize her father. She moved to the back door and cracked opened the screen. Bill moved again and she realized what had happened.

It was during one of his rare spells of drinking. He must have drank too much, and when he got home, dug the old sleeping bag out of the shed. Allison walked out into the yard and looked down on her father. His snoring seemed comical to her just then and she laughed with relief. Though he'd told her that he spent most of his time outside when he was younger, it was the first time in her life she had seen him sleeping out-of-doors. He was sleeping soundly and once she knew he was safe she looked up to the gaping door of the storage shed.

Until that moment the contents of the shed had not interested her. But the orange sleeping bag had come from in there and its brightness surprised her. She had thought everything in the shed was khaki, with cobwebs and a musty smell. She took a step closer and peered inside as if it was the cave of Ali Baba. Before her eyes had focused, she knew the shed held more than she had ever imagined. The dusty trunks and duffel bags were mysterious to her that day and there, on the floor, was the candy box with the lid laid aside and the pictures bared to the morning light. An old, black flashlight lay beside the box and she picked it up and pushed the switch. The batteries were dead and she imagined her father sitting on the floor in the dark going slowly through the pictures as the light failed.

Then she sat on the floor where her father must have sat and brought the mass of pictures out and into her lap. Here was her mother. Here was her father in another time. And she felt immediately stupid for knowing so little about their life.

The scenery in the background was as beautiful as the people; slate gray cliffs and deep green valleys, peopleless expanses and powder blue skies. The box of photographs gave Allison a glimpse of what her parents had been like before her time and suddenly she knew it was the loss of those times that had injured her father. She leafed through the photos, dazed; sagebrush flats dusted with snow, a helicopter hovering over a rugged cliff, campsites beside moving water.

Then she felt her father over her shoulder, watching the pictures turn in her hands. His voice didn't startle her. "I was always a poor photographer," he said.

She didn't look up. Her eyes would not come loose from the pictures. "They're beautiful."

"Snapshots," he said.

A thunderstorm over the mountains. Antelope strung out across snow-covered wheat stubble. Her father kneeling beside a camp stove, something frying in a skillet.

"You were pretty cute."

Then her mother with a blue backpack. Neither spoke a word until the picture of Jamie Eaton flipped to the top. The silence intensified and Allison felt the tension. Still she wanted to know who this was. "This guy," she said. "A friend?"

When he didn't answer Allison looked to her father. His eyes were set on the picture. They revealed a pain she had never seen before. When he felt her watching, his face relaxed. "Just a jerk," he said. Then, "No. He just didn't understand."

But Allison kept watching her father until he went on. "He was a rich kid. Had some connection with the Arabs. I was supposed to teach him about reintroducing peregrine falcons."

"And?"

Bill laughed. "He wasn't a very good student." He was trying to lighten up this discussion. His daughter felt him trying to wiggle free of her, and she wasn't going to allow it.

"And?" she repeated.

"And he had power." Bill turned away and went to where the sleeping bag was still rolled out on the ground. He picked up the stuff sack that lay beside it and began putting the bag away. But Allison followed him, the pictures still in her hand.

"I want to know about him," Allison said, but when her father looked up from the sleeping bag, she could see he should not be pushed.

"People like that see the whole world and everything in it as a commodity," Bill said. He was not angry but there was something frightening about the way he reached out and took the pictures from her hand. He found the one of Jamie and handed the rest back to Allison. Without looking up he slowly and deliberately tore the picture to shreds and tossed the pieces over the back fence. Then he looked deep into Allison's eyes.

"You've grown so big," he said. "Somehow I thought I could avoid talking to you. But you're too much like your mother to resist." A smile crept across his face. "You got time to hear a story?"

Allison nodded. "You bet."

"I'll put these things away. You go start a pot of coffee." He rubbed his temples. "I need coffee." But when he reached for the rest of the pictures, Allison would not give them up.

Now, as she lay in her bed, the memory of that day loomed in her consciousness. As on many nights before, it would not let her sleep. Her father told her a startling story. And as he carefully let it out, she came to see how he could be the way he was.

The falcons had brought them together. Allison imagined her parents falling in love in a green mountain valley as they watched young falcons developing their powers of flight high above, around a towering cliff. The image touched her and forced a sad smile even in her darkened bedroom. It was the falcons, she thought. Though she could not remember him training a falcon, she knew something about that process was vital for him. From his story, she learned what she had long suspected— the birds and the places they lived made her father's life worth living. When those things were taken from him, he sank. He lost his strength.

Now the tenuous nature of her father's strength frightened her. Some nights she lay in her bed paralyzed by fear. She came to think that her father could die, and her belief that she was the only one who could help him weighed her down. It was as if the tables had been turned. In her mind she was the parent and he was the child. She had been frightened for her father for years but tonight she was frightened for herself.

She fell asleep thinking of her father as a child. It was a thought filled with responsibility, but she felt up to it. She would keep doing what she must to protect him. It was like being a mother and she drifted deeper into sleep with that poignant desire to nurture engulfing her. But those thoughts would not stay.

Her mind turned quickly to flashes of light interspersed with penetrating darkness. Somehow she was still doing those good things but the world had gone mean and her dream took on a nightmare quality of evil happening, but with no focus on exactly what those evils were. She awoke with a lurch and was sitting up by the time she realized she was in her own bed. Bugs was curled tight on the pillow beside her. She stroked the cat and closed her eyes tight to drive away the dream. When she opened them, there was a faint glow from down the hall. It was the kitchen light and at first she thought it was morning. But when she looked at the clock she saw that she had only been asleep a few minutes.

The bathrobe was on the floor where she had dropped it, and she slipped it on as she made her way down the hall toward the light. When she saw that her father was in the kitchen she made as little noise as possible. She didn't want him to know that she was there because she seldom got the opportunity to watch him when he thought he was alone. He knelt on the floor near the cardboard box that held the hurt bird. He wore only his blue jeans and his stiff leg stretched out straight to the side. She knew there was a chance he did not intend to sleep in his bed that night. He had taken to leaving the sleeping bag on top of the dryer on the back porch where he could take it up easily as he slipped from the back door. She hoped he would stay in the house tonight. It would help her sleep to know he was there.

Allison wasn't sure if her father's habit of sleeping alone on the grass was good for him or not. But she knew that what she was seeing now was good. The box flaps were already open and he was lowering his hands slowly into the darkness where the injured merlin lay. His eyes were cast slightly to the side so the little falcon would not feel the added pressure of his stare. He moved his hands very slowly, with uncommon gentleness.

His reach seemed to take forever but Allison didn't mind. It was so rare that she got to see him like this that she wished he would take all night. It gave her a chance to notice the arms; the remnants of full, pulsing biceps and lats that could, even now, work for hour upon hour. And the skin—a few white scars gathered over the years and the frail transparency that results from long days in the sun, wind, and cold. If a stranger were to look at him there on the floor he might not see much. But Allison could see in her father's movements the wisdom of years. To watch him bring the injured bird from the box and turn it slowly in the pale light made her chin quiver.

He held the little falcon close and examined the head that was twisted back and up like a brain damaged child's. Bill's hazel eyes looked into the strickened falcon's black eyes and Allison could see that he was searching his memory for a clue. She wanted to keep watching him but if he turned and found her staring he would be embarrassed. She left him like that and moved back down the hallway and into her bed. But she lay awake, filled with worry and wonder. She tried to picture her father happy, as he was in the photographs. She tried to imagine him smiling and gathering her mother up in those aging arms, touching her as gently as he had touched the injured falcon.

6

BILL WOKE from a dream of walking a pasture edge to the sound of Allison calling in to him before she left for school. He felt heavy in the bed and grunted affirmation that he was awake. He used to like early morning, but in the last few years he had trouble finding the energy to propel himself up and out of bed. The last two nights' alcohol and the uninspiring day teaching freshman biology that lay ahead of him were conspiring to cheat him of a good morning attitude. All it took was one excuse— headache; boring day. Any one of a hundred other excuses could sour him on a coming day. He had to force himself to sit up in bed.

Allison was leaning into his bedroom and looked wide awake. She was smiling and he got the feeling that she was humoring him. They exchanged words—something about orange juice and bagels—then she was gone and Bill had to struggle to keep from rolling over and going back to sleep. But there was little choice. His first class was at ten o'clock, and even though he could give his lecture by rote, he wanted to go over it and try to find something new and interesting about the scientific method to which his freshmen could connect.

It wasn't an easy task. The week before a student had called the text "about as lively as a dead frog." That was a severe indictment for a biology text, but Bill had to agree. He spent the first two classes talking about his ideas of biology, how important he thought it was that everyone understood the similarities and differences among the species. But today he would have to begin going through the book, A Journey Into Life. It was a great title for a biology text, but a quick glance at the table of contents showed that its authors approached the journey into life quite differently from the way he did. There was this chapter on the scientific method, which Bill supposed was necessary. But then they began with cells. Hundreds of pages of cell biology, with almost no mention of the plants and animals that were made up of those cells. Bill believed more students would be hooked on biology if they started with species they were interested in and worked down to the cellular level. That is what he had talked about in his first lectures—how an intense interest in and relationship to some living thing, a hands-on experience, was possible and did more to foster an interest in how those things functioned than any other experience a person could have. If they listened to what he said, they were going to be as bored as he was wading through the cellular biology chapters.

Of course, he had been talking of his own experience. In his case it had been the birds of prey, but it could have been muskrats or white-tailed deer, tropical fish or snakes, trout. It could have been rhododendrons and azaleas for that matter. Who could fall in love for the first time with a cell? What eighteen-year-old gives a shit about mitosis? He was talking out loud now—into the mirror and shaking his razor to emphasize his point. There were a few dollops of shaving cream splattered across his reflection. But complaining about the textbook was useless. He'd been doing it since he got the job, and it had done absolutely no good. It had been selected by a committee when he was a very junior member of the department. The book was sacrosanct in the way committee decisions often became.

It had come as something of a shock that universities were run a lot like government agencies. His colleagues in the biology department were like the people he had known in the Park Service; they would do anything to keep from taking a chance—especially if their job security might come into question.

In the university he had to work closely with people like that, but in the Park Service he had been mercifully removed from the career bureaucrats. He had been only a field-worker. Margaret fought the battles for money. She stuck her neck out on several occasions to demand that the Park Service not sit on its collective hands and shirk its legal duty to reintroduce peregrine falcons to the national parks. Bill gave Margaret a lot of credit. If it hadn't been for her going to bat for private foundations focused on the peregrine's recovery, arguing the Park Service's responsibility in light of the Endangered Species Act, and hiring "less traditional" people to get the job done, the Park Service might have committed itself into inaction. Instead of aiding the recovery of an endangered species, they might have contributed to its extinction. He hoped he would fight just as hard for a new textbook when the time came. Of course, it might cost him his job the way it had finally cost Margaret hers. Bill shrugged. Maybe he'd end up with a better job the way Margaret had. But if he did, he hoped it wouldn't be in law enforcement. A job like that would kill him.

Bill was dressed now and was starting to feel better. He was in the kitchen and poured himself a cup of coffee. It was strong and rich with just a hint of cinnamon. Neither Allison nor he was much on flavored coffees, but occasionally he found this tiny hint of cinnamon in the first cup and it tasted good. He rummaged around looking for the morning paper. He wanted to read about what had happened at Mountain Air Estates but there was no paper. Maybe Allison took it to school. He sat at the table and from nowhere came thoughts of Margaret Adamson.

He'd thought many times of her over the years but in isolated snippets—the day they met during their freshman year, the time she nursed him through the flu. He remembered the way she kissed and the pain on her face when she saw the way he looked at Ellen. He had remembered a million little things about Margaret and they usually sneaked up on him. Seeing her again had shocked him and now she was part of that memory rush boiling in his mind. Had he not got to drinking he would have looked her up. She was sure to think he was still mad at her, sure to think he'd be madder yet for the things she had to say at the meeting. But he wasn't mad at Margaret. She was only doing her job. He had learned a lot about what it meant to do one's job. The agents that arrested him all those years ago probably didn't even know her, but when she called, he had been as cold as possible. That was a poor way to leave a relationship as rich as theirs.

Since he and Allison had had their heart-to-heart and he'd told her about the old days, she had been working on him to get back into falconry. Margaret's name had come up. She was a first love, like falconry itself, and Bill had a hard time separating the memories. They had done everything together in those early years. Margaret had been there for most of the really important events in his life.

Allison must have seen something in the way he talked about Margaret because she came right out in the direct way Bill loved and asked if they had been lovers. "But before your mother," he assured her. After Ellen, he had not thought of Margaret in that way. Now he wondered why that was so.

He sat at the table wondering for a full minute. Then a resolution came to him with certainty. After he was done at school he'd find out where Margaret was staying and look her up. They wouldn't talk about Brendan Prairie or the time he got arrested for trapping a gyrfalcon without getting a permit first. They wouldn't talk about Ellen or Jamie Eaton. They'd talk about the peregrine falcons they helped release in the Rocky Mountains. Maybe they'd talk about hunting grouse when they were both still students. They'd talk about the great Swainson's hawk migrations they had witnessed—when the fields and fence posts would be covered with birds for miles. He'd remind her of the day they had seen the whooping cranes at Grays Lake in Idaho. Yes. He'd go find Margaret and they'd get back on track. Right after his one o'clock class.

His one o'clock class.

By then he might have figured out how to make a lecture on the scientific method interesting. He rose to take his empty cup to the sink and saw the box that held the injured falcon. He hadn't forgotten, far from it. The truth was he'd been dreading to look at the bird. From his examination the night before he guessed it had a neurological injury. Just how severe was hard to tell. Like all animals, birds are poor patients. They can't tell you where it hurts. They wouldn't if they could. Their only chance

in the wild is to not look hurt. They keep up the charade until
they can no longer manage. They seldom recover from a serious
injury. If they do, they almost never regain the vitality needed
to be wild again. Out of the hundreds of hurt birds that Bill had
seen over the years he felt sure only those who had very short-
term injuries ever made it. It was usually best to leave them
alone and quiet for a day or so and, if they got better, to release
them as soon as possible. If they didn't show signs of a quick recovery, it was most humane to euthanize them.

He slowly opened the flap of the box and peered in as unob-
trusively as possible. The little falcon was only slightly larger
than a robin. It lay still on the floor of the box. Its head remained twisted but it was not dead yet. Its black eyes stared
brightly upward and Bill gently shut the flap. It was sad because,
except for the neck injury, the merlin seemed healthy. It was an
adult male with a slate blue back and a crisply barred tail. Bill
had been particularly taken by the pale mustache stripes and the
jet black eyes. They seemed to be a deeper black than most, like
gleaming drops of rich oil paint. The night before the merlin
had felt fat in Bill's hand. That meant he had been a good
hunter and Bill imagined him streaking over the prairie, following the contour of the earth at tremendous speed, hoping to surprise a bobolink or a horned lark. He touched the box softly. A
shame. He had probably been shooting along the front wall of
Cooney Jenkin's cabin when he saw the front window and decided to cut through. He might have hit the glass going forty
miles an hour. Now it was all over. Bill would put him down
when he got to the laboratory. He had syringes there and a bottle of potassium chloride.

IT WAS A nice morning for a walk, which was good because Bill
had to retrieve his car from where he left it the night before. The
morning air made him feel better and the first thing he did when
he got to the car was roll down the windows so he could continue taking it in as he returned to the house for the merlin.

He drove gently so the bird would not be bounced around in

the cardboard box. He crawled over the speed bumps in the university parking lot. There was supposed to be a parking place for him near the science building but there was almost always a jalopy of some kind parked under the sign with his name. Today was no exception. This time it was a be-chromed pickup truck jacked up so high that it must have required a ladder to get into the cab. A penismobile, Bill thought. He took a turn around the parking lot and finally found a place in nearly the last row.

A few students were wandering around the halls of the science building, but it was still a half hour before the ten o'clock classes began. There was just time to euthanize the merlin before he had to teach. He slipped into his office and cleared a place on his desk to put the box. He glanced around the room. Books were stacked to the ceiling in every corner. The tropical fish tank needed cleaning. Papers from last spring were scattered under a work table. A gerbil colony threatened to overpopulate itself. A box with two stale donuts, remnants of yesterday's breakfast. He shook his head then started toward the lab to get a syringe of potassium chloride. The classroom where he did his teaching was connected directly to his office and, as he passed through, he found a student already in his seat, pouring over the assignment for the day. The student was a tall, thin boy dressed in jeans and cowboy boots. He was almost certainly a rancher's son—a first-year student. The boy looked up at Bill and, although they looked nothing alike, Bill could see himself years before. "Morning, Mr. Malone."

Bill nodded. "Morning." He could not remember the boy's name but made a note to look it up as soon as he could.

When he passed the boy on his return from the lab he looked down at the book he was studying. It was that damned chapter on the scientific method, and the boy had highlighted almost every line. There was also a notebook open and an entire page filled with neat rows of small writing. The loaded syringe was in the pocket of Bill's shirt. He had determined to get his little execution over quickly, but the neatness of the handwriting and the diligence of this student fascinated him. He was suddenly compelled to find out just what this boy found interesting

in the chapter Bill thought monumentally boring. He stopped
and looked down at the boy. "I'm sorry," he said. "But I've forgotten your name."

"Cody Carlson, sir. I'm in your ten o'clock class."

"Yes, I remember you." He nodded toward the notebook.
"Really getting into this?"

The boy laughed nervously. "Yeah, it's interesting. We never
talked about this stuff where I went to high school."

"And where was that?"

"Perkins County High School. My dad rented a room for me
in Bison. We live too far out." He seemed embarrassed by this
fact, but when he said it he sat up a little straighter and his chin
thrust forward a fraction of an inch.

"And you never talked about the scientific method at your
high school?"

The boy shrugged. "I suppose they mentioned it. But if they
did, I never saw the logic. I mean, this makes sense. Step by step.
It's a plan for figuring things out."

Bill couldn't help staring at the boy. It was hard to believe
that approaching a problem scientifically was news to anybody.
Suddenly he realized that the lecture for today was not trivial or
theoretical, that if you had never thought about how to system-
atically solve a problem it could be the most important lecture of
your life. He stood gazing at the boy. For God's sake, he thought,
how dumb can you be? And he wasn't referring to Cody Carlson.

A rapid *ki ki ki ki* sound roused Bill from thought. Both he
and Cody were surprised. The boy because he did not recognize
the sound as the cry of the merlin in the box, and Bill, because
the merlin hadn't made any noise until that moment. A few
more students were trailing in so Bill hurried to his office and
took the syringe from his pocket. But it was too late now. He
was thinking about what he would say to the classes of students
he would face during the day. The key to making it relevant had
been in the eighteen-year-old's open face. He lay the syringe on
the desk beside the box and closed his eyes. He concentrated on
nothing for several minutes, then turned and reentered the
classroom.

By one o'clock, at the end of his second lecture, he was feeling good about his performance. The first class had been attentive. Cody Carlson had asked several insightful questions. The second class was even better. Their eyes had remained glued to Bill as he chronicled the evolution of scientific thought. They loved the examples of how nonscientific thought had led people to comic conclusions. Hummingbirds did not migrate on the backs of geese. Rain did not follow the plow.

The students were still asking questions when the bell sounded and Bill was on a roll. These kind of days, in the teaching racket, were not common. He intended to make the best of it by taking the comments that raised the most interest in the two earlier classes and using them in the last class. He was experiencing a rare teaching high as the students of the next class filed through the door. But when Allison walked in with her Kelty backpack over one shoulder and wearing her fleece jacket, he became self-conscious.

She was not a freshman and was not in his class. But she smiled at him and motioned to an empty seat in the back row. Would it be all right if she stayed to listen? How could he resist. All the boys in the class were twisted around in their seats to stare at her and Bill felt a pang of pity for them. The girls in the class looked miffed. Sure. Sit down. He nodded to her and wondered what the students thought. He didn't want them thinking this woman was there for the wrong reasons. "She's my daughter," he said. There were a few chuckles from the class. "Just checking up on me, right?"

Allison nodded and Bill began to speak. He had of course been through this lecture twice before and, though he was perhaps not as spontaneous as he would have liked, the class responded well. But he never forgot that Allison was in the back row. In fact, toward the end of the class, when the discussion had evolved beautifully into one student questioning another, Bill was able to glance up. He found Allison watching the students in the debate. Just then she looked so much like her mother that Bill couldn't take his eyes away. He heard the students talking but did not realize that the discussion had come back to him until Allison looked at him and made a face. That brought him back to the present and he fumbled with a paper on the podium as he figured out where things were. The class was nearly over and he felt a need to bring everything to a concise end, but as all eyes came back to him, the shrill *ki ki ki ki* sounded again from his office and the room went completely silent.

Bill was taken by surprise and someone said, "What the hell is that?" Students began to laugh and the clock ticked to the hour. A few students stood up to leave. He looked over their heads and saw that Allison had guessed that the sound was the merlin and for some reason that made him proud. She beamed at him when the sound came again. The bird was still alive and she was thrilled. Then the bell sounded and she stood for a moment smiling. Her face was smooth and young but the eyes were those of a much older woman. Students moved between them and she worked her way to the front of the class.

"The merlin is better?"

"He's still kicking." Bill had gathered up his notes and folded them into the textbook. They moved toward his office.

"Keep him, Daddy."

"Keep him?"

"You're still a licensed falconer. Keep him and fly him the way you talked about."

Bill laughed. "Train him to kill grouse?"

"No. Of course not. He's too small. Sparrows, starlings. Just fly him, Daddy. I think it would be good for you."

Bill exaggerated his limp as they entered his office. "You think I'm a little old for grouse hawking? Think I should go to sparrow hawking?"

Allison frowned. "I didn't mean that. It would just be fun to see a falcon hunt. Any falcon."

Bill was going to go on teasing her but what she said and the way she said it touched him. She was right, it would be great fun to see a falcon hunt again, and she wasn't just saying it for him. "Honey," Bill said. "He's a real sick bird. He probably won't make it."

Bill started to lay his book on the pile on the desk. But then he saw the syringe and put the biology text over it so Allison wouldn't see. "Oh, I feel so sorry for him," Allison said.

"I know, honey, it's sad. Don't think about it." He was about to say something that might take Allison's mind off the bird, when there was a gentle knocking on the door frame.

When they turned, Margaret Adamson stood not three feet away. "Maggie," Bill said.

But Margaret was looking at Allison. "My God, she's as lovely as Ellen."

Bill smiled and nodded. "Yeah, she sure doesn't take after me in the looks department." He was talking to cover his surprise. Here was Margaret Adamson. He needed to do something so he stepped forward and embraced her.

They held like that, very still with eyes closed. Then they pulled apart and looked at each other with smirks on their faces. "Sorry I stormed out of there the other night." Bill said. "I planned to get a hold of you today."

"Good to see you," Margaret said.

"You, too." They looked at each other for another moment then went embarrassed. They turned to Allison, who looked puzzled. "This," Bill said, "is Margaret Adamson."

"Oh, Daddy's told me all about you."

"And I held you when you were just a baby."

"A long time ago," Bill said.

"Yes, indeed." Margaret held her hand out to Allison and Allison took it with a smile.

"Whoa," Margaret said. "Strong, too."

"She pumps iron and runs," Bill said.

"Daddy."

"A runner? Me, too! That's good. Do you climb rocks and chase falcons?"

"No," Allison said. "But I'd like to. If I could get this old guy to show me how."

"If you could," Margaret said, "you'd have a great teacher."

They stood silent for an instant. Then Allison spoke up.

"I've got a study date at the grill. It's nice to meet you, Margaret."

"Call me Maggie. Your father always did."

"Okay. Will I see you again, Maggie?"

"Hard to say. I'm supposed to go back to Denver tomorrow. My business is about finished here."

"Well," Allison said, "I hope I do."

They shook hands again and Allison kissed her father good-bye.

Allison's smile was devilish. "You two behave, now," she said as she walked out.

That left the room a little empty. The old friends didn't look at each other. They were searching for the right thing to say. Finally, Bill spoke. "We should have kept in touch."

"Yeah, I tried to find you a couple times after I heard what happened to Ellen. No one seemed to know where you'd gone."

"I went back and stayed with my folks. They were a big help with Allison. We stayed with them a couple years, then I finished graduate school at South Dakota State."

"I figured if you wanted to talk to me, you'd call."

"I did want to talk to you but I wasn't at my best." Bill made his way to the other side of the desk.

"You were pissed about Mathews taking your bird away and releasing it."

"Releasing it?"

"Yeah, he confiscated it for evidence and after your day in court took it back to where you caught it and released it."

"Right." Bill sat down at his desk.

"God. You should have just forgotten about it." Margaret had moved around in front of him and bent down to look into his face. "You got fined twenty-five bucks. It was a technicality."

Bill looked up, hesitated, then began to nod. "You weren't in on it, were you?"

"No. Did you think I was? Was that it?"

"No, that wasn't it. Maybe part of it, but things went pretty bad for me for a while there. I cut ties with everyone."

They were looking at each other now and Margaret took a

deep breath. "I was so sorry to hear about Ellen." Bill nod-ded and, in a moment, Margaret said, "God, Bill, we got some history."

Bill nodded again. "We got history. It's good to see you."

"Good to see you, too. Now what happened to that leg?"

"A souvenir of those bad times. More history." He smiled the way Margaret remembered. "It's pretty stiff but it still works." He moved the leg, but the knee stayed rigid. His eyes stayed on the leg; he was thinking. "How would you like to go for a walk this afternoon," he said, "then over to a friend's house for dinner?" When he stopped talking the room seemed too quiet. "The big ducks are starting to move through and I think you'd get a kick out of my friend."

Margaret didn't let the room go quiet again. "I'd love it," she said. "I'd have to go back to the hotel for hiking boots. But I need the exercise. I missed my run this morning. A guy kept me up 'til after ten o'clock."

"Holy smokes, that late? What was the celebration?"

"No celebration. It was the sheriff. It was about Andy Arnold."

"What about him?"

"Don't you read the newspaper? He's dead, Bill."

"Dead?" Bill studied her for an instant, as if he was trying to decide if she was kidding him. "You're serious."

"Yep."

"He was the one that got run over at the construction site?"

"Yeah. I saw it. A machine crushed him."

"Up at Brendan Prairie." Bill spoke softly and his eyes narrowed as if he could see that high mountain meadow in his mind.

"It was awful."

Bill thought about it for an instant. "I'm sorry you had to see it," he said and shook his head. "Andy Arnold, Jesus."

"I spent a whole day with him," Margaret said. "He was an all right guy."

"I suppose." Bill shrugged. "I guess I'll never get used to chamber of commerce types. It's those polyester suits and the dreams of empire."

Margaret looked away from him. "He didn't know. He was just tying to get along."

Bill nodded slowly. "I'm sorry." Then he moved around to where Margaret had to look at him. "You're not going to let this jeopardize our walk, are you? There are more important things than Andy Arnold." He smiled.

"No," Margaret said without a moment's thought. "I'm not going to let anything jeopardize this walk. I've been wanting to go walking with you for fifteen years."

"Where are you staying? I'll pick you up about five."

"You got it. The Franklin in Deadwood. Five o'clock." They stood smirking at each other again. "Good to see you, Billy Boy."

"You too, Maggie."

AFTER Margaret left, Bill's mind was a jumble. Andy Arnold was dead. And Margaret saw it. Their lives seemed destined to tangle. Neither of them had mentioned the fact that she had been the one to sign Brendan Prairie's death warrant. He wanted to tell her that he understood. Not that it was all right, but that he understood. He was glad she'd heard about Ellen's accident. That was one thing he wouldn't have to explain. But he was amazed that she knew so little about what had happened with that gyrfalcon up in Montana. He shook his head. Of course she didn't know. How could he have thought otherwise. Then there was the way she and Allison had taken to each other. And Andy Arnold. Christ, Andy Arnold.

He nearly let his thoughts avalanche over him. But no, that wouldn't do. He shouldn't let himself slip into the past. It would ruin his walk with Margaret, spoil dinner at Cooney Jenkins's. He looked around the office for something to do. He saw the textbook and knew the syringe filled with potassium chloride was underneath. Here was something that would certainly take his mind off Margaret, Ellen, and Andy Arnold. He hated to think how many times he had had to use a syringe of potassium chloride on sick or injured birds of prey. It was a grim business and he especially wished he had never had to use it that first time, never had to see that wild gyrfalcon die the way it had in a strange and hostile land. But he had a responsibility that could not be shirked. He agreed with the poet, Robinson Jeffers; he would sooner kill a man than a hawk. But he didn't have that choice.

He opened the flap slowly, expecting to see the fierce little bird contorted as before with humiliating paralysis or, mercifully for them both, dead at the bottom of the box. But that was not the case. The head was still twisted but now the merlin sat up on his haunches, the feet balled in front of him. He had almost no control over his movements but Bill could see that the black eyes were trying to meet his own. The overhead light spilled into the box and Bill was sorry about that. It drenched the falcon in brightness, just the wrong thing at a time like this. But the light accentuated the bird's beauty. Its cere and feet were a waxy yellow, nearly orange. Its back was a dusky blue. Bill held the syringe in his right hand and intended to reach into the box with his left—it was important to do this with as little trauma to the bird as possible. But when he moved his hand the merlin's eyes shifted and the beak opened. Crippled as he was, the bird was defiant and a strident *ki ki ki ki* reverberated from the box.

Bill's hand retracted involuntarily. Here was raw and wild courage—resilience. It shook him and he laid the syringe back on the desk. What was more difficult than killing a bird of prey? He was not a silly, blind, lover of life for its own sake. He knew death was equally important and that, particularly for wild things, it was often preferable. But this refusal to yield—Jeffers's "implacable arrogance"—complicated the equation. He looked into the merlin's glittering eyes and saw a profound, fantastic belief in freedom. He knew this was one of the qualities that made the birds of prey magical. Even severely injured, the merlin had the power to humble him.

But because he loved such birds so, he felt obligated to protect them from the truth about their freedom. Bill had always seen it as a question of dignity. Without the majesty of precision flight there was no dignity for these birds, and precision flight was a function of physical perfection. The chances were almost nil that this bird would ever fly with the kind of power it would need to match the defiance in its eyes. Still, Bill reasoned its condition was not deteriorating. He rationalized that recovery was not impossible. He felt himself losing his stomach for killing hawks and hoped it was not simply cowardice.

But keeping the bird in captivity long enough for it to recover could hurt it as much as the impact with Cooney Jenkins's window. Falcons were not built to hit windows or live in boxes. Their feathers were delicate and irreplaceable, their feet and minds fragile. One damaged flight feather or a badly bruised foot could mean its life, even if the neurological problem cured itself. And there was the matter of food. This bird had not eaten for at least a day. Was eating even possible?

Bill lowered the flap of the box top. Time to decide. He didn't want the responsibility of keeping this wild thing. He had seen too many deteriorate beyond repair by fighting captivity. He had seen them beat themselves to tatters and had never considered that an acceptable alternative to a painless death. He looked at the syringe, then raised his eyes and surveyed his office. The mess disheartened him, but when his eyes fell on the gerbil cage his spirits rose.

This was it. A test. A way to see if there was any chance the merlin could survive. It was, after all, a fight that all wild things were familiar with. This merlin would have to find the strength to kill a gerbil. It would have to feed itself because Bill would not insult it by holding it and stuffing food down its throat.

The gerbil colony was a mass of seething rodents, and Bill reached down into the ball of movement and came up with a half-grown juvenile. He cupped it in his hand and carried it to the merlin's box but did not toss it in rudely. He gave the merlin every chance; he opened the box gently so the bird's eyes could get used to the light, then carefully lowered his cupped hand into the box and released the gerbil. Once the gerbil was loose, Bill moved his head back and watched from as far away as he could.

The gerbil blinked and looked around the box. It stood up on its hind legs and sniffed the air. Apparently it did not associate the smell of merlin with danger because it began to move casually, investigating its new surroundings. The merlin was still on its haunches with its head twisted cruelly back and to the side. Only his eyes seemed to be able to move and even though the gerbil was within his range of vision, he did not seem to be watching it. He may have been watching Bill, or he may have been staring off into space. It was not until the gerbil actually came up to him and sniffed his feathers that the eyes showed any sign that he even noticed there was a rodent in the box with him. The falcon had to be hungry. If he had the power to survive, he would take the gerbil now.

But the merlin didn't move, and Bill felt something slump inside. Now he had no choice. He reached slowly for the syringe, picked it up, and let it lay there in his hand. He looked down at the needle and the tube of poison and tried to see it as an instrument of mercy. He closed his eyes and wondered why humans alone understood the concept of mercy. It was a moment before he was ready to do what he must.

But just as he opened his eyes, he heard a shuffling in the box. When he looked down, one of the merlin's feet was firmly around the gerbil's neck. The rodent was rigid and still. The merlin was trying to overcome the paralysis of his neck and strained toward the gerbil. Bill watched as the little falcon battled to straighten its neck enough to do what it had to do. Slowly, a quarter of an inch at a time, the beak came within range of the vertebrae at the base of the gerbil's head. It seemed to take forever, but finally the notched beak found the sweet spot and nestled into the fur almost lovingly.

When the merlin finally broke the gerbil's neck, Bill sat back in his chair, exhausted, and stared at the ceiling. He knew the chances were still great that he would have to use the syringe. But he was thankful for the reprieve. He slid the syringe into a desk drawer and exhaled toward the ceiling.

7

IT WAS perfect weather for a walk in one of the high meadows in the central hills. But the only access to that meadow was over a rutted logging road, and Bill's car didn't have enough clearance. So before he left campus he went to the student union to find Allison and trade his car for her pickup. Allison was glad to give up her keys. She didn't say much. She just grinned at her father, holding the keys out to him, allowing him to use the truck.

Bill didn't take Margaret to Brendan Prairie. He took her to a similar place that he knew she would recognize as the same habitat type. The meadow was only a hundred acres but a small stream ran through the middle. Like Brendan Prairie, it was ringed with the Black Hill's sea of dark ponderosa pines, and fingers of aspen snaked up the hillsides from the island of grass. Autumn was further along at that elevation, and the aspen shimmered yellow-orange in the afternoon breeze. The first snow would soon come up here and the leaves wouldn't last long after it struck.

They gazed up the golden draws as they walked the edge of the meadow. Some leaves had already fallen, and the forest floor below the aspens looked as if they had been manicured, trimmed in a crinkly, orange shag. Juncos flitted in the aspen branches and, in the draws that emptied out onto the miniature prairie, thrushes bounced in the sumac and snowberry bushes. The only green left in the grasses was a subtle shading along the central vein of each blade. They knelt down in the cushion of vegetation and tried to identify all the species of grasses and forbes within their reach. Because Bill lived there, he knew many more than Margaret. He pointed out two sedges that she had never seen before. Then the native grasses—junegrass, little bluestem, grama grass, and prairie dropseed—all within a few feet of them. They giggled like two kids with each successful identification. It was as if no time had passed, as if a huge chunk of their lives had never happened.

Beavers had dammed the stream at the far end of the meadow—in fact, the ancestors of these beavers had probably created the meadow by flooding out the original trees—and a small flock of mallards came off the pond behind the barricade of mud and aspen branches.

Bill held his index finger to his lips then mouthed the words *brook trout* as he pointed to the pond. He motioned for Margaret to keep down and they crawled to the edge of the pond. The sun was behind them and the water completely transparent so they were able to see two blood orange male brookies laying on the bottom. The fish wore their breeding colors, and the white and black on their fins seemed too bright to be real. Bill and Margaret knelt on the bank until one of the fish moved sideways, elevated, then snapped the smoothness of the pond as it sucked an invisible insect from the surface. They both exhaled. "Wow!" And the fish were gone, the spell broken.

They made the whole loop around the meadow and walked the last few hundred yards, with the sun behind the pine forest but still smudging the sky with color and offering enough light to see every feature of the terrain ahead of them. Margaret walked easily. Bill remembered that she could always keep up with him. She had proved it many times. Now, of course, his knee was stiff. She could walk him into the ground.

Margaret was thinking the same thing. The tranquility of the meadow made it hard not to notice his halting gait and she thought again of asking what had happened. But the reunion was going so painlessly she didn't want to chance ruining it with too many questions. There would be time enough for talking at dinner. Now she just wanted to enjoy herself. She didn't get outside enough. She had gotten into wildlife work twenty-five years before—back when women were a rarity in the field. She had entered the field to work with and fight for wildlife, and because she enjoyed walks like this one. But with each passing year there had been less and less time for walks. There had been more and more time spent organizing sting operations. More time behind a desk, more and more opportunity to compromise in her fight for wild things. It wasn't long before she began to feel used, isolated from the objects of her passion.

With Bill walking beside her she couldn't help thinking that the only important thing she had ever done was their work reestablishing peregrine falcons after the DDT holocaust. What had she done since? Not much. A few highly publicized arrests of poachers, some undercover work with fur exporters. She had even gained some notoriety for her instincts. But nothing that would have a lasting effect on the world. The time she had spent—mostly with this man—doing prey species surveys, finding places to release falcons, walking like this for hundreds of miles, was the defining feature of her life. But now all that seemed like ancient history.

As they walked the last few yards to the car she admitted to herself that her life was unhappy. Moving to law enforcement had been a mistake. It had not been good for her. She had fought hard at first, but the weight of the bureaucracy had worn her down. Maybe Bill had been right to go a different direction. But he didn't seem much happier. Maybe the world just wasn't right for people like them. She felt some guilt lumping herself with Bill. He had always been a breed apart. Still, they might well share a fatal flaw. Maybe it was lethal to care so deeply about towhees and wheatgrass and brook trout. Maybe it was nuts to wonder how those things all fit together. Maybe people like her and Bill were anachronisms. Maybe they were as endangered as black-footed ferrets or California condors. That idea struck her as funny.

"We're a couple of old condors," she said.

Their walk was finished and Bill leaned against the car with his bad leg stretched out and no weight on it. He exhaled loudly. "Sometimes I feel more like an archaeopteryx," he said.

Margaret laughed and leaned against the car with him. They were silent. They passed the last fifteen minutes of the day with their minds blank, feeling no distance between them or between themselves and the pine tree darkness that grew to engulf the whole meadow. It was as if only yesterday was the last time they stood watching night come gently over a sea of solitude. As if there had never been an Ellen Mayhan.

COONEY Jenkins and Bill Malone had known each other since they were boys. Cooney was a few years older but Bill had passed him in grade school. They had been in the fifth grade together. But that spring Bill matriculated to the sixth grade, and Cooney was held back for his third try at the fifth. Because of Cooney's disabilities and because of peer pressures, they had never become friends back then. They hadn't gotten to know each other well until Bill came home to the Black Hills to take the teaching job at the university.

In the years since then, as unlikely as it seemed to others, they had become best friends. Cooney lived in a tiny log cabin halfway up Spearfish Canyon on land that his grandfather had homesteaded in the first few years of the twentieth century. Cooney was barely fifty years old but he looked older. He was physically strong, and despite what people thought, he was bright. It was only a small short circuit somewhere in his brain that made his words come slowly and made some common tasks difficult for him. In his early years he was classified retarded, so he never got much education. But after spending his early years as the village idiot, he found a tenacious streak inside himself. He came to understand that he could do anything other people could do—it just might take longer.

He cut his gray hair and beard only once a year—in the spring when it started to warm up—so by autumn there wasn't much of his tightly wrinkled, sun-baked skin to be seen. But Margaret could tell he was smiling as he waved from the porch of his cabin when they crossed the bridge over Spearfish Creek. A powerful yard light illuminated Cooney's ancient cabin, casting odd-shaped shadows across the yard.

They pulled up behind Cooney's old Datsun pickup. It was

one of several cars in the yard and it didn't look any more drive-able than the '52 Mercury or the '68 Chevy Impala up on blocks. There were six old, yellowing clothes dryers near the corner of the cabin. The doors had been removed and replaced with wire. A pair of chickens scratched and clucked inside each dryer. There were animal hides tacked to the log walls, evidently dry-ing in the sun. "Here we are," Bill said. He patted her on the back. "You'll like this guy, he's one of a kind."

Bill had prepared Margaret for Cooney on the drive down the canyon. She knew he lived alone and survived on what he made from odd jobs and from tying flies for fishermen. In his younger days he had trapped animals for their fur—hence the name Cooney—but he didn't have the heart of a trapper. He had never finished school, but Bill claimed Cooney was a self-taught naturalist. Looking at him come off his porch in green coveralls and a very ratty cardigan sweater, Margaret had her doubts. But she got out of the car and waited for her introduction.

When Cooney took her hand she tried her best not to let the surprise show in her face. He was a big man and slightly over-weight so she expected a large hand, but Cooney's was enor-mous. She felt like she was shaking hands with a polar bear.

"I've heard a lot about you," Cooney was saying slowly. "Good stuff."

The fact that Bill had spoken about her was nice to hear and Margaret wanted to think about that for a moment, but Cooney's sparkling blue eyes commanded her attention. The eyes were nestled in a plump, weathered, whiskery face. Cooney's cheeks were the deepest nut color she had ever seen, and she couldn't help thinking that the yuppie skiers in Col-orado would do anything for a tan like that. Anything but live the way Cooney was living.

He motioned them toward the cabin. "It's getting cold at night." He rubbed his shoulders as if he was chilled, but Mar-garet had a hard time believing he was actually cold. "Watch your step," Cooney said, "the top board needs some fixing. I got to get at it one of these days. Just jerk on that screen door."

They stepped through the door and into the damnedest mess

Margaret had ever seen. It was an unfathomable clutter. There were stacks of books and newspapers, a hundred potted cactus plants jammed onto a shaky bank of shelves by the only window, colorful chicken skins tacked along one wall, bits of fur, hair, and feathers everywhere. There was a tortoise in a cage made from the shelves of old refrigerators. The only neat thing in the cabin was a small tepee of kindling wood piled perfectly in the center of the sooty, stone fireplace. Cooney hadn't lit it yet, but it looked like he had spent some time getting it ready. Margaret moved to one of the half dozen plants hanging from an exposed beam. What caught her eye was a massive bloom, a gorgeous thing, and Margaret studied it for a instant, trying to recall the name of the plant.

The inside of the cabin had startled her. She looked around the room and tried to find some order. Then she looked back at the flower. Here the order was stunning. A blossom as big as her fist, trilayered with a white oval petal as a backdrop neatly dotted with nearly black spots, two horizonal rust petals trimmed in yellow, and a lighter, central petal that protruded like a puckish tongue.

"*Pa-phio-pedi-lum Gee-long,*" Cooney said. He was standing right behind her, his battered, bearded face animated as if he had just tasted chocolate for the first time. "It's an orchid," Cooney said. "This one is *O-don-to-glos-sum harry-anum.*" He reached out and touched the next plant. "It's almost ready to bloom, too. Look right there."

Margaret looked and saw a hint of purple in a delicate bud. She looked around in surprise and found Bill watching her with a delighted smile. He shrugged to say, *I told you so.* When Cooney turned his way Bill laughed out loud. "You got anything to drink around this joint?"

"I picked up some beer," Cooney said. "It's the perfect drink to go with my stew."

"Stew? Venison stew?"

"That's it."

Margaret looked around the room for evidence of a kitchen. There was a hot plate with a small pot boiling on top, a miniature refrigerator, and a microwave like in a convenience store. After her eyes had traveled around the room and, to her way of thinking, found no cooking equipment, they came to rest on Bill. He looked happy as he pulled three beers from the refrigerator. "Don't worry," he said as he handed the beers around. "It'll be great."

"Stew's cooking in a Dutch oven out back," Cooney said. "I'll bring it in as soon as the turnips are done." He pointed to the boiling pot. "But it will be awhile. Come here and look at this, Bill."

He directed their attention to his workbench. The two men hunkered down to look at a tiny fishing fly held in the jaws of a stainless-steel vise. Cooney's half-moon glasses were on a shoestring around his neck, and he pulled them up to the tip of his nose before he spoke. "It's a trico spinner," he said. "Guy that fishes the Big Horn River sent me a bunch he collected after they came down to the water. He wanted to know if I could make a fly that would imitate them. Said he'd tried everything in his box and the trout wouldn't go for it. Look here." He moved a pile of books and a few spools of thread so they could get at an old microscope. It was like the one Margaret remembered from high school biology. Cooney looked down his nose through his crooked glasses and shuffled through some slides.

"Here you go. This is the trico he sent me. Stout little guy, the bodybuilder of mayflies. You know how they're usually gray and white? Well, look real close at this one." He put it under the microscope and Bill adjusted the knob.

"It's more a reddish brown," Bill said thoughtfully. Margaret had moved up and was looking at Cooney's fly in the vise. It was nothing more than a very tiny hook with a fuzzy body and horizonal buff wings. The whole thing was no bigger than a mosquito. It seemed impossible that Cooney's big hands could have made it.

"That's what I thought," Cooney said. "More like a rusty spinner than a normal trico. I'm betting this little guy slays them on the Big Horn." They turned back to the fly in the vise and caught Margaret squinting at it. All three of them bent over the fly and were silent for a moment.

"I don't know how they could possibly resist it," Bill said in a whisper.

"It hardly seems fair," Cooney replied.

"They'll probably have to outlaw it," Bill said.

Margaret straightened up. "You guys are nuts," she said. She took a long drink from her beer.

"Salvation is in the details," Bill said.

"Salvation may be in the dinner," Margaret said.

"No salvation in this dinner." Cooney smiled devilishly. "A little sal-i-vation maybe." He laughed out loud at his joke.

Bill and Margaret groaned. Then, without another word, Cooney went to tend to the meal. Bill shook his head and turned to the fireplace. He pointed to the neat little pile of kindling. There was a single wad of newspaper in the middle and pieces of wood of gradually larger sizes piled around it. He called out the back door, "Cooney, is the kindling in the fireplace for decoration?"

Cooney called back. "No. Light it, if you can find a match."

Bill nodded. "You cold?" he said to Margaret.

She shrugged. "A little."

"Allison must have matches in her truck."

"I'll get them." Margaret motioned for him to stay put. She didn't want him waiting on her.

"Probably the glove box," Bill said.

Full darkness was just coming into the sky and stars were breaking through the blackness above the cabin. When she opened the pickup door and the overhead light came on, the stars faded several degrees of intensity. The contents of Allison's glove box was as soothing as the sky. Here, unlike Cooney's cabin, was order, and Margaret couldn't help being reminded of the way Ellen kept her things. Like mother, like daughter. A small box of Kleenex, a crisp leather case for car registration and insurance papers, road maps stacked neatly, a flashlight, a small plastic box with four or five tapes—mostly country and western—a plastic packet of what looked like tools, and, near the back, a pack of matches. Margaret smiled and moved the tools to get at the matches. But she moved the tools too far and they fell from the glove box, hit the floor of the pickup, and clattered onto the moonlit ground.

Margaret couldn't help smiling at herself. She was such a klutz. It was always worse when she was around Ellen. Now just being around her daughter's pickup was causing it. The packet of tools turned out to be a set of Craftsman wrenches, each size with its own pocket. Most had come out of the packet and in the poor light it took Margaret a minute to sort the half-inch wrench into the half-inch pocket and the quarter-inch wrench into the quarter-inch pocket. Finally she had picked up all the wrenches. But the largest one, the three quarter-inch, was missing. She checked the floor. Nothing. Then, thinking she'd missed it, she checked the ground again.

She found nothing. She had lost Allison's wrench. What a klutz. She wrapped the packet back together leaving the bright red craftsman insignia uppermost, the way she had found it. She let the truck door go shut behind her and when the dome light clicked off the stars came bright again.

She held the matches in her fist and watched the stars. It was a luscious night. She stood for a long minute before she started up the steps to the cabin.

Bill was ready to light the fire when Cooney came in to offer his advice. Bill was on his knees in front of the fireplace and Cooney stood over him with a large wooden spoon in his hand. It made Margaret grin. Men were so funny about building fires.

Bill touched a match to the newspaper and in an instant the whole pile was ablaze. Cooney nodded as if to approve of the job Bill was doing, then went back to his stew. Bill waited a moment then laid a pair of logs on the fire. He continued to watch the fire, and Margaret continued to watch him. Men and fire, what ancient connections were at work here?

They found places to sit. Bill settled for the floor, as close as he could get to the new flames. The couch that Margaret found was draped with woven cords that seemed familiar but strange at the same time. "That's where I spent the night before last," Bill said. "Just put those on the floor."

Margaret couldn't help noting what Bill said. In the back of her head she wondered if it could have been Bill who wrote the foul words on Mountain Air Estate's machinery. He'd been angry after the meeting. But he was a little old for such pranks. It was silly to even think of Bill doing something like that. Maybe it was her old training in police work, but still, it was nice to know he'd been asleep on Cooney's couch. When she picked the cords off the back of the couch, she realized that they were halters for horses. They were beautifully intricate and slightly slick to the touch. "Horsehair," Bill said, "another of Cooney's pastimes. He braids the finest horsehair halters and reins in the country. But he doesn't have a horse and says the halters are too much trouble to make except for special occasions. He won't sell them."

Margaret laid the halters gently on the floor. "I feel like I've stepped through the looking glass."

Bill was at the refrigerator again. "Maybe you have. Another beer?"

"Sure."

Bill swung his arm around the room. "Quite a place, no?"

"Quite a place, yes."

"Cooney was never one to mind a mess."

Margaret laughed, but it was more complicated than that. She wanted to think about the whole scene. To try to figure out what this gentle, odd man was doing living in this cabin. She wanted to try to figure out how Bill had been drawn to him and what that said about her old friend. But Cooney came rattling through the back door with a steaming Dutch oven held in one gloved hand and the wooden spoon in the other. All her thoughts were put on hold. "Ooh," Cooney said, "got a good one going here."

It smelled wonderful. Cooney put the Dutch oven beside the hot plate and took off the lid. Then he removed the pot from the hot plate, carried it to the sink, and drained off the water. He dumped the pot's contents into the stew and began to stir with the spoon. The steam from the Dutch oven doubled and the smell became richer. Both Margaret and Bill were leaning over Cooney's shoulder. The added ingredient looked like turnips and Margaret had to ask. "You grew them?"

"They aren't real turnips," Cooney said. "Indian turnips."

"Breadroot scrufpea," Bill said. "We spent a whole day digging them this summer. They grow on prairie hillsides." Their eyes caught before Bill went on. Margaret knew what he was going to say. "These came from Brendan Prairie." Bill left enough room in the air for a breath. "You have to boil them for about a week."

"But they're worth it," Cooney said quickly. He dished the stew into bowls of three different sizes then took a coffee can from the cupboard, inverted it, and whacked it hard on the bottom with the spoon. A cylinder of homemade bread bounced onto the counter. He tore it into three pieces and dropped a piece in each bowl. The biggest bowl got pushed toward Bill and Cooney took the smallest one. Margaret, who had always had to watch her weight, thought about trying to switch with Cooney but the smell was too good.

Then the room became nearly silent. There was some slurping from Bill and Cooney, a moan or two from Margaret. But no one spoke until all three bowls were wiped clean with the bread. The first word was from Cooney. "More?"

"I couldn't," Margaret said.

"Don't mind if do," said Bill. Margaret and Cooney waved off.

"So how's the little guy that ran into my window?" Cooney asked. "Did he make it?"

Bill wasn't sure he should talk in front of Margaret but decided to go ahead. "Cooney had a merlin slam into that window," he explained. "It's pretty banged up. I've got it in my office at school." No sooner had he said that than a queer feeling came over him. He hated to do it but added, "I've got a rehabilitation permit."

"So how's he doing?" Cooney asked.

"He's still alive, but I'd be surprised if he recovers. It's been a couple days. Even if his neck straightens out, something secondary will probably set in."

"Secondary?"

"Something from being in captivity," Bill said. He had another bowl of stew and was settling back down on the floor. "They get stressed out and that opens the door for all sorts of things. They get infections, dietary problems, broken feathers."

"But you used to be a falconer," Cooney said, "I bet you kept your birds in good condition."

"Perfect," Margaret said.

Bill smiled. It was nice that she thought highly of his expertise as a falconer. Maybe he shouldn't have said that about having a permit. "But those were healthy birds," he said. "It's a hundred times easier to keep them healthy than to make them healthy."

Cooney got to his feet and began collecting the bowls. "Does he have a chance then?"

Bill hesitated. He must believe the falcon had a chance or he would have euthanized him already. "I suppose he does," Bill said.

"You won't let him suffer though."

"No," Bill said, "I won't let him suffer."

Cooney smiled. "That's good," he said. "Suffering is for people who want to live forever." The smile never left his face. He put the bowls into the sink and turned back toward Bill and Margaret. But his eyes didn't seek out theirs. He kept his gaze slightly elevated and the smile went subtle behind the scruffy beard and mustache. It looked to Margaret as if he were thinking something pleasant. Perhaps it was the meal.

Margaret felt the coolness of the autumn night begin to creep through the cabin walls and, as if Cooney could read her mind, he went to the back door and brought in a load of firewood. "Green ash," he said over the armful of logs. And his eyebrows raised as if his burden was frankincense.

For the three who watched the flames flare and waver, it was as good as frankincense. They sat with the fire projecting their shadows to and fro on the wall behind them and told stories of things they had seen or heard. An hour passed quickly and they were into their second hour when Bill began to talk about the years before Ellen Mayhan. He didn't refer to those years in that way but that is the way Margaret registered them. Bill sat on the floor with his back against the couch near Margaret. His arms were behind him on the couch with his hands dangling. He stared into the fire.

Cooney told about a winter night he had spent in the cabin when the wind blew to fifty miles per hour and the temperature was thirty below zero. The power lines were smashed by falling limbs and all he had was the fire. They looked into the fire and the story made them draw closer. Bill nodded solemnly as Cooney described the feel of heat leaving his back at the same time his face seemed to burn.

There was a moment of silence when Cooney finished his story and the fire hissed and cracked as if telling its own story of cold. Then Bill began and Margaret knew the story he would tell when she heard the first words. "President's Day," he said. "It must have been nineteen seventy-four or -five." He didn't take his eyes off the fire. "Cold and windy. I probably didn't have any business out in it. And I wasn't out long, maybe forty-five minutes." He let the fire snap and brought his right hand up onto the couch and tapped his fingers as if he was thinking. Margaret watched the fingers touching the couch a foot from her thigh. They were wrinkled at the joints and veins stood out on the back of the hand. Then the fingers went still.

"There were a half dozen grouse in a draughty clump of Russian olives. I had to try them with the gyrfalcon." He squinted his eyes. "I can't remember her name or if she caught a grouse."

But Margaret remembered. Hyder. And, yes, she had baked the grouse that night, stuffed with garlic and sage.

"The flight went downwind and I went after them with the setter, I guess it must have been Lou. I remember picking the falcon up in a draw a mile from the pickup and not thinking a thing about the temperature until we started back into the wind. It was right in my face and building. The snow was a foot deep and hard to walk in." He smiled and shook his head. "It didn't bother Lou or the falcon much. I remember the bird laid down on my fist to keep her feet warm.

"I was numb when we got back to the pickup and had some trouble with my fingers when I was putting the bird and the dog away. But it wasn't until I was back indoors that the skin on the left side of my face began to hurt. By midnight the ear on that side had turned gray and was as thick as a boot heel. Frostbite."

Bill showed no signs of finishing the story. Perhaps he had forgotten. But there was more and Margaret couldn't help herself. "By five that morning the ear was black," she said. Bill looked up from where he sat with embarrassment on his face. His mind was struggling to remember. Margaret met his eyes. "It split along the back and drained into the pillow." Neither looked away. The room went silent again with Bill's right hand and Margaret's left a few inches apart on Cooney's couch. They both felt heat in their fingertips.

WHEN Bill dropped her off at the Franklin they sat in the pickup for a minute without a word. They started to talk at the same time, then fell silent and looked at each other. Bill tried to apologize. "I'm sorry about not remembering I was with you the day I froze my ear. I . . . ." But Margaret wouldn't let him go on. She held a finger to his lips and shook her head. Then she let her hand drift to that left ear and touched it where it was still hard and leathery.

"It's good to see you," she said. "Thanks." She slid out of the car before he could say anything. When she stopped at the top of the hotel steps, she turned and saw that he was still watching her. They smiled for each other and Margaret disappeared behind revolving glass.

As she undressed she reran the evening in her mind. She tried to keep it distant, tried not to think of Bill and the way his hand had been so close on that couch. She thought of the crazy cabin, the plants, the piles of feathers, the fishing flies, the meal, the books—but her focus continually switched back to Bill. Her feelings were still there. They had only been dormant, like winter grass. As she got ready for bed she wondered what it was about Bill that made people like her and Cooney—all people perhaps—love him so easily. It had something to do with the way he thought, the things he had said at the meeting about the plants and water and animals up on Brendan Prairie. There was something about the way he saw them all as one thing, and how that one thing included him.

But it wasn't only the things he said that drew people to him. Margaret was standing at the bathroom sink now, staring at herself in the mirror. It was simply who he was. What he did with his life. What he stood for. She shook her head and thought of Bill's crippled leg. She knew he had limped as they walked that afternoon. But just then she couldn't picture it. She saw only the two of them moving effortlessly, through the grass and along the bank of the tiny, glittering stream.

Margaret wanted her feelings to match what she saw in her mind but couldn't force it. She was uneasy about something but she wasn't sure what. Too long as a cop. She wondered how Sheriff Larson was proceeding with his investigation. She was still staring into the mirror but now she was laying out a plan for how she would proceed if it was her investigation. She'd check that machine out completely, she'd begin a list of who might have tampered with it, she'd . . .

"No." She brought her hands up and clasped her fingers over her head. "Leave it," she said and reached to turn off the bathroom light.

She moved through the dark toward her bed. Why spoil the night? Think of Bill. Think of his hand so close on the couch. She found the bed and peeled back the sheet. Enjoy this, she thought. It's a reunion. A day you've dreamed of.

8

IT WAS sixteen miles between the Franklin Hotel and Bill's house in Spearfish. The road wound and, though there were no tall cliffs lining the corridor, it reminded Bill of the Madison River Canyon east of West Yellowstone, Montana. That was the first site Margaret and he chose to release peregrine falcons.

The water in the Madison was warmer than might be imagined. Although it was high country and much of the water came from melting snow, there were warm springs in the river bottom that raised the temperature of the whole stream. But the water in the Madison River was still cold enough to take your breath away. Of course, that stretch of river was in Yellowstone National Park, so swimming was prohibited. Considering the water temperature and the regulations, it took a good reason for someone to strip down and plunge into the Madison River. In Bill Malone's four years of crossing the river to help release peregrine falcons on the other side, he only saw a swimmer once. He remembered the day as one of celebration.

Just west of Madison Junction a huge granite face appeared on the south side of the river. There were other granite faces along that part of the river, but there was one that made people gasp at its size. Its name was Mount Haynes. Peregrines like high places with great views and the sound of running water below. In fact, Mount Haynes was such a place and Bill remembered seeing the wild falcons streaking across its face and careening upward on the air currents that came down the river. Before the great mid-century pesticide poisoning, he saw them bank tight and assume the shape of a bullet as they shot for the mountain's top. The falcons were so high when they came to the top of this curve that they went out of sight against the granite and only the best eyes could pick them out when they broke the skyline at an altitude near nine thousand feet.

But that was early in Bill's life, when there was enough room between people to make a young man feel good about himself. Bill used to haunt those giant drainages were peregrines lived; the Madison, the Yellowstone, the Big Horn, the Shell, the Shoshone, the Wind. Peregrines were everywhere he looked then, and he would take a bird from one of the lower cliffs and hunt with it until, one warm October day, its inevitable urge to migrate overcame its training and the bird would speck out toward the south and be gone. There was a bittersweetness to standing on a sage flat swinging a meat-garnished lure to an empty sky. There was the sense of deepest loss but a vicarious exhilaration for the sights coming into the falcon's view even as Bill wound up the lure line and slid it into his hawking bag. He could content himself with the honor of having been a part of a three dimensional life, if only for a few months.

After the peregrines began to fall prey to DDT, Bill turned his attentions to the wintering gyrfalcons of the northern plains. The empty peregrine canyons made his stomach queasy and he missed the racket of breeding and feeding birds so much that after the mid-sixties, he avoided the shadows of those high cliffs, like the gregarious would avoid a ghost town. He was driven to those parts of the plains where he could continue to share the lives of falcons and their prey.

In some ways living with a gyrfalcon for a few months each year was a way to cover the pain of those silent canyons. It was a way to hide from all that, and when Margaret called and asked if he'd help reestablish peregrines in the Rockies by releasing captive-bred birds, he did not immediately say yes. He wasn't sure it would work and if it failed, seeing those old nest sights again, watching the lines of cars passing blindly under them, might be too much to endure. It was not until Margaret implored him to help, not until she made the argument that, if people like him didn't do it, the task would fall to government employees whose focus was too broad, that he began to listen. They would underestimate the care that was needed with birds of prey; they would never go the extra mile. "And besides," she said, "you know the old sites. You know where falcons belong." Later, Bill was amazed that Margaret had used the ineffectiveness of government argument to bring him to work. It was the fad even then to say that government agencies mismanaged everything they touched. Now Bill realized that if it weren't for government there wouldn't be anything left to manage.

But it was true that he knew where the peregrines belonged, and one of the first places Bill suggested was Mount Haynes. But Mount Haynes was just too much mountain. When the experts showed up and explained that, for the falcons' temporary home, they needed to bolt a six-hundred-pound hack box to the cliff face and that two hacksite attendants had to be able to observe the box and feed the young birds every day in all kinds of weather, the decision was made to put the hacksite on a smaller rock face a half mile upstream. It would have been nice to do the hacking on the historical nesting site but the rock they chose, while not as grand as Mount Haynes, was still a giant rock. If any of the falcons ever made it back from their winter migration, they would be only a few strong wingbeats from the historical site.

Bill learned fast that nothing about hacking peregrine falcons was easy. The site had to be accessible for the attendants, visible from a observation blind, and off the track of tourists, hikers, and climbers. Even more important, it had to be as free as possible from predators like owls, eagles, bears, raccoons, prairie falcons, martins, and mountain lions. Young peregrine falcons— in the weeks it took them to grow their feathers to full length, fledged, and gain the agility to escape predators—were as vulnerable as any babies. In the wild, the lack of parents is almost always fatal. A lot of experts said peregrines could not grow up at all, let alone normally, without their parents to defend them, but Bill and others who had experience knew people could fill the void if they were careful.

The work usually fell to college students or retired people, and many of them came to the mountains ill equipped to perform the job. Few had experience living for extended periods in the wild and even fewer had experience with raptors. In many ways, Bill's main job was to help them gain that experience as quickly and painlessly as possible. The high mountain sites were the least forgiving. That first site on the Madison was one of the worst.

They should have suspected it was unique when snow squalls grounded the Park Service helicopter that was supposed to sling the hack box to its perch on the cliff. Margaret had come from Colorado to help. They shouldn't have needed her. There were four other Park Service employees to help Bill. They planned to meet him at the top after they punched into work at the office. As it turned out, it was a good thing she was there. They had to cross the Madison River in a raft before they even started the climb to the top of the cliff, and as they were carrying the inflated raft down to the water a park ranger swung into the parking lot with lights flashing. He hit the siren and over his PA system told them to "hold it right there." The snow was kicking up at the higher elevations, and they had only two hours to get to the top and get ready for the helicopter. Margaret went back to talk to the ranger.

It took twenty minutes and several radio calls to headquarters to convince the ranger that they had permission to put a raft into the Madison River. He would have never believed Bill if Margaret hadn't been along. Bill might well have been in jail when the helicopter came dragonflylike up the valley with the heavy plywood box swinging below. Of course Margaret's efforts didn't make much difference because, by the time they got across the river and Bill and Margaret had gained the top of the cliff— it was two thousand feet of vertical rise—the snow had closed in and the helicopter had been forced to turn back. Bill and Margaret sat on the windy, snow-strafed rock and laughed. The temperature was falling, the valley below had turned white, and the river and mountains were gone. They could have been sitting on a rock in the middle of the prairie.

"Thanks for getting me this job," Bill shouted over the wind.

"What's the problem?" Margaret shouted back. "The truck is right out there." She pointed into the whiteness.

"It's the perfect job for you," she said as they retreated back into the trees along the ridge. "It's days like this that make me glad I hired you."

They got to spend the night together in West Yellowstone. The next evening they were supposed to meet one of the hack-site attendants who would work the site after they got the box set and the young falcons settled in. They stayed in Margaret's motel room and lay tangled into each other until just before dawn. It was an easy thing that they both took for granted.

Dawn brought only more snow squalls and they drank coffee until nearly noon. By two o'clock it was showing signs of clearing but there was not enough time left to set the box. Margaret postponed the helicopter until the next morning and they moved to a table in the corner of the Stagecoach Motel's bar. They nursed a pitcher of beer and watched out the window as the rolling gray clouds continued to thin. By late afternoon the sky was clear. Sunlight streamed into the bar from the windows on the west side and dust motes began to swirl through the beams. It was as if there had been no snow, no wind, no reason to cancel the helicopter.

Margaret began kidding about the Park Service, talking about how there seemed to be no one with authority to make decisions but herself and she made the wrong ones. It was comic because her face was stern. But when she looked up the sternness melted and she smiled. Bill let his eyes drift with Margaret's but the sunlight was at a bad angle and he saw only that someone was coming their way. It had to be the hacksite attendant they were supposed to meet. He followed Margaret's lead and stood up. When he rose, the angle of the sun changed and his vision cleared. He found himself staring, for the first time, into the strong, tanned face of Ellen Mayhan.

Bill had thought back on that first meeting ten thousand times. It started with the briefest of eye contact. There was no way to know for sure how it struck Ellen but he remembers a beat, a double pulse of time. Did something transpire that first instant or was that just what the two of them came to understand? Was it, as Ellen often said, the recognition of rogues? Or was that just something to say?

There is one thing that Bill was always sure of—she was a beautiful woman and he was attracted to her in at least the way any young man would have been. She was smiling, and she flipped the same sun-streaked hair that she was to pass down to Allison. "At last," she said. "Bill Malone. I've heard all about you."

Ellen's eyes sparkled when she learned the setting of the hack box had been delayed. She wanted to help with the helicopter. This was against policy, but the idea excited her and any shyness she might have had melted away as she tried to convince them that she could be useful. "I want to see you guys hanging off a cliff with the rotor wash bouncing you around."

Bill was wild with attraction. He looked at Margaret and made sure she understood that he would like this woman to come along. Margaret was thoughtful as she sipped her beer, but finally she gave in. Ellen laughed to hear she had permission. She reached for an empty glass with one hand and the pitcher of beer with the other.

THE SKIES were clear the next morning and the three of them drove out to the site in a Park Service pickup. It was a Saturday and the Park Service employees who had been ready to help two days before had the day off. Margaret cited their absence as an example of why the Park Service would never be successful at a project like the peregrine falcon recovery. She raved about how inefficient it all was. Ellen listened closely as if this was important information and she couldn't afford to miss it.

The plan was to meet the helicopter at the top of the cliff at eight o'clock. They wanted to finish bolting the box into the cliff before the wind came up or the usual afternoon lightning storms began. They were at the parking lot near the river's edge drinking the last of their coffee at six and pumping up the rubber raft by six-fifteen.

It was the first week in June, but there was a crust of ice in the low spots where the river had come out of its banks and flooded the slough grass just above its roots. The morning was still and cold and the sun was only beginning to creep down the canyon wall behind them. When they looked up to the rock that was their destination it was golden with sunlight and Margaret said what they were all thinking. "It's warm up there. Let's get to walking."

They were in high spirits and anxious for the physical day ahead. But first there was the Madison River to cross. They threw their packs into the raft and pushed off. They got their feet wet but that only served to make their senses more acute as they paddled perpendicular to the current. It seemed to take forever and they were continually tempted to turn into the current and paddle for a fixed point directly across. But they held to their course and skimmed across the water with aquatic vegetation waving below them like great green leviathan tails. Meaty cutthroat trout darted out from under the weeds and there was an instant, in midstream, where all three were looking into the six feet of pellucid water as if it was a giant television tube. They had lost fifty feet before Ellen spoke up. "Hey," she said unhurriedly, "unless we want to end up in Montana we should probably get back to paddling."

They touched the south side of the Madison several hundred feet below their mark but it made little difference. Part of the permit to release the falcons said that the raft had to be hidden so it wouldn't encourage people to break the rules and navigate the Madison. They pulled it up and into the brush and shouldered the packs filled with ropes, tools, and foul-weather gear. Margaret took the lead with Ellen right behind.

In his lighter moods, Bill wondered if it wouldn't have been better, that first hike with Ellen, if he had not been in a position to watch her move from behind. He remembered thinking, before the climb took the power of thought away, that this was an extraordinary day. With country like Yellowstone, a good friend, and a beautiful new woman walking ahead of him, it seemed an extraordinary day indeed. Even now he saw it as an extraordinary day. A day like that is extraordinary, no matter what it leads to.

The going was tough with a lot of vertical to overcome and slippery scree to traverse. They had barely reached the ridge and were cruising on the flat toward the hacksite when they heard the *whup whup whup* of the helicopter. They quickened their pace so the pilot would not have to wait for them. But their concerns were unfounded because the helicopter was still far down the canyon, and it was only the granite walls and still, crisp morning air that made it sound so close. They were above the broad ledge where the box was to go, with their rope secure, before the helicopter came into view. They rappelled down the rope and were on the ledge in time for Bill to reach over and check to be sure Ellen was clipped fast to a rock bolt. She had seemed surprisingly strong and confident on the way up and neither Margaret nor Bill had the heart to tell her she had to stay above while they worked. It would be like leaving a Labrador pup home on opening day. But, as Bill jerked to test the rock bolt, Ellen's eyes were wide with anticipation. He watched her as the helicopter approached, and when she caught him looking at her she burst out in a smile of pure exhilaration.

Then there was no time for playful smiles. The helicopter pilot was hanging a hundred feet off the cliff, taking a good look at the task before him. Bill took two feet of orange flagging from his pocket and let it flutter in the breeze so the pilot could get an idea of the wind close in to the cliff. He nodded from behind his dark glasses and moved the helicopter up and inward. The box hung thirty feet below, from the cable attached to the ship's underside. It pendulumed slightly and the weight made it irresistible and deadly dangerous.

Now everything was above them and the pilot stretched out of his door to see what he was doing. With her thumb, Margaret signaled for him to move over and begin to ease the box down. Like a ponderous hummingbird, the helicopter followed her directions. When the rotor wash hit them, they grabbed their safety lines with one hand and reached up to touch the descending box with the other—to guide it and to know where its vector of power was directed.

Down it came. Five feet, three, two. A foot to go. Margaret and Bill guided it with both hands to the right place on the ledge. The rotor wash was intense now. It was too loud to make conversation. When the load settled and the cable went slack they looked at each other over the box, wondering who would reach up and unhook the cable. Ellen moved first. Before Bill or Margaret could speak she was leaning over the box. She kept one hand on the safety line but reached over with the other and unsnapped the hook. When she swung back she looked up to the pilot and gave the thumbs-up as if she had done this a hundred times. The helicopter rose up and clear. It swung out, a hundred feet off the cliff, then the pilot slowly rotated the ship to bid them good-bye. He nodded and peeled off and down, into the canyon, west, toward the Montana line. In an instant there was just the distant *whup whup whup* of the rotors. In another minute it was quiet enough to hear the pine siskins in the fir trees above.

Ellen was smiling giddily. Margaret shook her head and laughed. "You like this, huh?"

"I like it. I like it!" Ellen said. Then she looked at Bill. "What do we do now?"

"Level her up and bolt her in." He unsnapped his pack from the safety line and put it on top of the box. It made a good workbench. He started pulling out tools and cable.

Margaret crawled inside the box through the hinged side door and began drilling holes through the plywood so they could wrap the cable around the two-by-two frame. There was plenty of room for her to work. She lay out on the clean gravel substrate that would be the young falcons' bed until they were grown enough for the barred front of the box to be removed. Bill laced the first cable through the holes that Margaret made and Ellen, after seeing what was needed, laced the second cable through the holes on the other side. She did it deftly, and both Bill and Margaret saw how able she was, how willing she was to put all her energy into action.

Bill had brought a level to be sure the box was placed perfectly. When he pulled it from the pack, Margaret raised her eyebrows. "What do you think we're building, a piano?"

"You want it to be here for a while, don't you?"

"No sense doing this more than once."

They leveled the box three different ways. When they were

finished they stood back as far as they could and admired their handiwork. It made them grin.

"Let's get inside," Bill said.

"All of us?" Ellen said.

"Yeah. Let's see if it's fit for falcon habitation."

It was a tight squeeze but they did it—Margaret and Bill on the ends and Ellen in the middle. They giggled as they settled in, and Margaret suggested that they looked like "see, hear, and speak no evil." But when they looked out over the Madison River bottom, fifteen-hundred feet below, they all went silent. The sun was fully up now and the river corridor radiated green upward against the canyon walls. The Madison, artery of North America, snaked through the valley it had created. There were side channels, switchbacks, oxbows, beaver ponds, and the varied greens of vegetation zones. Elk, as small as toys, grazed along the meadows. A pair of swans, tiny specks of pure white iridescence, circled in a back eddy. And the granite of Mount Haynes was dwarfed under the enormous western sky.

"Wow," Ellen whispered from between them.

Bill nodded. "They sure know where to live, don't they?"

The three goofed off on the way back to the raft and, before they launched it for the return trip across the Madison, Ellen announced that she had a surprise. She pulled a six pack from the icy water where she'd hidden it. "Let's celebrate," she said. Just then an otter surfaced near the center of the river. They watched in amazement as it held in the current then submerged to swim closer for a better look. Seeing a fur-covered mammal so at home in the river seemed odd. When it moved past the waving vegetation on the bottom it looked unreal and only when the slick head popped out, not six feet away, did it become recognizable again. No one spoke.

In the years to come, Bill got to know this otter well. Bill crossed the river perhaps fifty times taking care of that hacksite and most times he saw the otter. He came to expect it. But that first day it filled them all with awe. "I want to swim with it," Ellen said and they laughed. But Bill noticed that she watched it longingly as it slipped back out to midstream and was gone.

They passed the beers among them as they slid the raft to the water's edge and in. "This is the beginning," Margaret said. "We're going to put peregrine falcons back in the national parks." They were paddling hard for the other side then. "It's going to work," Margaret said.

And, in fact, it did work. It took a long time. They ended up releasing a total of twenty young falcons from the site over the next four years without a sign of a returning bird. But on the first visit to the site on the fifth year, Bill looked down at the ledge from the cliff top and saw a bird sitting on the box. There was still a trace of snow behind the box, where the sun rarely reached. A yellow glacier lily pushed its way through that little snow bank, and for some reason Bill let his eyes swing to that smear of yellow clinging to the ledge high above the Madison River. He froze and, only after taking a few deep breaths, shifted his vision back to the bird and slowly brought up his binoculars. He had in his mind that this would be a prairie falcon or, at best, a peregrine in immature plumage. But when the bird came clear he was focused on the gun-metal blue back of an adult peregrine. It watched Bill over its shoulder, aiming its deep black eyes over a fully mature, bright orange cere. Bill stepped back out of the bird's view and turned to his wife.

"It worked," he said to Ellen. And she took the binoculars from him and stepped up to see for herself.

"I knew it," she whispered. "I knew this would be the year."

And it must have been true that she had known because when they got to the raft that afternoon she took a bottle of champagne from her backpack. And when the otter appeared, she swam with it as she had wanted to that first day. She stripped naked and slipped into the water as smoothly as the otter itself. Bill never forgot paddling the raft above them both, two slick figures moving through a world removed, playing against the background of wild weed beds and washed river rock.

9

EVEN A garish gambling town like Deadwood is serene at five-thirty in the morning. A few neons still burned into the darkness but seemed desperate now. There was no noise or activity to buoy them up and give them meaning. It was cool and Margaret noticed the air on Main Street had a lightness that was missing or was masked when the street was filled with gamblers. A beer truck moved far down the street but it was silent. There was only the hollow sound of her running shoes against the sidewalk.

The historic courthouse was to her right as she left the hotel. She ran the entire length of Main Street, past the gambling halls and saloons. Past signs for tourist traps, the Wax Museum, the China Doll Restaurant. She passed two places that claimed to be the place Wild Bill Hickok was shot. Then she was on the lower side of town, near the highway that fell away to the prairie ten miles north. She crossed a bridge and took a left on a gravel road that followed the creek that would soon owe Mountain Air Estates' golf course a million gallons of water a day. Behind her, on the main road she had just left, the traffic was beginning to move up from Rapid City to service Deadwood. She heard big trucks downshifting to make the grade.

But then she was alone in the dark canyon beside the creek and the road noise faded as she moved downstream. Soon she could hear only the creek in the darkness to her left. She ran on, savoring the feel of the cold air against her skin. It became darker as she ran deeper into the canyon, more and more like a dream. Her legs were pumping but she could not see the trees beside her and so had no way to be sure she was moving. It was as if she was in a different medium, water perhaps. Black oil. She loved the feeling and continued pumping her legs.

Her legs. She liked the way they could work, even if she wished they were not so heavy. She wished her rump was hard and narrow, too. But it wasn't. Her rump was a dumb thing to waste this thinking time on. Running, like driving a car on a lonely road, made Margaret's senses more keen. It forced her to think and often these thoughts were prophetic. Now she focused on Bill.

The night before made it seem like no time had passed, as if he had never lost his mind over Ellen, as if events had not conspired to push them apart. Running through blackness, she tried but failed to understand what had happened. Things had simply changed. She wondered if they could change back and couldn't help feeling it was possible. Maybe they had already begun to slip in that direction. She wondered if Bill had noticed it, too. She answered her own question, out loud. "Yes," he felt it, too. She knew it. Why else had he looked at her the way he had? Why had he asked her to meet him for a late lunch after she'd finished her work?

If Margaret squinted she could now detect grayness in the direction of the creek. She could hear the water tumbling. Then there were a few shapes. Shadows. A hint of light on the canyon rim. She glanced at her watch, the face still glowed green. Almost thirty minutes, probably three miles. She ran another half mile in the building light, hoping thoughts of Bill would return. But they didn't. By the time she turned and started back toward town, the canyon was dull green and she had begun to think about her day ahead. She would likely be finished with her job by afternoon. It was Friday and she could stay the weekend if there was a reason. But Monday morning she needed to head back to Denver. She wanted to be happy about that but she wasn't. Denver was just an apartment at night and a desk in the Federal Building during the day. Occasionally she got to go out in the field like this but not nearly enough. Mostly it was just pushing papers across her desk. It was the price of success, and Margaret smiled to think that success had led her to feeling lucky to be staying for a few days on the third floor of a gambling casino.

She left the gravel and recrossed the bridge and faced the traffic on the way back to the hotel. She was at that point in her run where her legs actually felt good. It was time to lengthen her stride, put it on autopilot and let her legs coast. But her mind wouldn't coast.

One of the troubles with her job was that she was only partially a biologist. Her title was Senior Special Agent, which was much more romantic sounding than it was. For starters, there was nothing special about being a special agent. Really, all she was was a federal game warden with some biology responsibilities. She did more biology than most because she was interested in it. She did almost no law enforcement anymore but as Larson had pointed out, she had some expertise, she had taken all the courses.

In fact, a lot of her fellow special agents had come up through law enforcement. Only a few had been biologists and there was always some friction between the two groups. Though she kept it quiet, she disagreed with the law enforcement attitude that permeated Fish and Wildlife. A lot of the agents were frustrated CIA rejects who thought they were on some sort of eco-SWAT team.

It was a stupid way to look at the job. Enforcing most wildlife regulations was nearly impossible; infractions almost always occurred in the most remote places and had little biological effect on wildlife. The price of carrying on a sting operation was a national scandal, especially in light of the conviction rate and the fines levied. She had argued long and hard that Fish and Wildlife's energies could best be spent in education and habitat improvement.

Now she was letting herself go, physically and mentally. She carried on a monologue in her mind as she passed the opening saloons. Every enlightened person in the field agreed, but the law enforcement mind-set had a firm foothold and would die hard. Most special agents watched too much television. Rambos in green. She shook her head as she ran past a woman in a showgirl outfit smoking a cigarette outside the Dakota Territory Saloon. The woman watched her with dull eyes.

Occasionally her fellow agents got out of hand. She had been called a tree hugger on many occasions and, for her part, had been known to call more than one colleague a duck detective. But because of her work with the Park Service she'd come into the Fish and Wildlife Service with several years of federal service and now she had that senior status that got her out of almost all of the service's paramilitary drills.

Margaret was nearly back to the Franklin Hotel when she began thinking about some of the busts she'd been a party to. The truth was she'd been good at law enforcement. She'd made some tough cases and had to admit she liked the work when the case was important. But too many were not important. Too many were like the fiasco with Bill and the gyrfalcon. She could have been an unwitting player. When Mathews asked her if Bill trapped gyrfalcons she had said yes. It never occurred to her to lie. Who could say what use Mathews made of that information.

She slowed gradually and began her cooldown walk for the last hundred yards to the hotel. A gust of embarrassment and shame buffeted her. It was only right that it should come back to haunt her again now, the day after she had seen Bill Malone again. She wondered if the watering down of their friendship was due to him falling in love with Ellen as she had always told herself, or if he might suspect that she was the one who let it be known that he trapped a passage gyrfalcon every January on the plains of Montana.

She shook the rancid thought from her head. Perhaps she had mentioned it at coffee, she really didn't remember. Even if she had, it was a small thing—a technical error in the paperwork he filed that made his trapping the bird against regulations. She'd poured over the report from Mathews. She was enraged that he had confiscated the bird. But she was out of the loop on that case. And besides, according to regulations, Mathews had done a great thing. Bill had broken the law, he'd filed for a capture permit two days late.

As she started up the steps of the Franklin she swung her

arms pretending to loosen her shoulder muscles after the run, but she was really trying to shake the embarrassment and frustration away. She hoped Bill didn't think she was involved and, if he did, she hoped he hadn't been mad at her all these years. The report said the falcon had been released. It would have gone on with its life as if nothing had happened. Still, she wished she had been able to talk to Bill when it happened.

She scowled as she entered the hotel and started for the stairs. But a man caught her arm. He was tall and thin and stood just inside the door. His grip on her arm was not rough but he pulled her to one side. They looked at each other and Margaret found something familiar in the face but she couldn't place it. The man looked tired and had not shaved. Margaret let her eyes shift to his hand that still held her arm. When she looked back he let go immediately. "I'm sorry," he said. Then he licked his lips. "You're Margaret Adamson. The federal agent."

"I'm with the Fish and Wildlife Service."

"You were at the job site day before yesterday."

"Mountain Air?"

"Yeah." He nodded and his eyes narrowed.

It was then that Margaret placed the face. "Your name's Bass," Margaret said. "You were the guy driving the loader."

Bass nodded. "I was the guy driving the loader." He swallowed and Margaret could see cords along the side of his neck. Then he wiped his face with his hand and she could hear the sound of his whiskers. "I'm trying to talk to everyone that saw it." He shook his head and looked to the floor. "It wasn't my fault."

"No." Margaret knew now that Bass's starved look was due to stress, lack of sleep. "It was a terrible thing but it wasn't your fault."

Bass nodded again. "The brakes failed. I did everything I could." Then he looked up and his eyes focused beyond Margaret. His expression went neutral. He stood up straighter.

Margaret followed his gaze and her eyes fell on Sheriff Larson, sitting on a stool in front of a bank of slot machines. He nodded but didn't smile. "Everything I did was consistent with the safe running of that machine," Bass said. He was still looking at Larson. "There are guys here from the state. They ask questions but they don't listen to the answers."

Margaret looked up at his face and could see that he was frightened. "It must have been awful."

Bass was still looking at Larson. "Yeah," he said. Then he looked down at Margaret. "I'll never forget the sound. The way Andy screamed." This detail surprised Margaret. She had heard nothing and thought the machine drowned out any noise Arnold might have made. She wondered if Bass had heard Arnold's scream as the bucket hit him or if he had heard her try to scream a warning.

"I just wanted to talk to you." Bass said. "It wasn't my fault."

Margaret nodded. "Sure."

"He's coming this way."

Margaret looked and saw that Larson had pushed off his stool. When she looked back to Bass he was just disappearing out the door. Then Larson was there. "Morning, Miss Adamson."

"Sheriff."

"Could I buy you a cup of coffee?"

"I haven't had any yet." She looked down at herself, still dressed in running clothes. "I need a shower."

"I'm not busy." Larson smiled and Margaret started to say something about Bass. The old sheriff nodded. "Go get dressed. I'll be in the café."

THE SLOT machines were ringing and flashing when Margaret reappeared in the lobby twenty minutes later. The morning was gone. Business had begun in Deadwood. She could have sworn that the lady at the second machine along the wall had been there the night before. Perhaps even the day before. Margaret looked hard at the lady. She wore white tennis shoes, an orange muumuu and purple slacks. Her right hand was covered by a dirty white glove. That was the hand she used to feed the coins into the machine and to scoop them into her plastic butter dish when she won.

Larson was sitting at a booth next to a tall window above the street. People were passing, heading for their favorite gambling establishment. They were dressed in every imaginable way and the new daylight gave the procession a surreal air. Larson seemed even older to Margaret. He slumped in his seat. His cap, a jumping fish on the front, sat on the table beside him. When Larson turned to meet her the first thing he asked was if she wanted a cup of coffee.

Margaret sat down. "You drink too much of that stuff." She pointed to his cup and winced to think how she must sound. "But yes. I'll have a cup."

"My doctor says he doesn't think it can hurt me," Larson said. "Says I should hold it down to a couple pots a day to be safe."

"You drink a couple pots a day?"

"Maybe three." He called the waitress by name and asked her to bring another cup. Then he settled in, put both thin, white arms on the table, and looked at Margaret. "What did Bass have to say?"

"Not much. That man is scared." Larson nodded in his exhausted way. "What's going on, Sheriff?"

Larson didn't look at her. He watched his cup as he brought it up to sip. He swallowed and sucked at his front teeth. "He killed a pretty important man."

"The brakes failed. You told me that yourself."

"He's not going to get thrown in jail. They just want an end to it."

"They?" Margaret crossed her arms and squinted one eye. "Who the hell is 'they'? And what were you doing hanging around here this morning anyway?"

Larson shrugged and glanced at her. " 'They' are the people who make things happen in this state. Arnold's partners and friends of Arnold's partners. They just want an answer to why Andy is no longer among the living. And I don't know the answer to your second question. You seem like a nice person. You're easy to talk to."

"You don't know me."

"I know a little. I know you're a fed. The word is you're a good cop."

"Mostly a biologist now."

"Once a cop, always a cop." Larson nodded his head. "And I know you're a friend of Bill Malone's."

"And how do you know that?"

"I am the sheriff. For another few months."

"So Bill's an old friend. So what?"

"So nothing," Larson said. "You said I didn't know you. But I know a little. I know you seemed interested in my retirement. I suspect you've figured out that I've had it with being sheriff. I'm on the way out and not many people show an interest in my retirement plans." He smiled. "Maybe 'cause when I find someone who does I bore them to tears."

Margaret squinted at Larson. He was wrestling with something but she couldn't tell what it was. She smiled back and shook her head. "I don't cry easily." It occurred to Margaret that he might just be lonely. She tried for something that would let him talk if he wanted to. "You don't bore me. I like fishing."

"Really?" Larson said. "Do you fish?"

"Used to. Used to flyfish before the yuppies discovered it."

Larson sat back. "Flyfishing, huh? I never got the hang of that. I do some spin casting for bass in the ponds around here. But what I'm nuts to do is fish in the ocean."

"Have you ever tried it?"

Larson shook his head. "No. Never took the time. Busy raising a kid and being sheriff. But the kid's long gone. My wife, too. Died six years ago. And now the job."

"You been planning this retirement for a long time?" Margaret asked the question lightly. She expected to get Larson talking about his plans. But his eyes went back down to his coffee cup and he pursed his lips. He exhaled before he spoke.

"I been thinking about fishing in the ocean for a long time. But no, the retirement has come on suddenly." He glanced at Margaret and saw the question in her eyes. "It's not completely voluntary. The party didn't back me in the last primary. They don't think I'm up to running a county where there's big-time gambling."

"I thought it was low-stakes gambling?"

"That's the deal that was made with the legislature to get the casinos built. But in a few years they'll claim they're going broke. Everybody knows that. They'll scream about losing all those jobs and the bet limits will go up. The big boys will get the kind of town they've wanted all along." He shook his head. "No, my days around here are numbered. I'm definitely a lame duck sheriff." Larson's face was deadpan. "*Quack!*" he said.

Margaret was surprised. She stared at Larson. "A joke," he said.

They sat silently for an instant. Then Margaret asked the question Larson hoped she wasn't bright enough to figure out. "These people who make things happen in the state. Did they have anything to do with who was supported in the primary?"

Larson nodded. "They have something to do with about everything. A guy by the name of Lonzo will be running in my place. He's as good as in. He has very strong backing from the gambling lobby at the capital. Particularly a guy in the attorney general's office by the name of Hemmingford."

"And he's the guy who's coming to handle this Andy Arnold thing," Margaret said.

Larson nodded and smiled. "You're sharp," he said.

Margaret smiled back. "Once a cop, always a cop. When's Hemmingford coming?"

"He's already here," Larson said. "They're down at my office right now."

"That's why you're here."

Larson shrugged. "I'm not in a hurry to see them," he said. "But I did have one little routine question that's been bothering me and that I know Hemmingford is going to ask."

"Yeah?"

"Do you have any idea where your friend Malone went after that meeting the other night?"

Margaret smiled. "He wasn't with me but he was with another friend. He spent the night with a guy named Cooney Jenkins."

Larson nodded and rubbed his face. "Jenkins. I know who he is."

Margaret shook her head. "And I thought you came to see me because I was interested in your retirement."

Larson let himself chuckle. "I'm going out to take one last look at the accident scene before I have to face Hemmingford. If you want to talk about my retirement, ride along." He stood up. "It's coming right up. Real soon I'm going to pull out of here and not look back."

Margaret rose, too. "You won't miss the place at all?"

"I already miss the place," Larson said as he pulled on his hat. "It's been gone for years. Ever since they rolled in the first slot machine. Come on a ride with me."

Margaret thought she would never want to go back to where Andy Arnold was killed but something about investigations attracted her in spite of herself. "I have to be in Custer at eleven."

"It's on the way."

"I'd have to take my own car."

Larson shrugged. "Come on out and wander around with me. I could use the company and I promise not to talk about fishing."

THERE WAS A yellow crime tape around the front-end loader. Larson held it up and waved Margaret underneath. They walked to the bucket of the big machine and looked down to where the lip had pinned Andy Arnold to the ground. There were still blood stains on the rusted steel and the ground.

"Pretty grisly deal," Larson said.

Margaret agreed but she didn't say anything. She touched the heavy metal of the bucket and felt that it was already warm from the sun.

Larson walked slowly along the side of the machine and reached up and touched the words that had been sprayed on the engine cover. "'S'pose whoever wrote this was at that meeting of yours?"

Margaret looked up at the scrawled words. They were ugly and she could feel the hate that was behind them. "Maybe," she said. "I thought you were treating the two events separately."

"Events?"

"The vandalism and Andy's death."

"Oh," Larson nodded his head. "Yeah, yeah. Two separate crimes."

"Crimes?"

"Well, events."

Larson moved to the back of the machine and pointed to the ground. There were a few dark spots on the soil. "Brake fluid," he said. They backtracked the machine to the place it had spent the night before the accident. There was a large puddle of oil. "This is where he lost the fluid," Larson said. "He was freewheeling from here on."

Margaret stood beside him and nodded. She continued to look at the oil-stained ground. If this was where the bulk of the fluid drained out, there should be a plug of some kind. She surveyed the ground and found nothing. "You find anything in this puddle?" She said.

"Just brake fluid," Larson said. He looked back at the machine.

Incredible, Margaret thought. She wondered if Larson had any control in this investigation or if it had already been taken over by the people waiting for him at his office. She looked at Larson and saw that he was gazing off toward the timber. "Now the kids that did the painting must have just driven up here same way we did."

"Maybe," Margaret said.

"Had to," Larson said. "The nearest other road is a logging road a mile through those trees. Not likely anyone could make it through there at night."

"Hard to say," Margaret said. She looked in the direction Larson indicated. "Is that north?"

"Yeah. The closest place would be a little west of north but it would take a good walker and some luck to do something like that. I'll bet they drove right up here." He pointed to where their cars were parked. Margaret wanted to say it would be stupid for someone to do what Larson was saying, but she didn't speak. She looked across Brendan Prairie to the north. There was a quarter mile of grass before the trees began. Beyond that the terrain got rough. But it was hard to tell how rough.

"Well," Larson said, "I guess I can't put it off any longer. I'm going to have to face the big boys. And I don't have anything to tell them that they don't already know." He opened the car door but didn't get in yet. "You know how to get to Custer. Right out to eighty-five and right. Forty-five minutes max."

Margaret nodded. "I know how to get there." Larson was in the car now and Margaret moved to his window. "We didn't get to talk about your retirement," she said.

"No, I promised," Larson said. "But I'll have you over to look at my fishing lures sometime. I may get you crying yet."

Margaret laughed. "That would be good," she said. "Go ahead. I'll be right behind you." She waved him off and he made a U-turn and headed out on the dusty road.

But Margaret did not follow him. She waited a few minutes to be sure he was out of sight. Then she set the elapse time feature on her watch and set off in a straight line a little west of due north.

Thirty-one minutes later she stepped out of the forest and onto the logging road Larson had mentioned. The undergrowth had been tough but overall the walk was not nearly as difficult as Larson had supposed. Almost anyone could make it in the daylight. It would take someone with experience to do it at night.

10

BILL MALONE was not a complete fool when it came to knowing himself. All that Friday morning he had noticed his lightness of mood. He realized his jokes to his students and colleagues bordered on silliness. And he realized it all had to do with the fact that he was supposed to meet Margaret at three o'clock.

But the day didn't drag. He taught an early class, then took a half hour to feed the little falcon. It was still in the cardboard box and Bill kept thinking it would begin to deteriorate and die. But it was holding its own. It ate another gerbil and, in a way, that did not please Bill. He was beginning to fear that it would survive as a cripple. That would be cruel indeed. When it finished eating the gerbil, Bill closed the flaps gently and moved it into a dark corner of his office where a crossing breeze from the open window would keep him cool.

He finished his second and last class at two o'clock and rushed home to change his clothes. He wasn't sure why he was changing clothes. The ones he wore to class were plenty good for a late lunch at Turgen's Steak House. But he felt compelled to change. He took off his shirt and pants and stood in front of his closet trying to decide what to wear. Almost everything was the same as the clothes he had just taken off. Finally he settled on a pair of Dockers, a crewneck shirt, and Top-Siders. But when he looked into the mirror it was all wrong. He took them off and rehung them. When he left the house for Deadwood he was again wearing jeans, a blue work shirt, and boots.

Margaret's government car was parked in front of Turgen's and as Bill walked past he glanced into the backseat and found no luggage. He thought that might mean that Margaret had not checked out of her hotel, that she wasn't planning to get on the road for Denver anytime soon. He tapped the hood of the car and started up the steps to the restaurant.

Coming from the bright afternoon made it impossible to see inside the dark building. Bill could see the lights over the bar and the ubiquitous flashing lights from the video machines but it was a full minute before his eyes had adjusted enough to realize that Margaret was standing beside him. "You're right on time," she said.

Bill smiled as Margaret came completely into focus. "Have you been here long?"

"No. It worked just right. I finished all the paperwork about an hour ago. I can't say I'm unhappy about being done." She was dressed in civilian clothes and looked a little tired but pleased to be where she was. She looked like any woman after work on a Friday afternoon. "Let's get a chair and a drink."

"Good thinking," Bill said. "You want to sit outside?"

"Sure."

Margaret followed Bill through the bar and out the back door. It opened onto a rickety redwood deck with steps down to the alley. There were three empty tables with bowls of peanuts at their centers. "It ain't The Ritz but they serve finger food and drinks."

Across the alley, to the west, the land rose dramatically. The sun was already behind the ridge. The deck was quiet and cool. They'd been standing, looking up at the hillside, for only a few seconds when a long-haired man with an apron around his waist came through the door behind them. They all looked at the hillside—to where the sun's rays were cutting across the canyon. "This is nice," Margaret said as she moved to the nearest table. "Just what I had in mind."

The waiter stood staring up at the ridge even after Margaret and Bill were seated. His hands hung straight down at his side. He had no order pad or pencil. Finally he lowered his eyes and smiled. "What can I bring you?"

"Wine," said Margaret. "It's an afternoon for wine."

The waiter's smile broadened. "You like wine?"

Margaret nodded. "Yeah."

"What kind of wine?"

Margaret shrugged. "Red. A light red."

The waiter's smile twisted. "Like rosé?"

"No. No. No."

The smile returned. "Like Beaujolais?"

"It depends. You have some French stuff back there?"

The waiter sat down on the bench beside Bill. Bill moved over. "Yeah, we got some French stuff back there."

Now Margaret and the waiter were both smiling and Bill was wondering why. "You don't have any Brouilly back there, do you?" Margaret bit her lip and raised her eyebrows.

"You can't be from here," the waiter said.

"No. I'm not. Answer the question."

"We got it."

"All right," Margaret nearly shouted. "Bring a bottle."

The waiter was as pleased as Margaret. He stood and bowed. His ponytail flopped over his shoulder and he flung it back when he stood up. "Immediately," he said.

"And some chislek," Bill said quickly.

The waiter stopped in his tracks. He didn't face them. He thought for an instant. Then, "Perfect. Perfect," and disappeared.

"Chislek?" Margaret asked.

"Deep-fried sheep meat," Bill said. "It's Czechoslovakian." He shrugged. "If we're going to drink wine, I got to have something to eat."

They drank the Brouilly and ate the chislek on the deck as the canyon darkened. No one else came outside to eat or drink. The waiter looked in on them occasionally but mostly left them alone. They didn't talk about old times. They talked about politics, religion, the state of the world. They talked about football and novels. Only once did they come close to Brendan Prairie as a subject. That was when Margaret asked if Bill knew Sheriff Larson. "What's his story?" Margaret said.

"Old guy. Been around forever. Things are moving a little too fast for him these days. He's just putting in his time."

"Was he a good sheriff?"

"Yeah, I'd say so."

"Honest?"

"I guess. Yes, he's honest."

"Is being sheriff around here a tough job?"

Bill shrugged. "Not until now. Why? You thinking about running for the job?"

Margaret laughed. The wine was nearly gone. A single piece of chislek lay in the bottom of the basket. "No. I don't think so."

"You don't like our hills?"

"I love your hills." She reached for the last piece of lamb. "May I?"

"It's yours."

She bit the chunk of meat in half. It was rare and tender and juice began to ran down her chin. She caught it with her tongue and was reminded of the stew Cooney had fixed for them. Then she moved her wine glass in a circle until the ruby liquid was spinning and sipped it as it spun. When she looked up Bill was watching her. Except for a single light above the door the deck was dark. Shadows fell diagonally across Bill's face. They watched each other without saying a word, then a band struck up inside the building.

That brought them back and Margaret looked at her watch. "God, it's nine o'clock." The music was country swing. Lively and upbeat.

"You're not going to turn into a pumpkin are you?"

"I already have."

Bill laughed. "I know you like to drive and think. But you're not planning to go back to Denver tonight."

Margaret shook her head. "No."

"Then we might as well dance."

"Dance? You're joking."

"Slow ones. If I get going too fast this leg becomes a lethal weapon."

"About that leg . . ."

Bill held up his hand. "Just an old injury. You want to dance or not?"

"Yes, I want to dance."

They danced to all the waltzes, the two-steps. They danced with Bill's hand firm, but tender, in the center of Margaret's back and her cheek against his collarbone. Bill didn't apologize for his halting steps and Margaret came to anticipate and wait an extra instant before she moved with his bad leg. They danced until nearly midnight and were both surprised to hear the band leader say it was the last song. When the lead guitar began, they turned to each other and were already moving to the music when Bill pulled Margaret close.

When they came out into the parking lot the air was cool and dead calm. "You're going to stay the weekend?" Bill asked.

Margaret started to say that she might. But it had been too long since she had felt like this and she didn't want to play games with the feeling. "Yes," she said.

They walked with their shoulders nearly touching to Margaret's car and stood looking at each other without a word. Then Bill took her face in both hands and kissed her gently.

It was not a surprise. The emotions that make a kiss welcome had been with them both for hours and as they stood close in the dark, a heartbeat before he said it, Margaret realized that Bill wanted to be invited back to her hotel room. "It's been a long time since I've asked this of a woman, but I think I want to spend the night with you."

It had been a very long time since a man Margaret cared about had asked and she laid her head against his chest, savoring the moment and ready to say yes. But something nagged at her consciousness—a premonition. And she spoke without thinking. "Not tonight," she said. "Not yet."

Then she needed to get away from him. "Tomorrow," she said. "I want to see you tomorrow."

Bill nodded in the dark and leaned to kiss her again. But she had to move away. He straightened up and nodded again. "Tomorrow," he said.

THE VISION of Bill's hazel eyes sparkling in the half light would not leave Margaret. The eyes, along with the crooked smile, was the Bill Malone she remembered. When she stopped at the first stoplight she nearly denied her premonition and turned back to find Bill. But it was too late. She drove dazed into Deadwood and found a parking place across the street from the Franklin. Before she pushed the car door open she sat for a moment and shook her head.

Her feelings were jumbled as she began to climb the stairs to her room. There were all the old emotions but something more. It felt like someone was watching her and she turned at the first landing. One man played a slot machine in the lobby and did not look up. Margaret squinted at the entrance to the café. Someone could have been standing in the doorway and pulled back when she turned. But it was probably nothing but an overload from seeing Bill again.

Now her mind was back on Bill and she continued up the stairs. They hadn't kissed for over twenty years but it felt just the same. Or did it? Her footfalls made no noise in the carpeted hallway, but her weight made the floorboards squeak. Bill was strong in her consciousness, but there was something more. As she turned the corner and approached her room, that something more became intense. When she came face-to-face with the Calamity Jane sign on her door she again had the sensation that someone was watching her. No. Following her.

A floorboard squeaked behind her as she unlocked the door and stepped inside. There were footfalls as she shut and relocked the door. But whoever it was did not go past. Margaret's face was only inches from the door when the knock jerked her to attention.

"Who is it?" she whispered.

There was a pause. Then faintly from the other side, "It's Allison."

Margaret exhaled and unlocked the door.

Allison stood in the hallway in jeans, boots, and a goose-down vest. "I came to talk about Daddy," she said.

Margaret was dizzy with déjà vu. It was as if the years had peeled away and Ellen Mayhan was standing in front of her. Here was this woman, bold as her mother had been, asking her about a man. The difference was Ellen Mayhan had wanted to know about the dashing, strange young man she had just met on a cliff over the Madison River. Allison Malone wanted to talk about her father.

Margaret motioned Allison to come in and sit down in the only chair in the room, then backed up until she came to the windowsill. She leaned back and felt the coolness of the glass against her shoulders.

"I waited for you," Allison said. "I thought you might be with Daddy."

"I was."

Allison nodded and the room seemed very quiet for a long time. Then Allison began. "The years have just battered him," she said.

"Time is hard on us all."

"But not just time. Look at him. Was he like this before? Was he moody and disconnected?"

Margaret thought about disputing that description. But she knew that the evening she had just shared with Bill was an exception. She had to agree. When she had known Bill Malone well he had not been moody—distant perhaps—but not disconnected. The fact was that he had always been engaged. That had been one of his real strengths and when she thought back to the man who had stomped out of the Mountain Air Estates meeting, Margaret had to admit that he was different. "It was the loss of your mother," Margaret said, mechanically. "The death of a spouse can change a person."

Allison leaned back into the chair, holding her chin with one hand. A finger lay diagonally across her mouth. She studied Margaret hard. "How much do you know about the circumstances," she asked. "I mean, about my mother's death?"

"Just that there was an accident. Driving too fast I suppose. She was thrown from the car, wasn't she?"

Allison nodded. For an instant, Margaret thought Allison was going to tell her something. But she decided against it. "There's nothing I can do about that," Allison said.

"Of course."

"I'm looking for something I can do. I owe my father every-thing. I know he went back to school and got a degree, then a job and a house he hates, and has lived like that for fifteen years because of me."

"Now wait a minute . . ."

"No!" Allison's eyes flashed. Oh yes, this was Ellen's daugh-ter—capable of instant anger. "Don't you see that he's in hiding, like some three-legged old wolf? To him it seems like everyone is after him."

Allison's words frightened Margaret. "What do you mean?" she said. "Do you know something you should tell me?"

"About what?"

Margaret wanted to let it go, but she couldn't. "About what might have happened up at Mountain Air?" Allison's hand came away from her mouth. Her eyes drifted from Margaret's and her arms folded across her chest. "Did you come to tell me some-thing about your father and the accident?"

"No." Allison nearly shouted. She turned her eyes back to Margaret. "I just said, to Dad it seems like people are after him."

Allison was flustered and Margaret wanted to say something that would take the fury out of her voice. But there was nothing to say. Though there was something very wrong with the way Allison was thinking, what she was saying was hard to dispute. Bill probably did feel like something hunted. Hell, Margaret felt that way herself sometimes. So she moved from the windowsill, came down from that position above Bill and Ellen's daughter and sat on the bed across from her.

"Okay," she said. "What do you want from me?"

"I want to know what parts of my father are missing. Not Mom, he's told me all about that and I understand it. I want to know the essential ingredients that he's let slip away." Allison spoke passionately, as if she was finally getting to say things she'd been thinking about for a long time. "I've seen the pictures. He was something, wasn't he?"

Margaret had to nod. "Yes, Allison, he *was* something."

"What gave him that glow?" Allison said. "What gave him all that life?"

Margaret surprised herself. She gave the question no thought. She didn't need to. "Wild things," she said. "He was drawn to them. The birds."

"He's always liked birding."

"More than that, Allison. He loves birds. That's where his energy comes from." Margaret nodded her head to give this emphasis. "Especially the birds of prey," she said.

"The hawks. He gave me a book about them once. They used to hunt for him."

Margaret had to laugh. "You're understating it," she said. "They hunted with him. Together."

"Until he met mother?"

"Always."

Allison shook her head. "I know he was a falconer, but he's never had a bird that I can remember."

That bit of information surprised Margaret, but it was consistent with some of the other things that surprised her about the contemporary Bill Malone. His drinking had been a shock. She never thought he could abide a job in a bureaucracy as rigid as a university. It seemed impossible that he could live in a tract house inside city limits. Not having a falcon was perhaps another way to leave what he really was behind. "Well, he used to have falcons. He was very passionate about them."

"It was his hobby."

"No, much, much more." Margaret said. "He was extremely skilled with them. He understood what they needed. His birds weren't pets. Somehow he could keep them so they never seemed compromised. They were like wild birds that he had made a deal with. They had consented to let him watch them do what wild birds do."

"And what had he consented to do in return?"

"I'm not sure," Margaret said. "Respect them? Dedicate his life to them? Know them for what they are? See them as symbols for all the wild things?" The words were coming from nowhere and it occurred to Margaret that her subconscious must have been sorting and searching for words for a long time. "He was so good, Allison. Where most people would just keep a bird to have it, your dad would strike up this partnership. The ones that he trapped, he always released after the tough part of the winter was over. They went back on their own stronger and smarter than when he'd caught them. Their minds are as fragile as their feathers and they have to be kept perfect. He could fix an abused falcon's mind or mend its feathers."

"Imping," Allison said. "That's how you fix a feather."

Margaret nodded. "You must have read that book he gave you."

"It was a long time ago. I was a little girl. I don't remember much."

When she talked like that, Allison was still a little girl and Margaret couldn't help a tiny maternal twinge. She had held Allison when she was just a baby. But, on the other hand, this person who sat on the chair in front of her was clearly not a child. She crossed her legs like a woman and set her jaw like a woman. "The world has been rotten to him," Allison said.

"He's had bad breaks."

"More," Allison said.

"It's a bad time to be a person with your father's sensibilities."

"He's even lost the ability to fight for what he thinks is important."

"You should have heard him the other night at the hearing for Mountain Air Estates."

"I did," Allison said. "I was standing at the back. It made me cry."

Margaret puffed a little with pride. It was nice that her old partner could move his daughter to tears. The thought of it gave Margaret hope and made her realize that her hope had been on the decline. "He was fighting that night. Fighting for that piece of ground and all the animals and birds that live there. He was fighting for you, and your children. He stopped everyone cold. He made them listen."

"But they went right on like they didn't understand. They treated him like an old nut case."

It was hard to tell if Allison was about to cry or swear. Margaret reached out and touched her shoulder. "I think those people treating him like that is what made him give up," Allison said. "They cheat him and bully him because they have money and this world runs on money." Margaret removed her hand. She could see that Allison didn't need comforting. "I want to give him everything that's been stolen from him. I don't want anyone taking a part of him again."

"Then start with the birds." Margaret said. "He'd do better if he were reconnected."

Now Allison looked tired but she smiled. It was a small smile that played differently on each corner of her mouth. It was a smile Margaret recognized. Here was a tough cookie with a honey frosting. Here was moxie. It didn't escape Margaret that in some ways she was trying to fill in for Ellen, trying to help this young woman understand a little more about life, the way a mother should.

It was the smile that connected them as a family. Ellen had smiled like that when she vowed she would have Bill Malone. "He's got what I want," Ellen had said. Then she smiled the way her daughter was smiling now. But Ellen's smile had stung Margaret because she knew Ellen would get what she wanted. Bill couldn't resist wildness no matter where he found it. Margaret could never compete with what Bill would find in Ellen's heart. She knew even before Bill did that he would give Ellen all the love he'd been hoarding. And twenty-five years later, by looking at Allison, Margaret saw that the daughter loved the father the same way.

11

JAMIE EATON was supposed to work with Bill the summer of the fourth season of peregrine falcon release. Margaret had moved on from her Park Service job to the higher-level job at the Fish and Wildlife Service. She performed her duties mostly from a desk in Denver, but, in a way Bill never understood, still had some say in the Park Service's falcon recovery efforts. In fact, Margaret was the first to approach Bill with the idea of "training" Jamie. The way she explained it, Jamie's father was an eastern oil man who had spent years in the Persian Gulf. Jamie had done some of his growing up there and had become a favorite of one of the Saudi sheiks who was passionate about falconry. He told Margaret he wanted to go back to Saudi Arabia and bring some western ideas with him. Arabs were notorious for having a poor concept of conservation and Margaret thought it would be a good idea if Jamie spent a summer with Bill. It was a good deal. The sheik was paying Jamie's wages and expenses.

"I can always use the help," Bill said. And that was true. In the last two years the number of hacksites had grown to the point where some days Bill was supposed to be in two places at once. The season had gotten progressively longer—it was pressing up against the beginning of the fall semester which was the only semester of college Bill was attending. The work began early in the spring and he was still trapping, training, and hunting for a month with a gyrfalcon each winter. "Another hand would be great."

In years past, Bill wouldn't have minded day after day of driving all night to hike the next morning. But by then, he and Ellen had been married for two years and Allison was already a year old. Ellen had worked a couple of hacking seasons but, after Allison came, had taken a summer job in Bozeman, Montana. That was the center of Bill's activities. He was seeing his new family a lot but Bill wanted more. He found himself longing to be with them as he drove, found himself thinking of them when his mind should be on other things. He was glad to have some help for that summer.

But it didn't work out as well as he had hoped. One of the first days Jamie rode with Bill they were supposed to pick up a half ton of the gravel that was used in the bottom of the hack boxes and haul it to the shop where boxes were being readied for the cliffs. Bill and Jamie had been together for only two days and were still being overly polite to each other, but when Jamie found out they had to shovel the gravel into the pickup truck and drive it a hundred miles, he scoffed. "Is this the only gravel in the Rocky Mountains?" Perhaps Bill was being a little finicky but this particular gravel was as smooth and round as peas. He believed ordinary gravel could hurt the young falcons feet and that there was no sense in taking a chance.

Bill laughed at Jamie's comment. "No, not the only gravel in the Rockies but it's the best. Nothing but the best for our falcons." Then he took up a shovel and, thinking that Jamie would laugh too and take up the other shovel, Bill started to pitch the gravel into the pickup box. But Jamie did not grab the other shovel. Bill pitched a few shovelsful then stopped and looked at Jamie. He was younger than Bill, good-looking, smart. But now he was pouting like a spoiled teenager.

"So what's the problem?"

Jamie gestured to the shovel still stuck in the gravel pile. "This isn't what my employer had in mind for me," he said. "The sheik has people to do this kind of work."

Bill glanced around. "Did you bring a few with you?" Then he looked back at Jamie. "Look," he said. "I'm supposed to be training you. Shoveling gravel is part of the job."

"I'm here to pick up ideas not shovels. They'd laugh at me in Saudi."

Bill looked around again. "Don't worry, no one is going to see you." He tried a smile to coax Jamie into the work. But Jamie only smirked back at him. Bill leveled his gaze. "Pick up the fucking shovel," he said. "If you want to ride with me this summer, pick it up and start shoveling."

They stared at each other for only an instant before Jamie reached out and jerked the shovel from the pile. His eyes remained contemptuous but he sunk the shovel into the pile of gravel. He was a strapping, athletic young man, but he shoveled daintily and only one shovelful for Bill's three. After a few minutes Bill smiled, trying to let Jamie know that he wouldn't hold this against him. "Fill the back of that shovel, Jamie. We'll make a laborer of you yet." They glanced at each other as they worked. Jamie's eyes finally lost their defiance, but he never did move much gravel.

Working together in such close proximity is always difficult for two men who do not know each other. Everyone has idiosyncrasies and in this case there were social differences that neither really understood. Jamie had obviously lived a cosmopolitan and privileged life. He was gregarious, easy with language and Bill's habit of going sometimes for an entire day without talking drove him crazy. He liked to talk about everything that popped into his mind and would sometimes jabber for hours, stopping occasionally to ask Bill a question that never got answered. It was not that Bill was trying to be rude. In fact, the first couple weeks he listened intently to what Jamie talked about. But when he realized that mostly Jamie talked about his relationship with powerful people in Saudi Arabia and what a great opportunity he had, Bill lost interest.

"Why don't you ever talk?" Jamie said.

"I don't believe in breaking the silence unless I can improve on it."

The whole summer they worked together Jamie asked only a few questions about the falcons they were releasing. He laughed. "In the Gulf we catch them. We don't let them go." The only time Jamie showed any real interest in falcons or falconry was when he questioned Bill about the gyrfalcons that he trapped and trained in the winter. Bill knew gyrfalcons were highly regarded in the Arab countries. Even though they were Arctic birds and seldom remained healthy in Arab hands, they were big and flashy. They were status symbols and some of the princes paid unbelievably high prices for them. Bill suspected Jamie imagined himself going back to his employer in Saudi Arabia and posing as a falconer who knew all about the elite North American gyrfalcon. Bill tried to put a halt to any such idea. "They're the hardest birds to keep healthy. In inexperienced hands they can deteriorate fast. It takes a good facility."

Jamie laughed. "I can assure you that the Saudis are experienced falconers. And the sheik is bankrolling a building for me in New Mexico. State of the art."

This was the first Bill had heard of Jamie's place in New Mexico. In the weeks to come Jamie would drop more hints about the thirty acres his father had bought and the falcon facility the sheik insisted that he have. "It must be nice," Bill told Jamie.

Jamie smiled and sat back in the passenger seat of the pickup. "I'll tell you, Bill, a guy's got to plan ahead. Life doesn't just fall into place on its own." He put his hands behind his head and stretched out. Five miles down the road he was asleep.

After a while, Bill came to expect no real work from Jamie. Like a beautiful, overgrown kid he tagged along, sleeping every chance he got, getting out of as much physical work as possible, and generally saving himself for going out at night. It became a sort of joke. If, after they had done what needed to be done at a given hacksite and they found themselves near a town with a bar, Jamie, who had likely slept a few extra hours that morning while Bill drove, would argue sincerely that a couple beers would be good for them. Of course, Jamie did not drink beer—he usually asked for some single malt Scotch that no one had ever heard of and finally settled for something like Chivas Regal. He only mentioned beer because he knew that was what Bill liked after a day out of doors. Jamie would raise his eyebrows and repeat the word *beer*, then say with a straight face that a little relaxation would help them sleep and they'd wake up refreshed and ready to work even harder the next day. He had a perfect, winning smile and when he flashed it he was quite irresistible.

THEY HAD been two days at a hacksite in one of the huge canyons that run west from Jackson Lake up into the Teton Range. One of the falcons had been chased by a young red-tailed hawk a few days after release and had not made it back to the hack box for that first critical feeding. It had been gone from the site for three days when Bill and Jamie arrived. The site had been plagued with black bears. They raided the camp all summer, and even though Jamie had never seen a bear, he didn't like them. It was always a battle to get him to hike in country that was known, or even rumored, to have bears.

At this trailhead, Bill had to coax Jamie out of the pickup. Jamie was particularly goosey because of a discussion they had had with a Forest Service employee the evening before. Eighty miles northwest, in Montana, near Hebgen Lake, there had been a grizzly bear incident. A camper had been dragged from his tent in the middle of the night. The man's partner had driven the bear away then gone to get help for his seriously injured friend. When help arrived, they found the bear had returned and not only killed the camper, but eaten a large portion of him. The Forest Service employee had helped track the bear down and kill it. He had also been in on the autopsy and described in vivid detail the condition of the body parts found in the bear's stomach.

"But these are black bears," Bill said.

"A bear is a bear," Jamie said.

It was the first day Bill could remember that Jamie did not fall behind on the hike. In fact, he stayed right with Bill as they tracked the missing falcon. Using radio telemetry they finally found the bird far up the canyon. It had taken up residency on a ledge three-quarters of the way up a five-hundred-foot cliff. The bird was hungry and sat puffed up in a miserable posture, screaming for its nonexistent parents to come feed him. He was only a half mile up the canyon from his hack box where attendants had

spread food. But the scare from the red-tailed hawk had disori-
ented him and he did not recognize that the hack box was home.
By this time he was probably weak from lack of food and would
have to eat before he would have the strength to join the other
young falcons. If he could be fed where he was, Bill was sure that
he would be all right. But if he got no food or flew off and down
into the canyon, he would surely die.

Knowing what to do was easy. They had to get a couple
freshly defrosted quail near enough to the falcon so he would
recognize them as food, go to them, and eat. The tough part was
how to do it. The falcon was on the west end of a ledge no more
than two feet wide, but nearly fifteen feet long. If they could get
the quail anywhere on that ledge without frightening the falcon
he would probably see them and eat. But the ledge was ninety
feet down from the top of the cliff. There were a couple hundred
feet of broken rock and timber above the lip of the cliff. Just to
get to within quail-tossing distance would require some difficult
rope work. To do it without disturbing the falcon would be
tough.

But there was no other option. The hacksite attendants
stayed below where they could see the falcon. They would be
able to let Bill know if the bird was getting nervous. They had a
flat spot off to the side of the face where they could be comfortable for the hour and a half it would take Bill to climb up above
the face and find something solid enough in the broken rock to
tie his rope to. It was a long up-hill climb but not dangerous. Bill
wanted some help at the top, so as he shouldered the pack with
the climbing gear, he looked around the flat spot where the
hacksite attendants were setting up their spotting scopes. "Be
careful," Bill said as he started off. "This little flat spot is a perfect place for a bear to come for an afternoon nap." The hacksite
attendants looked at Bill as if he had lost his mind. But Jamie
scurried along after him.

They made their way up and through the jumble of shattered
boulders. Here and there a hardy ponderosa pine pushed its way
up between the rocks and afforded them brief shade from the sun
that was nearly overhead. By the time they got above the cliff

face, Bill could feel that he had soaked through his shirt where the backpack allowed no evaporation. When he looked back, Jamie was right behind. Perspiration beaded on his forehead, and Bill couldn't help thinking that was the first time he had seen Jamie sweat. It looked good on him. In fact, he looked generally good—a little nervous about the height perhaps, but that was the way it should be. Bill was nervous, too.

They signaled to the hacksite attendants and got an indication that they were above the east end of the ledge. Then they found a tree that was solid enough to hold Bill's weight and secured the rope with a bowline. Bill was stepping into his harness when he noticed that Jamie was looking at him incredulously. "You're going down?" he asked.

Bill nodded. "Need to get close enough to toss some quail to that falcon. Can't do it from here. Don't worry, no bear will bother you."

"I'm not worried about bears. No bear would be stupid enough to come up here." He looked at Bill and shook his head. "You're a crazy man."

Bill couldn't help laughing. "You're probably right, Jamie." He wound the rope around his figure eight and clipped it into the carabiner on his harness. He stood on the edge of the cliff, ready to go down. "And I'm going to ask you to help me in my madness. Crawl over here and take a look." Jamie's eyes got bigger. "Really, I need you to help. I'm going down here and I'm going to try to stay out of the falcon's sight and pitch quail around the corner. You're going to have to tell me how I'm doing."

Jamie looked like he wanted to argue but he knew it was no use. He moved toward the edge of the cliff, got down on his knees for the last few feet, and peeked over. He could see the falcon. "I'll be even with him but I won't be able to see him," Bill said. "Tell me where to throw the quail."

Jamie looked frightened but he nodded. He was laying flat, with only enough of his head over the edge to see what was going on below. Bill slid off backward, into the cliff's updraft, and was gone. He rappelled slowly, trying his best to keep a huge column of rock between the falcon and himself. If the falcon saw a clumsy human clattering down the rock toward him he might fly and never be seen again. Bill could hear the hungry falcon pitifully begging for food. When he was about level with the bird he looked down to the hacksite attendants. They waved their arms and he knew that he was down far enough. He swung as close to the falcon as he dared. Then he clipped into the rope with his ascenders and reached over his shoulder and into the pack.

There were a dozen defrosted quail in the pack and he took out two. He swung ninety feet below Jamie, but the updraft carried his voice that far with ease. "I'm going to give it a try, Jamie. See where this one hits." He figured the falcon was twenty-five feet to his left and if he got a couple quail within ten feet of him he'd be doing well. It was too bad he had to toss with his left hand, but there was no other way. He leaned out a little more and blindly made a gentle underhand pitch.

"You missed the ledge," Jamie's voice was faint and hard to hear over the wind. "It fell clear to the bottom. Throw it harder."

Bill tried again.

"Short. Throw harder."

Bill dug in the pack for more quail. He gave the next quail a higher trajectory. An instant after he let go of the quail the falcon's persistent food-begging suddenly stopped. Bill grimaced. He was afraid he'd frightened him. But then he heard Jamie. "You hit the ledge right in front of him. He looked at it but it bounced off. Do that again."

Bill tried to duplicate the last toss. He tried to recall just how he'd done it.

"It stayed on," Jamie called down, "but it's not close enough. Throw farther."

Bill put a little more on the next quail and Jamie yelled, "Yes, good one. He's looking at it. Throw again."

By the time Bill was out of food, four quail had stuck on the ledge, three in plain sight of the falcon. "He's watching them," Jamie called out as Bill began his ascent. "He's watching."

And sometime in the few minutes it took Bill to ascend back to the top of the cliff the falcon flattened his feathers against his body and made the three hops to the quail closest to him. By the time Bill had pulled himself back over the lip of the cliff Jamie had raised to all fours and was supplying a play-by-play. "He's got a hold of it. He's plucking the neck. He took a bite. There. He's eating it."

And Jamie turned with that winning grin. "We did it," he said.

Bill was sitting on a rock facing into the fresh wind and taking deep breaths. He smiled back. "We sure did," and took Jamie's outstretched hand. "Nice work."

IT WAS late afternoon when they got back to the truck. The schedule called for them to release falcons at another Teton site in the morning, so all they had to do that night was find a place to pitch their tent. Bill had planned it that way. Ellen was coming in from Bozeman. Allison was with a friend. It was perfect. They were feeling good about saving the stranded falcon, and they had nothing to do until morning so they headed directly for Dornan's restaurant on the outskirts of Moose, Wyoming, where they would meet Ellen.

Jamie had never been to the Jackson area, so had never been to Dornan's. But Bill had been stopping there ever since he had gone to work for Margaret. Dornan's had a great barbecue, but Bill and Jamie went straight to the bar with its deck that looked out at the Tetons. In the early evening of summer nights like this, it was a very good place to be.

When they walked onto the deck a woman dressed in a sweatshirt, shorts, and hiking boots waved them to a table. It was Ellen. She was tanned and her sun-streaked hair flew around her face as she jumped up. She came and wrapped her arms around his neck. They laughed and Bill introduced her to Jamie. Bill could see that Jamie was taken by her, and was surprised to see that Ellen was impressed with Jamie. They shook hands and stared at each other for an instant before they spoke. At the time, Bill thought they were simply interested to finally meet each other. Now, of course, he knew it was something else.

They drank as the sun went down and by the time it was

dark they had worked up terrible appetites. "We'll go to the Mangy Moose for dinner," Ellen said. "Rebecca is working tonight. You like Rebecca, don't you?" She was talking to Bill.

"Sure, I like Rebecca." He was playing along. He barely knew Rebecca but knew she was an old friend of Ellen's and had been lined up to be with Jamie.

"Good," Ellen said, " 'Cause I'll bet she'll like this guy." She watched Jamie for a bit before she patted his cheek. A smile spread across Jamie's face and he tilted his head as if the pat had been a slap.

Bill rode with Ellen to the Mangy Moose and Jamie followed in their pickup. They stopped off on the back road to set up a tent. It was peak tourist season and there would be no vacant motel rooms in Jackson. Bill knew they would need sleep, and this particular place was a favorite of his. Strictly speaking, it was a no-camping zone but he usually set up his tent after the rangers had gone to bed, and he was up before they got going again. It was a quiet place, with the Grand Tetons towering up black behind and a creek running twenty feet from the tent. He probably should have just sent Jamie on and stayed there with Ellen. But Jamie had no idea where he was. Besides, they all felt like a party.

Things were slowing down in the restaurant but going strong in the bar by the time they arrived. They were waiting to be seated and Bill told Ellen they'd be right back. Jamie and he stepped into the bar because Bill knew Jamie would get a kick out of it. The walls were covered with old mining tools and stuffed animal heads. There was a loud band so Bill just poked Jamie and pointed toward a bear head over the doorway. Jamie only smiled.

They got in just before the kitchen closed and Rebecca seemed glad to see them. "The place is dead," she said as she took their order. "I mean nothing but Iowa hog farmers on vacation. I-O-W-A—Idiots Out Wandering Around. We're talking dollar tips. Get the prime rib. It's rare and I'll get you double portions."

The menus clapped shut, one, two, three. "And a Watney's," Bill said.

"Two," said Ellen.

"Glenmorangie," said Jamie.

"You're shitting me." Ellen said. "Are you from Iowa?"

"Leave him alone," Rebecca said. "We got it. He can drink whatever he likes." She put her arm around Jamie's shoulder and Jamie straightened up and nodded his head.

"At last," he said. "A civilized bar."

The food was delicious and they drank a bottle of Merlot along with it. They were the last ones in the dining room and they teased Rebecca as she set the tables for the next day. Finally she chased them into the bar. "I'll be off in ten minutes."

It took her less that five minutes to join them. She was from Texas originally and had come to Jackson skiing three years before. She met Bill and Ellen waiting on them one night when they'd come dragging in from one of the Teton hacksites a couple years before. She and Ellen had become friends when Ellen worked one summer at a hacksite on the elk refuge near Jackson. The band was already into their last set when they ordered their first round. Rebecca ordered a double to catch up and everyone danced while the waitress was bringing the drinks. They ordered another round when the first was half finished and Rebecca and Jamie continued to get friendlier. "You didn't tell me he was so cute," Ellen whispered to Bill.

"And rich," Bill whispered back.

Ellen watched Jamie and Rebecca as they nuzzled each other on the other side of the table. "Rich? Perfect."

"Not quite," Bill said.

The tape deck replaced the band and the waitress cleaned up around them. Of course, both Ellen and Rebecca knew the bartender and so the drinks kept on coming until he had to go home.

"Let us finish, Brad," Rebecca said. "We'll close it up."

Brad frowned.

"You owe me," Rebecca said. "You do."

Brad shrugged. "Make sure the door is locked. Pay for what you drink." Jamie looked slightly indignant, as if Brad had insulted him. But Brad paid him no mind. "Have fun," he said.

They turned the lights down low and danced to the tape deck. They had two more drinks and it was three in the morning. Rebecca and Jamie were very friendly now, and she had already agreed to come to their camp.

Jamie went to the men's room and Bill explained to Rebecca how to find the tent. He had his arm around Ellen as he talked. "We'll close it up," Bill said. "You guys go on."

Rebecca took Jamie's arm as he stepped from the men's room. "Come on, we're going to the tent." Jamie smiled stupidly and followed.

When they were gone Ellen turned to Bill and kissed him hard on the mouth. "Could you drink one more drink? I've got something to show you."

"Sure. What?"

She changed the tape to Neil Young and turned off the bar lights as she brought the drinks around to where Bill stood. She twisted his drinking arm through hers and they drank like in the movies. "Look," she said and turned him around. The west wall of the bar was mostly glass and, though Bill knew that, he was surprised that he had never paid much attention to the ski hill lights running up the mountain behind. It was beautiful. The top lights mingled with the stars. When "Heart of Gold" came on, they danced. Bill slid both hands down into the back of Ellen's shorts and she growled in his ear.

It was nearly five when they made it to the tent. The night was still black with a perforated top. It was cold and the stream sounded brittle in the hollow woods. They had made love on the floor of the Mangy Moose and Bill had brought the mounted bear head along with them. He stalked Jamie and found him just the way he had hoped—stretched out facedown and naked on the sleeping bag with Rebecca beside him. They both snored lightly. The light was poor in the tent but there was enough to make out shapes. Bill began making a sniffing noise before he eased the bear head into the tent.

He pressed the nose to Jamie's leg and sniffed loudly. He moved the head and sniffed the back of Jamie's knee. Then twice in his butt. Jamie stopped snoring and Bill made a couple sniffs on his back. He felt Jamie stir. When he rolled over, Bill sniffed his chest and was moving for a nose-to-nose sniff when Jamie exploded.

It was a terrible scream and he hit the end of the tent with enough force to break through. In no time he was outside, naked and running hard for the pickup. It took a lot of coaxing from everyone to get him to come out.

12

By six-thirty Saturday morning, Margaret had already put in a mile of uphill running, and she was doing it on little sleep. Allison had been in her room until nearly two o'clock. All the time they talked, Allison's hands had continued to move from her lap to her face and back again. Her eyes were sometimes placid, sometimes tortured and the dark shading underneath made it obvious that she had spent other late nights wrestling with her perceived responsibility for her father. But on those other sleepless nights she had done her wrestling alone, and Margaret couldn't help feeling honored that Allison had treated her as a confidant.

By the time Allison finally left, Margaret was exhausted. Staying up until two-thirty in the morning was a colossal rarity for her and she thought she would sleep hard and late. But her mind was racing. There was Allison to think about. And there was the dancing. There was the feel and smell of Bill Malone. There was the recurring shiver at the back of her neck and the quiver and shift in her abdomen that she had nearly forgotten. Very early she found herself studying the shadows cast by a streetlight over the metal ceiling of her hotel room. None of her muscles were tired. Her arms wanted stretching and her legs twitched. Her mind was going over things for the hundredth time, blowing things out of proportion, formulating outrageous responses. At one point she thought about calling Bill, going over to his house. For awhile she concluded that she should not spend the weekend and that she should get dressed and leave for Denver as soon as possible.

Finally, she threw the blanket aside and jumped from the

bed. She dressed in her running clothes without turning on the light. She didn't bother to stretch. Suddenly the most important thing was to get outside, to find some cool air, and start her blood circulating.

Nothing was moving on Main Street and she crossed without looking. The air was as cool as she had hoped and her skin turned to gooseflesh. Behind her a motorcycle was kicked to life. It roared for only an instant then backed off to a resonant and measured popping. It faded altogether when Margaret turned her first corner.

A good hill was what she needed. Three times she had noticed the sign for Boot Hill where Wild Bill Hickok was buried. It was still dark in the deep gulch that cradled Deadwood but Margaret found the sign on the road that came in from the town of Lead. She followed the arrow and immediately began to climb a twisting street through an old residential section. The homes were Victorian. Monsters dressed in gingerbread. Here and there a light shone in an upstairs window as if the houses, and not their owners, were waking for the day. But the darkness at the street level was complete; black between the streetlights, cool and deep.

Margaret leaned into the hill, shortened her stride and breathed deeply. She thought she might be able to get back to the thoughts that had kept her awake. She had hoped the running would clarify things. But this part of the hill demanded too much. The houses were thinning out, the pines were gaining dominance. There was still not enough morning to illuminate pigments. The Black Hills were black. The grade was steep. The graveyard somewhere ahead. She focused on what she was doing. One foot in front of the other, smaller steps, breathe. A chill at the back of her neck but not from the mountain morning. She concentrated on the breathing, the sound of her running shoes on the asphalt. Metered, steady, pistonlike. She ran another fifty feet before she sorted the sound of her running from the popping of the motorcycle.

She glanced over her shoulder and saw the headlight weaving up the hill behind her and involuntarily quickened her pace.

But the hill was steep and she knew the motorcycle could out climb her easily. She made herself slow to let him pass. The light swung onto her back and she held her breath waiting for it to slide away and move on toward the graveyard. But the light stayed on her back. Closer. Louder and closer. And Margaret knew she should not be afraid but she was. She couldn't help speeding up and, when she did, the motorcycle accelerated.

The road had wound out of the residential district and now there were only the tall black spikes of ponderosa pines to the side and her laboring shadow projected on the asphalt ahead. When she came to where the road branched she was running as hard as she could and the motorcycle engine was cracking only a few feet behind her. Her lungs burned and her chest heaved. She had to make a decision. She took the right turn and prayed the motorcycle would go straight. But it didn't.

It took only an instant for the headlight to swing and find her again. This time her puny shadow shown on the wrought-iron fence of the graveyard. An instant later she was at the fence, with her hands clutching the iron railing and her whole body gasping for breath.

When she turned, the headlight was on her face. The beam was so strong she could feel its heat. Her wind was coming back but she was breathing hard and blinded by the light. The motorcycle popped somewhere beyond and Margaret knew it was senseless to run anymore. Then the engine shut down. There was an instant of silence before the light went off. Then nothing. No light, no sound. But Margaret still could not see. She rubbed her eyes. "Who are you?"

Then she could make out the outline of the motorcycle. The shadow of a man as he swung his leg over the gas tank and separated himself from the motorcycle. "Who's there?" Margaret forced her voice not to break.

"Don't be afraid," the man said.

Margaret tried to place the voice. She waited with her back against the graveyard fence. The shadows had lightened to gray. The man took another step toward her. "It's only me. Troy Bass, the guy from Mountain Air." The face did not come clear until he was three feet way. When it did, Margaret could see that there was no malevolence in the eyes. "I didn't mean to scare you."

"Well, you did."

"I just needed to talk to you."

"Did you think about calling me on the telephone?" Color was seeping into pine trees. The black iron fence at Margaret's back showed a hint of reflected light at the periphery of her vision. There were headstones too, green with moss.

Margaret pushed away from the fence and stepped closer to Bass. "What the hell is the idea?"

"I'm trying to be careful. I don't want them to know I'm talking to you."

"Hold it, Troy." Margaret waved her hands. She took two more deep breaths and swallowed. "You're paranoid. I talked with Larson. He's not blaming you."

"No. It's his buddies. They're trying to say we didn't maintain the equipment right. They're trying to say we forgot to put the plug back in the master brake cylinder."

"Did you?"

Bass looked down and exhaled. "I don't know. How can you know?"

Margaret walked past him, halfway to his motorcycle. She left her back to him. "Why tell me this?"

"You were there."

"I was there. A lot of people were there."

"You're a cop. You saw me. You were looking right at me when the brakes failed."

Margaret still had her back to Bass. She shrugged. "So?"

Bass caught her arm. It was the second time he'd touched her and it frightened her. But when she spun around he let go. His face made the apology. "Look," he said. "I live here. I'm a good construction foreman. People know I'm good. That's why they hired me to do Mountain Air Estates." He looked away from Margaret. "I wish I'd never heard of Mountain Air Estates."

Bass looked down at the ground. It was bright enough to see well and Margaret took the time to look closely at him. He was no older than thirty-five, not bad looking. He hadn't shaved for a couple days but it looked all right on him. He rubbed the stubble as if he were reading Margaret's mind. Then he looked up and stared directly into her eyes. "I got a wife," he said. "I got two kids. Little girl four and a boy six. My whole family's here. Four generations of Basses. We used to hunt up there on Brendan Prairie. My grandfather, my dad, my brothers. We used to hunt deer. And I was hoping my boy could do it, too." He hesitated, embarrassed at what he was saying. "When the development came in I wasn't for it 'cause of the deer hunting. But I'm a builder. That's what I do. So I got behind it." He shrugged and shook his head. "I helped them lay it out. Survey. The whole bit. I convinced myself there'd be more good come out of it than bad. Now they're turning on me. All I got's my reputation. They're selling me down the river."

"They?"

"Larson, Lonzo, and that Hemmingford. I think they just want something easy. They tried to get me to sign a paper that it was my fault."

Margaret squinted at him. At first she had thought he was overreacting, letting things get blown out of proportion the way she had let things expand in her mind the night before. But a signed statement? "They actually wanted you to admit that it was your fault?" Bass nodded and Margaret found herself chewing her own lip. "Do you have an attorney?" she asked.

"No. They said I didn't need one."

Margaret wanted to stop chewing her lip, but she couldn't. "Maybe they're right," she said. "I'm going to find out for you." Now she was nodding her head. "You let me finish my run," she said. She started to jog slowly along the graveyard fence. "I'll call you," she said over her shoulder. "I'll call." Bass only stood there looking after her.

Margaret felt sorry for him. He seemed like the kind of guy who made the world work. But he'd made a mess of her run and now she tried to regain some equilibrium by striding at a measured pace. When she came to the graveyard entrance she glanced at the signs. They were crudely painted and posted by the chamber of commerce. There was a one dollar fee to get inside. She slowed to read another sign and heard the motorcycle start up. Almost immediately the sound began to recede as Bass turned down the hill. Margaret thought seriously about climbing the fence and running through the graveyard. Wild Bill Hickok was buried inside. So was Calamity Jane.

She had her hands on the top rail before she decided against climbing the fence. It was daylight now, not the best time for running through graveyards. She'd run along the ridge for another mile instead, then turn and let gravity help her get back to the hotel in time to catch Larson before he finished his first pot of coffee.

FOR THE first time in years, Bill Malone woke up with a woman on his mind. He lay in bed staring at the ceiling, feeling the friction of the sheets against his skin, and trying to remember if Margaret had ever affected him this way before. They had been lovers but in a too-young, offhand, easy kind of way. Neither of them had ever paid dues that would make them privy to what love really was. Back then they had no idea how rare it was. Bill pulled the sheets down to expose his bare chest. A thin film of perspiration began to evaporate and the cooling made him want to breathe deeply. When he thought of Margaret he could not see that she had changed and he concluded two things: first, that the feelings passing over him now had always been there and second, that he might well have been a fool for letting her go.

He took a deep breath, flung the covers away, and sat up on the side of the bed. It was a Saturday and there was a full week's work to be done around the yard in preparation for winter. The thought of cutting grass and mulching shrubbery depressed him. He wanted to go outside, but not alone and not to tidy up a suburban lawn. He wanted to be out in the real outdoors and he wanted to be with Margaret.

They had agreed that she should stop by in the afternoon. She mentioned that she wanted to see Cooney again and thought she might go out to see him and learn to braid horsehair.

He looked at his watch. It was not yet eight o'clock. Four hours at least. He stood up and took a pair of sweatpants and a T-shirt from the back of a chair. Already he had made up his mind to call Margaret and ask if he could ride along to Cooney's. He pulled on the clothes and slipped into a pair of tennis shoes as he made his way to the phone in the kitchen.

But there was no answer at Margaret's hotel room and Bill was immediately worried that she had gone back to Denver. But he knew she wouldn't go without telling him, probably out for her run or perhaps already at Cooney's. She'd come over in the afternoon the way she said she would. Now Bill felt a sag of depression. He couldn't spend this Saturday working in the yard the way he knew his neighbors would. He moved to the counter and poured himself a cup of coffee.

He hated yard work. Trying to take care of Kentucky bluegrass in the middle of the great American desert was lunacy. He wanted to go walking on Brendan Prairie, but in the back of his mind, behind yard work and Margaret Adamson, he was thinking about the merlin in the box. He had brought it back from his office and put it in the garage where it would be cool and quiet. It had eaten another gerbil the day before and Bill was tempted to say that its condition was improving. But over the years, Bill had found the best attitude to have about injured birds was skepticism. The merlin couldn't go on like this for long. Today might be a good day to make a decision. The bird couldn't live in the cardboard box. Its tail was already showing signs of fraying against the bottom of the box. It needed proper perches and fresh air. He would either have to euthanize it today or start taking care of it right.

He fully expected to give the injection of potassium chloride and he wasn't looking forward to it. The little falcon had begun to get under his skin. He was a tough little guy and Bill had always liked that kind. Its personality was one of the reasons for wanting it to live, but it was also a reason for not wanting it to live any other life but that of a perfect, flying falcon. Bill looked out the kitchen window and stared at the tops of the trees to check the wind. Just a hint in the yellow cottonwood leaves.

Another glorious autumn day; too bad the roofs of his neighbor's houses were in the way. He took the last sip of his coffee and stepped from the kitchen to the garage.

Allison had a Saturday morning class so her pickup was gone. He had left his car parked in the driveway. The garage was empty except for Allison's mountain bike and the lawn mower. Just the sight of the lawn mower made him sad and angry. Along the far wall, under the cupboards where they stored everything they didn't have the heart to throw away, was his workbench. On the bench, pushed back away from the edge was the cardboard box. On top of the box was the syringe.

His workbench was reasonably neat. There were a few tools scattered around but most of them were on the pegboard where they belonged. There were two rusty nuts beside the vise, left from a month ago when he'd put a new bracket on Allison's tailpipe. Only a little light came in from the single windows in the upper half of the side doors, just a hint of the bright, warm day outside. Suddenly the garage seemed oppressive, and Bill stepped to the near overhead door and flung it open. Sunlight shot halfway across the floor and the temperature seemed to jump a few degrees. It felt so good that he flung open the second door.

Standard procedure was to close all doors when opening a box with a bird in it, in case the bird flew. But Bill was sure this merlin would not be getting loose. When he'd last looked at it there was no chance of it flying anywhere. If he did have to use the needle he would just as soon use it in fresh air and sunlight.

Now he was sitting on one of the stools at the workbench with the cardboard box in front of him. He reached up to take the syringe from the box so he could open it and look inside, and the instant his hand touched the plastic plunger he thought of the first time he had ever killed an injured falcon. He felt queasy. This memory had been just on the edge of his consciousness for days now, and fear of rousing it had been part of the lethargy that had plagued him since he first woke up. He picked up the syringe and let it roll back and forth in the palm of his hand. Light and lethal. He looked up, continuing to roll the syringe back and forth, and the bright sunlight stung his eyes. It was powerful and its source felt close. It reminded him of sunlight in New Mexico and the heat from it reminded him of that horrible day seventeen years before. His garage was not plush like Jamie Eaton's falcon compound. Bill glanced around, assuring himself that he was not in the desert mountains above Santa Fe. No, this was still his garage. No leather-upholstered furniture, no air-conditioning, no locks that he had to break to get inside. But the weight of that poisonous syringe, the too-bright sun outside, and the proximity of a crippled and tortured falcon created the same taste in his mouth.

Back then he drove for eighteen hours straight—down the spine of the Rockies from Missoula, crossing the divide twice before dropping into the Great Salt Lake basin. Then he angled through the canyonlands to Cortez, Colorado, crossed the divide again east of Durango and into the dry mountains of northern New Mexico. He navigated by dead reckoning, concentrating on every conversation he had ever had with Jamie about the building the Saudi sheik had built for him. An hour drive from Taos, gravel road winding up a mountain, Tierra Amarilla the closest town. It was easier than he had imagined. When he thought he was close, he asked at a café and the waitress nodded her head. "Falcons? You bet. Arabs, too. Right up Old Post Road. You can't miss it. Only new thing that's been built in this county in years."

He should have slept before driving the last few miles. Should have timed his visit for something other than the middle of the day. But he'd come too far and now had to find out if his hunch was right.

Two days before, he'd come home from the courtroom where he'd gotten off with a small fine and found Ellen still wasn't home from what she called a vacation break. She'd been gone for a week, off to New Mexico as she'd done twice before that winter to spend time with Rebecca and Jamie. According to Ellen they were living in luxury on the Saudi's payroll—dinners at Santa Fe's finest resturaunts and parties with famous people.

Allison was at kindergarten and there wasn't much for Bill to do. It was January and his plans to fly a gyrfalcon were obviously scrapped. The house was lonely and cold, and when the phone rang he jumped for it. There was a chance it was Ellen calling from New Mexico. But it wasn't Ellen. It was Rebecca.

Bill hadn't spoke to her since that night in Jackson and instantly thought something had happened to Ellen. "What's happened? Is it Ellen?"

"Is what Ellen?

"Is she all right?"

"That's what I'm calling for. Wondered how you guys were doing."

"She's with you."

Rebecca hesitated. "Let's start over here, Bill. I called to talk to Ellen. Ellen is *not* here."

Bill was stunned. "But she's visiting you and Jamie."

She snorted. "Jamie? I haven't seen him in a year. I'm in California." Rebecca went on talking but Bill wasn't listening. He stood with the telephone to his ear, trying to sort things out. Finally, he just hung up.

Early the next afternoon he drove up Old Post Road in the mountains of northern New Mexico. He might not always know where his wife was, but he had a sixth sense when it came to finding falcons.

The grounds of the falcon facility were like an oasis in the barren mountains—irrigated—with cedars and junipers lining the walk beyond the chain-link fence. He drove past and parked his pickup a half mile down the road. When he got back to the gate he tried it and found it locked. Then he hopped up onto the chain-link and over the barbed wire at the top.

Bill did not use the walk. He veered off under the mesquite trees that afforded a small amount of shade to one side of the building and to a side door. The building was just a pole barn but designed with a roof that hung four feet over the side walls for extra shade. Air-conditioners hummed from somewhere above.

The lock was good and difficult to jimmy with his pocketknife. The entryway was carpeted and well kept. The temperature was thirty degrees cooler inside. The first room he came to

was an enclosed courtyard with a half dozen prairie and peregrine falcons perched calmly on highly decorated blocks. Bill
was impressed and took a little pride in thinking that Jamie was
at least doing a good job of caring for the falcons. But he was also
tense with anger. His hunch was right. Jamie was collecting
North American birds to ship to Saudi Arabia. He peeked
through a window into a second courtyard and there were two
dark-skinned men lounging with falcons on their fists. The Pakistanis Jamie said were employed by the sheik. Bill ducked below
the window and went on. He had hoped to find the gyrfalcon in
exquisite condition standing on one of the blocks in the front
chambers. The fact that he hadn't was not good. If the bird was
at the facility and well kept, it would be blocked out with the
others.

He passed a well-stocked veterinary lab and on the other
side of it began to find the birds that had been injured or abused.
There were four closet-size chambers and in each one there was
a battered falcon. The first chamber held a prairie falcon
hunched on its perch with splinted wings but fiery eyes. The
next bird was a merlin with broken feathers. The bird was wild
and threatened to fly against the bars when Bill looked in. The
next room held a peregrine with bandaged feet, and she looked
droopy and dull. There was even a tiny kestrel, North America's
smallest falcon, in a chamber of its own. The only species missing was the gyrfalcon.

Bill found her in the last room. She lay on the gravel floor
with her head slumped and eyes glassy. Her flight feathers were
broken from bating against her leash. And Bill knew, because he
knew these passage gyrs, even before he leaned down to look,
that her feet were ulcerated balls of puss—that she had pounded
them with her frantic bating until they were bruised, swelled,
split, and had become hopelessly infected. He knelt as close to
her as he could without frightening her. Then he cried.

But he did not cry long because he did not want to be discovered. From the vet lab window he saw that the midday break
was over. The Pakistanis were now outside, the falcons still on
their fists and Bill couldn't help thinking that those birds looked

healthy and well trained. It was a numbers game in this world; birds made it or they died a painful death. He remembered Jamie saying that his boss never allowed a falcon to be killed, even if it was in great pain. Only Allah could take a life.

The Pakistanis blocked the falcon out beside a project they were in the middle of. They were planting shrubs. Bill saw them go back to work digging in the rocky dirt. He found the bottle of potassium chloride on the third stainless-steel shelf and the syringe in the cupboard above the sink. When he stepped back into the hall he heard someone open a door and start to come his way but he didn't hesitate. He walked quickly to the chamber where the gyr lay on the floor, entered, and closed the door behind him. He knelt again beside the falcon and she looked up at him with clouded eyes. It made him sick. He made himself remember how she had looked at him on that frozen sage flat in northern Montana. He held the syringe lightly in his hand and heard the footfalls approaching in the hall. "I'm so sorry," he said as he slipped the needle into her thigh. He was holding the bird in his lap, thinking of how she was meant to slice through frozen air, and feeling the life fade mercifully from inside her when he realized someone was standing at the door.

THE WEIGHT of another syringe in his hand. The light shining through the garage door and blinding him. The knowledge that someone was standing there, watching him.

"Is the merlin still in the box?"

Bill squinted at the voice. The September sunshine made her hard to see. Yes. September and the air was cool and kind. And this was his own garage. Bill knew it was Allison, but before she stepped inside and out of the sun's glare he thought it could be Ellen, or Margaret. Yes, it would have been nice if Margaret would have been there. But it was Allison and that was good, too. She was in jeans. The hiking boots. The dark blond hair a little wild from the wind. "Is the bird still in there?" She gestured toward the box.

Bill nodded. He felt the syringe in his hand and was embarrassed by it. He made a quarter turn toward the bench, opened a drawer, and dropped the tube of poison into the tangle of assorted wire and hose connections.

"So how's he doing?" Allison had come closer while his back was turned. "Is he going to make it?"

"I don't know," Bill said. "He ate yesterday. I was just going to take a look."

She was very close now and smiled as if Bill had made a joke. She pointed her thumb over her shoulder. "Not with the door open. He might get loose. You don't want a crippled falcon out on its own, do you?" It was something she'd read in that book he'd given her years before. She had spent the rest of the night after her talk with Margaret rereading it.

"You're absolutely right." Bill got up to close the doors. As he walked he tried to shake the ghosts out of his head. This was Allison, it was Cooney's merlin in the box.

He switched on the lights over the workbench, put his hands on the merlin's box, but did not open it. He looked at Allison who had moved to where she could see into the box when it was opened. "Let's have a look," Bill said. He eased the flaps open and they looked down at the merlin. Bill was amazed to see him spread his wings and hiss at them. Some of his feather tips had fecal material on them and the number-two primary on his left wing was bent. Living in the box was no good.

"He's gorgeous," Allison said.

"Must have some nerve damage. His head is twisted."

"It's not so bad."

"You sound like a bird worshiper," Bill said. "This guy doesn't need romance. He needs the truth." He tried to be as matter-of-fact as possible but as he looked at the bird, he could see that it had improved. It was no longer sitting on its haunches and the head had straightened a little. Bill began to close the box flaps again. He was thinking about what he should do.

"Are you going to jess him up?"

Bill looked at her, surprised she knew the jargon and that the merlin would be better off out of the box. But he didn't comment. He wasn't sure the merlin was ready to be treated like a healthy falcon. "We don't really have a place to keep him jessed."

"You could build a shelf perch."

This was too much. "Where are you getting all this?"

Allison shrugged. "It's interesting. I've been reading up." She tapped the workbench. "We could build one right here. There's some old carpeting in the attic." She pointed to the crawlway that led to the garage's upper level. "It wouldn't take long." Bill smiled at her. "You have to," she said.

Bill did not want to do what she was asking but when she nodded her head, as if there was no doubt about what had to be done, he gave in.

A half hour later they had a semicircular padded platform bolted to the wall eight inches above the workbench, which had been cleared of everything, and a carpet, complete with soft underpad, laid over the bench's entire surface. The garage had a door that opened into the front yard and one that opened into the back. They had tacked burlap sacking over the windows in each door so when Bill turned off the light over the workbench, the room was completely dark. When he turned the light back on Allison was grinning with delight.

"That will keep him quiet," she said. "He'll get well on this perch. Now how about jesses, swivel, and leash?"

Bill raised a finger in the air. "For that we have to break into an ancient treasure chest." He took a ring of keys from a nail beside the garage door and began sorting through them. There were a half dozen keys whose locks he had long since forgotten. But the small oval brass key with the lion's head on the side was as familiar to him as his first baseball glove. He let the rest of the keys on the ring fall into his hand and held the special key between his thumb and first finger. He moved his fingertip over it and could feel the lion's head rising to meet his touch. "Follow me," he said to Allison.

They walked out the side door, into the backyard, and crossed to the storage shed against the back fence. The shed was not locked but the huge leather steamer trunk was. Bill pulled it from under a broken lawn chair and a boxed croquet set. He dragged it out onto the grass and, suddenly very excited to open it, grasped the heavy buckles that held the two leather straps and jerked them free. Then he found the small brass key again and inserted it in the tarnished lock on the front of the truck. The lid opened with a creak and for the first time in many years the contents felt the warm yellow light of a high plains afternoon.

The inside of the trunk had been turned into a sort of cabinet with two rows of hooks across the top and compartments of varying sizes in the bottom. Bill was on one knee in front of the trunk with his bad leg stretched out to the side. He felt Allison settle on his other side and together they gazed at the richness of oiled leather and polished wood tucked neatly away in the trunk. A gauntlet of tan doe skin, trimmed in dark brown kip, lay over the largest compartment. Under the gauntlet were two wooden blocks, the size of large flowerpots, turned from laminated walnut and maple. These were falcon perches, rubbed to a deep shine and fitted with cork tops to protect the falcon's feet. Another compartment held a worn leather hawking bag with brass fittings and darkly oiled cowhide leashes of different sizes, coiled and stacked conically in the compartment's corner. In another compartment there was a balance-beam scale with a padded pan designed to give the birds a better grip as they were weighed. Other compartments held small boxes, a few gyrfalcon primary feathers, a pair of binoculars in a battered canvas case.

There were twelve hooks on the top of the trunk and each held a leather hood of a slightly different size. They were crafted of three pieces—sown with tiny stitches—and a plume of sharptailed grouse feathers protruded from the top to form the handle used to slip the hood over the falcon's head. Allison reached up and unsnapped one from its hook. She rolled it in her hand and looked carefully at its design. "Did you make these?" she asked.

"A long time ago," Bill said. He took out one of the small wooden boxes and it made a muffled tinkling sound. He laid it in the grass between them, opened it, and the sunlight reflected off a half dozen pairs of silver bells. There were also stainless steel swivels of varying sizes and Bill selected the smallest of the lot to hand to Allison. "Hold this," he said and reached for a second box. From that box he took strips of oiled kangaroo leather and a few brass grommets. He passed those on to Allison and dug back into the trunk for a small brown metal toolbox from which he took a leather punch, a pair of scissors, and a small pair of vise grips with the two parts of the grommet set welded to its jaws. "That should do us," he said and gently closed the trunk lid.

They spread everything out on the bench and Bill went to work with the leather punch and scissors. He said nothing, and Allison only watched him as he prestretched the leather, measured it, and cut carefully. Here was the Bill Malone she had seen in the photographs. Finally he began to rearrange everything on the bench so that everything would be at hand when he needed it. "We need a glass of very hot water," he said. "One of the big glasses above the toaster. Let the tap run for awhile."

By the time Allison was back everything was in place. "Okay," Bill said, "You've never cast a falcon so we'll take it slow." He was enjoying this and that made Allison beam. They were feeding each other's joy, both loving the intensity of it all. "Just remember," Bill said, "he's a delicate thing. Hold him firmly but not hard. It's important that we do it all as fast as we can because being held puts them under a lot of stress. But we have to do it right. I'll pick him up and I want you to raise the hot water up so his tail and wing tips are in the water. Soak off all the crud. Swish them around slowly. The hot water will straighten that bent feather. Then I'll hand him to you and you just hold him the way I hold him, up in the light where I can work."

Allison was tense and afraid to speak but she nodded with a nervous grin. "Now just hold your hands up around the box while I reach in," Bill said.

She did as he said and from her vantage point saw that the bird had again spread its wings and was holding its mouth open. But it didn't offer to bite. Bill moved his hands down over the wings and slowly brought them into the bird's sides. He made sure his hands encased the bird completely and that all its feathers were in place before he gently squeezed and raised the little falcon into the light.

Allison had the hot water ready, and she slipped the glass up and around the soiled feathers without the bird even knowing it. She sloshed the water around in the glass and the tail and wing tips went a slick black. "That's good," Bill whispered. "Now put your hands over mine and I'll transfer him to you. Easy."

They were both intent on what they were doing but the touch of their hands couldn't help but register on Bill. There was a contrast of weathered, hard-used hands against those still smooth and youthful. There was a wonderful friction as the falcon slipped from Bill's hands to Allison's. But they were focused on the falcon, trying to make the transfer without scaring the bird more. "Not too tight now." Bill's hands slipped completely away. "Hold him like you love him."

Allison nodded and mumbled, "I do. I do." And that was the first time Bill smiled since they had first opened the box. He took an instant to notice how beautiful they looked—the bright defiant little falcon held by the young woman. But there was just that instant to squander. He took up the first small strip of kangaroo hide with the holes punched in each end and wrapped it around the falcon's soda-straw leg. It was a good fit and he pushed the first grommet through the two holes and crimped it flat with the vise grips. It made a perfect bracelet but Bill rotated it around the leg to be sure it was not too tight. He did the same on the other leg, then threaded a five-inch-long kangaroo-hide jess through each grommet. A leather button on the end of each jess held it in the grommet and the slit at the other end accepted the swivel. When the swivel was in place he pulled the leash through the free swivel loop. He attached a tiny silver bell to one leg with a quarter inch strip of leather, then he looked up at Allison.

"He's done."

Allison's grin had widened. "He didn't even struggle."

"He's a good boy. Now I'm going to tie the leash to the perch and I want you to put him down on it, but don't let go until I turn off the light. We don't want him to bate."

"Got it."

Bill tied the leash and moved to the light switch on the wall next to the outside door. "Just set him there and see if he'll put his feet down."

"He's trying to grip the perch."

"Okay. Let go slowly." Bill turned off the light. The garage was completely dark. He waited to hear if the bird would bate. But there was no sound. "I'm over here," he said but the room remained silent. The darkness had weight, and Bill reached behind him for the doorknob to anchor himself. "Over here," he said again.

"I'm here," Allison said and Bill felt her hand touch his chest. "He stood up on the perch like a pro," she said.

They were standing inches apart in the total darkness. "That's great." Bill twisted the knob and let a crack of light come across Allison's face. Now her grin was bursting and her eyes sparkled with exhilaration.

"We did it," she said.

Bill let in a little more light and they moved so they could slip out and still look back at the merlin. The last they saw of him, before Bill took the light away again, he was standing up tall, his jesses and swivel hanging below him properly and his head perhaps straighter that it had been only a half hour before.

They spilled out into the sunny front yard laughing at their success. "He's going to make it," Allison said.

"If he stays quiet, he's got a chance." Bill was smiling with Allison, and at first he thought it was all because of her. But there was more. He held his hands to his face and smelled the neat's-foot oil from the jesses. It was a rich and poignant odor that he had always loved. He breathed it deeply and it smelled so good that he took one hand and held it up to Allison's face. "Breathe," he said.

13

By the time Margaret showered and dressed it was nearly nine o'clock. If Larson was going to be in his office on a Saturday, he should be there by now. She thought of calling first, but she wanted to find out what Larson and his friends were thinking and didn't want to lose the element of surprise.

The door to the sheriff's office was open but there was no one in the outer office. The room had no windows and was painted a pale institutional green. The receptionist's desk was clean, with only a picture of three small children in a wooden frame left in sight. Margaret stood in front of the desk and ran her tongue across her front teeth. Then she heard voices in the next office. The door was closed so she tapped three times with the first knuckle of her right hand. The voices stopped and Margaret heard someone move toward the door.

When the door opened Margaret found herself looking up at a tall pale-faced man in a yellow polo shirt. The man stared at her. "I'm looking for Sheriff Larson," Margaret said. The man nodded and stepped aside.

Larson sat behind his desk and another man sat across from him. When he saw Margaret he started to stand but didn't find enough energy to complete the move. He tipped forward and an uneasy smile came to his face. "Miss Adamson," he said.

"Sheriff." Margaret nodded. "I'd like to talk to you when you get a chance." She started to back out of the office and this brought Larson to his feet.

"Margaret," he said. The use of Margaret's first name startled both of them and an instant of silence followed. "This is Barry

Hemmingford." He indicated the man sitting across the desk from him. "And that's Danny Lonzo."

Margaret shook their hands. So these were the guys that were pushing out old Larson. Lonzo looked like a Italian golf pro and Hemmingford looked like your garden-variety chubby politician. These were also the guys that were hassling Troy Bass. Margaret knew she should come back later and talk to Larson alone but she couldn't pass up the opportunity. "You're here about the Andy Arnold accident," she said.

Lonzo didn't answer. He looked to Hemmingford who was now on his feet. "We're interested. Just trying to make sure things go smoothly."

Margaret nodded and thought she might leave it at that. But she'd come here because she felt something dangerous about this investigation. She figured she might as well ask. "What's the deal with Bass?"

Hemmingford shrugged. "He was the man on the machine."

Margaret looked back to Hemmingford. She knew now who was in charge. "Bass just climbed onto the machine. Andy Arnold was simply in the wrong place." She looked back to Larson.

The old man was still. She looked at Hemmingford. His nod was patronizing. "I was just curious," she said. She started to leave the room again, but hesitated and turned back to the men. "I told Sheriff Larson," Margaret said. "But just so you know, I saw Bass very well when this thing happened. No one was more surprised when those brakes failed than Troy Bass. I saw his face."

She didn't wait for a response. Hemmingford repulsed her, Lonzo was too spooky. She had to get away. And Larson. How spineless can a man be? Bass was right. They wanted to pin this on someone. They could never stick it on Bass, but from spending two minutes with these men Margaret knew they'd find someone else.

She pushed out onto the street and into another beautiful autumn day. Forget it, she told herself. She didn't want to worry about these small-town politics. She wanted to think about enjoying herself. She wanted to concentrate on visiting Cooney. She wanted to think about seeing Bill Malone that afternoon. But of course, her uneasiness was tied to Bill. He might be the next person they'd try to blame.

The Franklin Hotel was visible from where she stood and she headed that way. But before she reached the first intersection she heard her name being called. When she turned she saw Larson hustling along the street after her. She thought about going on toward the Franklin—Larson could never keep up. But he looked pitiful shuffling along the sidewalk and so she waited. By the time he caught up, the light had changed. Margaret started across the street and Larson came along like a child.

They said nothing for half a block. Then Larson said, "You and Bass got it figured about right. They need a scapegoat."

"Sticking Bass is cheap and stupid."

"Maybe. It was the first thing that popped into their minds. They thought he might roll for accepting some blame. He didn't."

"What happened to the idea that it was an accident?"

She thought Larson would have something to say to that. But he didn't. He hung his head and squinted as if he was in pain. But when Margaret started to look away Larson found his voice. "Look," he said. "I think what you said about seeing Bass's face made an impression on them. He's off the hook. No easy way out for Hemmingford." Larson seemed suddenly exhausted. He shrugged. "The thing is, the master brake cylinder was empty. There's no getting around the fact that *somebody* drained it." Margaret stopped and stared at him. "They wanted it to be simple." Larson said. "But maybe it wasn't."

Margaret understood what Larson was trying to say. She nodded and saw Larson purse his lips again. She thought he might say something more. But all he did was shrug again.

COONEY JENKINS spent the whole morning trying to figure out how to get the fuel filter off his Datsun pickup. He'd been having trouble getting it started for months. Sometimes it worked fine, other times nothing. The week before he had determined that it was getting good spark so it had to be fuel. The fuel filter was the first thing that came to mind and he'd changed it. But the catch was that model of Datsun pickup has two filters, one in the fuel line and one at the fuel pump. He didn't know that until this morning when he was lying under the pickup, getting ready to take the fuel pump off as a last resort.

There it was, a dollar-and-a-half plastic gizmo held on with two hose clamps. A piece of cake—if you have hands the size of an average Japanese mechanic. Cooney's were at least three times that size. But, after a lengthy search, he found a pair of needle-nose pliers and a screwdriver in a cardboard box under the sink. Another half hour and he was finally getting somewhere. There was a minor sense of urgency. Cooney didn't have to get the pickup going immediately, but he would need it the next day or so. He had talked to Agnes Barsky three days before and learned that her *Paphiopedilum actaeus* was blooming. He'd woken up that morning to find that his *Paphiopedilum astarte* had begun to bloom. That meant that if he was going to produce a *Paphiopedilum* F.C. Puddle FCC, he'd have to get his *astarte* to Agnes Barsky's house for fertilization soon.

In a way, this was a chance of a lifetime. The first *P. F.C.* Puddle FCC was produced in 1932 in England by one of the orchid legends—F. C. Puddle. Cooney had never seen one in the flesh, but to his way of thinking, the pictures proved that *P. F.C.* Puddle FCC was the prettiest of all the white orchids. To his knowledge none had been produced on the high plains of North America, certainly none in the Black Hills. So cleaning the damned fuel filter was important.

Finally he worked the hose clamp around to where he could squeeze it and slide it up on the hose. When the end of the hose came loose, a thimble full of dirty gasoline dribbled on his forehead. "How can the Japanese stand it?" He got a good grip on the filter with the needle-nose pliers and pulled. It came off. Another splash of gasoline in his face.

He came out from under the pickup coughing and wiping his face with the sleeve of his coveralls. His eyes were closed and when he opened them there was Margaret Adamson. She scared the daylights out of him.

"Jesus!" he shouted as he jumped back against the pickup. He dropped the fuel filter in the grass.

"Sorry," Margaret said. "I thought you heard me drive up."

"Jesus. Jesus. No. I didn't hear a thing." Cooney looked at her, took a deep breath, then went back down on his hands and knees to look for the fuel filter.

"You said if I came out you'd show me how to braid horsehair."

Cooney found the fuel filter and held it up as if it were a gold nugget. "Soon as I get this baby cleaned out."

Margaret watched as Cooney walked to the back of his pickup and dug out a can of gasoline. He rooted around in the trash under the topper until he found a pop can. With his pocketknife he cut the can in half and filled it with gasoline. He swished the filter in the gasoline and then, to Margaret's horror, put one end of the filter in his mouth and blew. A wad of black crud shot out and Cooney laughed with glee. He swished the filter around in the gasoline again and held it up for Margaret to see. "Clean as a new nickel," he said. "Hang on a sec. I'll just hook her back up."

While Cooney laid on his back and wrestled with the fuel filter, Margaret walked around his yard. It had been dark when she was there before but in the daylight it didn't seem much more orderly. In fact, now she could see that there were ten or fifteen five-gallon buckets of what looked like engine parts stored under the front porch. And the yard was not pine needles from the surrounding trees, as she had thought, but wood chips. There was a chopping block with an ax stuck into its top and Margaret deduced that Cooney split his wood in the front yard. But the chips must have come from years past because there was only a small pile of wood ready to be burned. It was late September and the nights were getting cold. She wondered when Cooney planned to cut his winter wood.

The sound of the Datsun coughing to life spun her around. Cooney sat in the driver's seat with the door open and one leg still out on the ground. He wore a big smile and revved the engine a few times out of sheer exhilaration. "Like a Zviss vatch," he shouted over the engine noise.

An hour later, Margaret was sitting cross-legged on the front porch with five bunches of horsehair tied to the railing, trying to remember if the third bunch in her left hand went over the first bunch in her right or the other way around. Cooney reached around her and put his big hands on hers. "Left over right," he said. "Pull tight. A little twist. Outside over the left." He took Margaret's hands through all the motions and amazed her with the gentleness of his movements. He was a big, solid man and, though it was obvious that he didn't bathe often, with Cooney it didn't seem to matter. He smiled as he inspected the braid she had made.

"Tight," he said. "Tough." He unfastened it from the railing and tied the ends for her. Then he made a wrap around each hand and jerked it hard. "Stronger than rawhide." He handed it to Margaret. She let her fingers run over the silky surface of the horsehair. It was truly an amazing material.

" 'Course, if you use bundles of different colored hair you get a pattern." Cooney handed her a bridle he had made. It was tan and black and the braid had come out with tan star patterns on a black background.

Margaret glanced up from the bridle. "Thank you," she said.

"No problem." Cooney picked up the extra pieces of horsehair and stroked them. He looked at them hard through his half-moon glasses and Margaret thought he was concentrating on the hair. "But that's not the only reason you came up here today," Cooney said. He looked over the glasses. "There's another reason, isn't there?" Margaret looked quickly at him and saw the disconnection in his eyes that could make people wonder about what was going on in his mind. But of course he was right. There were other reasons.

Cooney's perception took Margaret by surprise. Originally the braiding was the only reason for her visit. But after spending the evening before with Bill she woke up craving someone to talk to about him. Cooney was the natural choice. Then, after her encounter with Hemmingford, Lonzo, and Larson, she had become worried. It didn't take a genius to figure that if Bass were let off the hook, someone would have to take his place. Whoever they suspected of vandalizing the machinery might be next in line. In just a couple hours she was supposed to meet Bill at his house. She was nervous about just meeting him. Nervous about being alone with him. And now there was a sense of foreboding that told her he was in jeopardy.

Cooney stood watching her with his head cocked to one side. He smiled. "Well?"

"Yes," Margaret said. "I suppose braiding wasn't my only reason for coming here. I might have been wondering about Bill. You said he spent the night after the Mountain Air Estates meeting here on your couch."

"Yeah. Right there." Cooney pointed through the front door, toward the couch. "Why?"

"Probably nothing," Margaret said. "Just a feeling I'm getting."

"Feeling?"

"Like the sheriff might start thinking something crazy." She spoke slowly, trying her thoughts out loud for the first time. "Like he might start thinking someone sabotaged the machine that killed Andy Arnold."

Cooney was looking at her over his glasses again. He thought for a moment about what she had said then began to nod. "He was here," Cooney said. "All night. Slept under the old quilt, right on the couch." His expression was flat until a devilish gleam came into his eyes. "Alone," he said.

"Alone?"

"That's what you're wondering isn't it?"

"Not exactly."

"But kind of."

Cooney was leading the conversation in a different direction. Margaret knew what he was doing and, in a way, she was thankful. She was curious, too. "Not that night. But in a general sense, maybe."

"He was alone that night and alone every night since he came back to the hills. Far as I know."

Cooney shrugged in a conspiratorial way and it made Margaret smile. "What makes you think I care who he's sleeping with?"

"Just thought you might be interested."

"Oh you did, did you?" Margaret was enjoying this. It had been a long time since she was last teased about a man. "You wouldn't make something up to make Bill come off better, would you?"

"I might," Cooney laughed. "But I haven't yet."

Margaret picked up the braided horsehair. "May I keep it?"

"You built it. It's yours."

Margaret held the braid thoughtfully. She was thinking that she might not see this man again, that the Black Hills might simply fall into the great void of her past. She should be back in her Denver apartment in a couple days. There was another environmental assessment going on somewhere in Utah. She couldn't remember where. Just then it seemed unimportant. She doubled the braid over and struck her left hand with it lightly, the way a person deep in thought taps a pencil on a book. She was halfway to her car when Cooney called after her. "Drive slow," he said.

At the car Margaret hesitated, then held her hand up in a passive wave. She hoped this wouldn't be the last she saw of Cooney. The big man waved back to her and she couldn't help being reminded of Smoky Bear.

A SMALL Maglite flashlight lay on the workbench of Bill's garage. The light shone against the near wall. Except for the twelve-inch spot of brightness on the sheetrock, the room was dark. Bill's form was gray and murky as he sat motionless on the stool set out away from the workbench. Beyond him, in even darker shadows, sat Allison. Bill wore the old gauntlet from the trunk and the merlin was perched on his fist. With the gauntlet,

Bill held the upper half of a fresh-killed sparrow at the falcon's feet. He squeezed it rhythmically and with every pulse the merlin's talons tightened on the meat. Everyone was stone still, mesmerized by the eerie light.

But the merlin knew there was food at his feet and only his wildness kept him from bending over and feeding. The humans did not seem threatening but the falcon knew that many predators were masters of patience, and he had known even when he was a chick in the nest that a wrong move could mean his life. Still the food was tempting, he had only eaten twice in five days, and it was so close, so easy.

They sat like that for ten minutes. Then Bill pursed his lips and chirped like a distressed bird. The merlin could not resist. His beak came down in an uncontrollable response to the noise and crushed a vertebra of the already-dead sparrow. When he realized what he had done and that there had been no ill effect, the merlin tasted the meat. It was luscious, warmed in the sunlight so that the blood was a familiar temperature. He pulled at the exposed meat, then at the feathers of the sparrow's neck. In another minute the falcon was engrossed in plucking feathers from his meal. The feathers cascaded into the air and made Bill grin. He began to whisper the story he had promised to tell Allison if the falcon decided to eat.

"I was a couple years older than you are now." He spoke in a monotone, trying to lull the falcon and convince him that there was nothing to fear in the human voice. "In those days I had a dog named Lou. A silky setter bitch with orange ticking and big brown eyes that she could turn on you and make you understand." The falcon had pulled most of the feathers from the sparrow and now began to eat the meat. Bill revealed only a little of the sparrow at a time so that the association between food and humans would be prolonged. "She was a sweet dog in the house but all business in the field. She ran with her tail high and curved to the left. She'd had a thousand grouse and pheasants shot over her but her specialty was working with the falcons.

"Lou would lay quietly at my feet in that first week when I'd feed the gyrs on the fist like we're doing now. She'd move carefully. She knew it was important not to frighten the bird. And when I'd first bring the gyr out into the daylight, that old dog would stay clear until the bird had adjusted to the sights and noises of civilization. By the time we were ready to go grouse hunting, she would have narrowed the distance between herself and the falcon." Bill paused and slowly raised his hand to adjust the sparrow so the merlin could get at the tender meat at the base of the wings. The merlin froze when he saw the hand coming and Bill moved that much more carefully. When the hand came away the merlin brought a foot up and delicately scratched at the tiny feathers under its chin. The dainty silver bell sounded brittle in the darkened garage and the merlin went back to eating.

"In those days I prayed for Januarys without too much snow. Now it doesn't matter so much, but back then the weather might have been the most important part of my life. On the high plains everything depends on weather. The grouse, with their spiked tail feathers and silver breasts, are the great masters of that climate. They're camouflaged for winter and can stand the coldest weather. They have feathers to their toes. They can burrow into snow banks for warmth. They group up in winter and if the snow is too deep, they eat tree buds. On frosty mornings the cottonwood branches can droop with their weight."

Allison wanted to ask questions. She wanted to know how big they were, if they flew like crows or like pheasants. But she had promised not to say a word. So she sat quietly on her stool and watched her father and the merlin, silhouetted against the dully illuminated wall. The bird bent and pulled at its meal as predictably as a metronome. There was no threat in the small movements her father made. When he spoke it blended with the silence and did not intrude.

"But there is almost no chance of catching a sharp-tailed grouse that's in a tree. They're just too alert. They see the falcon when she leaves your fist and they fly only when they know she is out of position enough that they can escape. If the falcon is silly enough to try for them in the trees, they only hop behind a branch where she can't get at them. In January there are no grouse left that have not escaped from at least one falcon. It's the way they make a living. So Lou and I would try to find them in the edges of hay fields or the tops of draws where the wind blows away the snow and uncovers the grasses they prefer."

Bill smiled as he recalled those days. Allison wanted to ask what he was remembering, but she had promised. It was the trade-off for being allowed to watch this part of the merlin's training. "There's a particular ridge along the edge of a huge bench above the Missouri River. There were miles of wheat land on the bench and, if the wind had cleared some of the stubble, the sharps would come in and spend most of the day gleaning the ground of spilled wheat. The ridge ran generally east and west and since the wind was usually out of the northwest, I'd run Lou from the east so the breeze would be quartering. I'd stay right on the brink so Lou wouldn't drift into the wind and end up a half mile out in the stubble. From where I walked with the gyr, I could see twenty miles of Missouri River breaks and not a sign of any people.

"If you're wondering if it was cold, the answer is yes. It was a tough way to spend a day, but God, did I see some flights out of that wheat.

"When Lou caught the scent of grouse her tail would start to wring. It would go from a constant wagging as she ran, to a circular motion and the long hair would whip to a cone of white as she worked to locate the grouse. They're always jumpy and hard to get pointed that time of year so if Lou looked hot I'd unhood the gyr and cast her off. That would freeze the grouse, they wouldn't try to outfly the gyr unless hiding failed. And with Lou on the case, it was bound to fail. She'd zero in on the scent and lock up like a statue—head and tail high and absolutely still. When she went on point, no matter how many times I'd seen it, it took my breath away. I can see it in my mind now—Lou's long white hair shimmering in the wind and the gyr fifty yards upwind of her and mounting higher and higher. Then I'd be scrambling—I could run in those days—to get into a position where I could flush the grouse crosswind and down toward the Missouri. By the time I got to where I should be, the gyr might be a thousand feet above, facing away and into the wind and watching the dog over her shoulder. Rarely would there be a single grouse. Often the whole wheat field would lift off and a hundred football-size birds would rifle out at unbelievable speed for the river bottom. And when the grouse came off the wheat, the gyr would swap ends in a heartbeat and be flying straight down before you could see. It was always best to keep your eyes on the falcon. It was impossible to watch her and the grouse at the same time and, if you tried, you'd end up missing everything.

"She'd be stooping right at me and coming so fast through the snow-reflected light that the speed was hard to register. In a moment she would begin to flatten out and the grouse would come into my vision. Only then did her speed register. The grouse would already be a hundred yards from the flush and barreling for the river bottom a mile and a half away. But if things were right, one grouse would not make the sanctuary of the cottonwoods."

The merlin pulled the last mouthful of meat from between Bill's fingers and swallowed it with a gulp. "Sometimes," Bill said as he picked up the miniature hood, "she would hit them so hard they would fall dead from the sky." He brought the hood up with a steady motion and deftly rotated it onto the merlin's head. "They'd tumble another hundred yards toward the Missouri." He stood up with the little falcon upright on his fist. "That's the way I like to remember it, at least. Grouse for dinner." Bill grinned. "And the gyrfalcon ate first."

Allison stared straight ahead for an instant. Then her eyes moved to her father and after another pause she raised her eyebrows to ask if it was all right if she moved. "He's hooded," Bill said. "Now he needs to hear conversation."

"That was great," she said. "And he ate like a champ." She moved close. "May I pet him?"

"Sure, gently on the front." Bill guided her hand and the merlin hissed but not with much ferocity.

Allison stroked the bird slowly, again and again. She spoke without thinking. "Did Mother ever go with you to hunt grouse?"

It was still dark in the garage and the shadows made Bill's face more angular. "Oh, a time or two. But she was not as interested in what they really did as in the romance of it all. Truth is," Bill said, "your mother was a sucker for romance."

MARGARET ADAMSON pulled up in front of Bill Malone's house and slid out of her car. It was a grand late afternoon and she looked Bill's yard over well. There were a group of robins, no doubt migrants stopping over for a few hours, spread out working the lawn for earthworms. They were intent—hop, hop, listen, hop, hop, listen, stab. It was amazing.

Margaret moved up toward the house along the garage and sensed, even before she saw the burlap covering the window, that something important was going on in the garage. She paused at the door and heard a sound that she had not heard for many years. The delicate silver bell sounded inside the garage and a flood of memories rushed down on her. Instantly she knew that Bill was in the garage and working with the merlin. For years this cloistered ritual was part of his life and she learned to respect it and even to understand how a person could sacrifice those hours to solitude and darkness. She moved closer to the door. She would not go in, but she held her ear close and was surprised to hear Allison's voice.

"And is that the reason Mother went to New Mexico?"

"I think so," Bill said. "Romance, adventure. Jamie was attractive. He had money and a kind of power. I think he showed her a wonderful time and in a way I can't blame her. She must have found him much more attractive than a man who would follow a bird dog all day in a frozen wheat field. I don't think she could help herself."

"But she must have loved you."

"I think she loved the idea of me."

Margaret pulled away from the door. She was stunned and stood trying to process what she had just heard. Then there was movement behind the door and the knob began to turn. She stepped back and tried to compose herself, but this new idea, this image of Ellen Mayhan with Jamie Eaton did not shake easily from her head.

When Allison and Bill, with the falcon on his fist, came through the door she pretended she had just come up the walk. She smiled and made a feeble comment about the merlin's health. Bill laughed and said it was the first falcon he'd had on his fist for eighteen years. He was giddy with his reconnection and didn't notice that Margaret was feeling sick, insensitive, and stupid. But Allison saw it in an instant. She looked at Margaret with a touch of pity in her eyes. For the first time, Margaret was realizing that she had no idea of the depth of Bill's pain. She was only beginning to understand the forces that drove him.

THE FALCON never left Bill's fist as he started the charcoal fire and readied the T-bones for grilling. It was amazing to watch—with his right hand he hefted the charcoal bag, dumped it into the grill, and sprayed starter fluid. Then, most amazing of all, he held the matchbox against the picnic table with his left elbow and struck the match. As he did these things one-handed, the memory of him doing them before came to Margaret. He talked the whole time and she knew that it was partly to make the bird more accustomed to his voice. But there was something young and ditzy about the things he was saying. It was totally charming.

While Bill worked and talked on the deck, Allison was in the kitchen making a salad. Margaret volunteered to help but no one needed her. Bill told her to relax. So she sat at the picnic table, the sliding glass door to the kitchen open behind her, and joined in the conversation.

The air was absolutely still, the light from the setting sun thick and yellow. Margaret commented on the quality of the light and Bill agreed. "If people only saw the world in that light," Bill said, "they would never think of plowing up sagebrush or strip mining." He laughed. "Or strip malls, for that matter."

Bill's comment made Margaret think of Barry Hemmingford. He would never notice such light. "Do you suppose Andy Arnold ever noticed this kind of light?"

"Who knows?" Bill said.

"He must have been a pretty important man. Nobody wants to say that his death just happened. Seems like they want to blame someone."

Allison came to the kitchen door and stood with her shoulder against the jamb. "How do you mean?" she said.

"I think they don't want any questions about what happened." Margaret didn't want to say what she was about to say. She didn't want to be suspicious. But she couldn't help it. "There's a guy here from the state attorney general's office." She watched Bill's face. "He's investigating." Bill went on poking the steaks with a fork.

He shrugged. "How close are you with the salad?" He turned to Allison, but she was gone. She had gone back into the kitchen and now stood leaning against the counter. "How close with the salad?" Louder this time.

"A couple minutes."

Bill turned to Margaret. "A couple minutes," he repeated. He continued to look at her. "You look great," he said.

"It's this autumn light you like so much."

"Isn't it fantastic?"

Margaret had to agree. She kicked herself for being suspicious, for questioning. She closed her eyes and let the light wash her face. When she let herself, she felt luxuriant.

They were just sitting down to eat when the phone rang. Bill was nearest and picked it up. He laughed at what the person on the phone said. "Yes. Yes. Okay. I'll get her." He laid the phone on the counter. "It's Cooney," he said. "For you." He pointed to Allison.

The falcon was still on Bill's fist and he had to swing it out of the way to let Allison pass. He made a complete pirouette and ended up at the table beside Margaret. The food was getting cold and so they began without Allison. She was only ten feet away and they could hear half of her conversation with Cooney. "Nothing," she said. "No, tomorrow is Sunday. You know that." "Tonight? I don't know." Then she went silent as she listened. When she spoke again, her voice was lower, impossible to make out.

Bill tried to dish the salad with one hand. This he could not manage and Margaret took the bowl from him. She put salad on all their plates. "Would you like me to cut your steak?" she asked.

"I could put him down," Bill said. But Margaret knew he didn't want to put the falcon down. Besides he looked happy and boyish with the bird on his fist.

"No. I want to cut your steak for you."

"Then, please." He motioned toward the plate with his free hand.

He watched her cut the meat. Pieces small enough for a child. All the best parts, cut off close to the bone. She felt his eyes on her but did not look up from her work.

"I'm going out tonight," Allison said. She had already sat down and was wolfing her meal. "Cooney had this great idea." The salad was gone. The steak was being cut into pieces four times the size of those Margaret had cut. "He invited me for dessert. Ice cream."

Bill was surprised at the way Allison was eating. The steak was half gone. "She's always liked ice cream," he said to Margaret as a sort of explanation.

"Then we're going to try calling owls. Cooney has a tape."

"An owl-calling tape?"

"Says he just got it. Said he tried it and it worked good."

Bill looked at Margaret and squinted one eye. He looked back to Allison. She was almost finished with the meal. "This is sort of a new interest for you, isn't it?"

She stood up and moved around the table. She stroked the merlin's breast. "I won't be home tonight," she said. "I'll stay at Cooney's." Then she smiled, first at Margaret, then at her father. "You two will have the house to yourselves."

14

COONEY HAD known Allison since she was six years old. That was the year Bill came back to Spearfish to teach at Black Hills State University. Bill's roots were in the Black Hills but his mother and father had retired to Arkansas, and Allison had spent most of her time with them while Bill went back to school. But when he got the job, he wanted her with him. She stayed in Arkansas only until Bill was settled into a rented house on Pine Avenue. Allison came at Christmas and by then Bill and Cooney had become friends.

Allison's arrival came after much anticipation. She was a main topic of conversation that first autumn of their friendship, and Bill expected Cooney to be there when he brought her home. It was a cold December night and Cooney hadn't known what to bring for the occasion but he stopped at the grocery store and bought some ice cream. Bill told him that Allison liked ice cream but it didn't seem like enough of a present. After buying the ice cream, Cooney walked to his pickup parked near the rear of the grocery. He heard a squeak and had to get down on his hands and knees to peer under a car. It was a tiny kitten, thin and frightened. This seemed like a more appropriate gift than ice cream and Cooney decided it was fate.

There were only two chairs in that house—Bill was broke after three crash years of graduate school—but there was a nice braided rug that his parents donated to the cause and that is where the three of them sat. Cooney brought a whole gallon of ice cream because Bill had made a big deal about how Allison loved it. Cooney had no idea how much a six-year-old would eat but he wasn't taking any chances. They sat on the floor with three spoons and the gallon of chocolate chip. When the kitten stuck his head out of Cooney's shirt, Allison screamed with delight. "He looks like Bugs Bunny," she said. The cat became Bugs and they took to each other immediately. Bugs was a hit. And so was Cooney.

There was an old radio on the floor between them and it played Christmas carols. The only other things in the room were books. Stacks of them.

It was books that brought Bill and Cooney together. They re-met as adults in the university library where Bill was preparing for a class. Cooney was trying to figure out how to find a book that might tell him about a beautiful little flower he had found growing in a deep gulch that ran into Spearfish Creek just a mile from the cabin.

He had moved into the cabin after his grandparents died. His parents had tried to get him to stay at home in the town of Spearfish, but he hated it there. He had no friends because of the way he looked and the fact that he seldom spoke. There were people who knew him and knew that he was not dangerous, but they were older and had families by then. When he lived with his parents it was rare that he saw anyone he knew except them, and they were ashamed of him. They had raised him and fed him and clothed him and tried their best, but they were ashamed. He wasn't like other people and when Cooney was still young, they gave up. Early mornings he walked out to the edge of town where the forest began and disappeared for the entire day. When he did come home he spent all his time in his room. He had a box turtle named Jake and he hid him under his bed. He would talk to Jake for hours at a time, practicing saying his y's and o's so if he talked to people, they could understand him.

But he didn't talk to people often. The town kids made fun of him. They thought he was too stupid to know when they were playing a joke. Early in his life he had pretended not to know what they were up to just so they would play with him. But as they grew older the jokes became more cruel and it ended one day when the Catholic priest happened by when Jim Evans and his friends were being particularly mean.

It was springtime and Cooney had been caught lying on his back watching Canada geese veeing over on their way back north. "Watch out, Bobby!" Jim Evans had yelled. They called him Bobby then—he was still too young to be a coon trapper. The boys were coming back from school, the eighth grade. Cooney had quit school two years before and though he was older than these boys they had all been in the same grade at one time. "Watch out," Jim said again. "Those are flamingos!" His buddies exploded into laughter and Jim was encouraged to go on.

"Deadly birds," he said. "They go for your nose." More laughter and Cooney laughed, too. He knew the birds passing over were geese but he played along by holding his hands over his nose. Now he cringed to think that he needed the company of these boys that bad, but they were laughing and slapping him on the back.

"You need some nose protection," one of the boys said and Cooney saw Jim's eyes light up.

Cooney could tell that Jim was about to burst out in a smile but his voice was very serious. "We got to protect that nose," he said. Then, as if he had just thought of it, he snapped his fingers. "I've got just the thing."

The other kids gathered around as Jim dug into his gym bag. Everyone watched as Jim rummaged through dirty gym clothes and everyone went wild when he pulled out his jockstrap. Cooney wasn't sure what it was but the boys, who had just learned about jockstraps themselves, giggled with nerves and delight. "It's your basic patented nose protector," Jim said. "Guaranteed to work against mosquitoes and particularly," he pointed upward, "flamingos!"

Now Cooney couldn't imagine what made him go along with them. He knew those geese were not flamingos and he knew that a jockstrap was not a nose protector. He knew they were making a fool out of him but he couldn't stop himself. He let Jim put the elastic band around his head like a hat and let him lower the cup down over his nose. "Every time they fly by, just flip this baby down." The other kids were rolling on the ground and Cooney was smiling as if he were grateful.

But then Father Morgan was among them. He had come up unnoticed and when the boys saw him they went completely still. He let his granite stare swing over everyone. Jim had already removed the jockstrap and was zipping up his gym bag. Several boys were mumbling apologies as they backed away. But Father Morgan didn't speak to them. He was silent until they were gone. When it was just the two of them he stepped closer to Cooney. "You poor child," he said. And though Cooney was fourteen and not really a child, he felt like one that day. He looked at the priest and knew he was going to cry. He didn't sob but tears rolled down his face and gathered at his chin.

Cooney was filling the bird feeder in his backyard as he thought of the years before he had gotten to know Bill Malone. The feeder always made him think of Bill and Bill always made him think of those days. Now it was autumn and that was the time to get the birds coming into a feeder. That was what Bill had told him that first September. It was warm in the backyard but still a chill ran down Cooney's neck. Not long after that incident with Jim Evans, Cooney had withdrawn altogether. He found that he could hitchhike to his grandfather's cabin and that is where he spent most of his time. It was fine with his parents and in a couple years they moved to Sioux Falls. He lived with his grandfather, learning a little about trapping animals for their fur until his grandfather died. Then he was completely alone.

He knew very little about how to get along in the world, but somehow he got by. He lived in the cabin and sold his furs. It was his only means of support and several times the county people came to try to get him to come into town. But he wouldn't go. He didn't know it at the time but he had fallen in love with Spearfish Canyon. He walked the river and the side canyons for days at a time and came across things that fascinated him. It was years later that he decided to try to find out the names of some of the plants and animals he found. That is when he became friends with Bill. When he thought back on the luck of that day he had to shake his head. If it weren't for Bill Malone he probably would be living in the county home. He would never have gotten a driver's license, or found out that he could read any book in the library. He wouldn't be pouring the birdseed down behind the glass partition of the bird feeder. He had gotten a fourteen-year reprieve and enjoyed every day of it. He had never realized how good life could be. It struck him as ironic that a man with his own deep sadness had been the one to show him how important the small things could be.

Cooney often told people that he was never one to mind a mess. That was a euphemistic admission that he was a world-class slob. He was a slob now, but he was worse when Bill met him in the college library. Now his untidiness was confined to his cabin, pickup truck, and yard. In those desperate days, when he felt himself constantly on the edge, he had neglected everything about himself, his clothes, his hygiene, his attitude.

Bill had nearly run over him as he came around the corner of the book stack where Cooney knelt on the floor trying to find a book that might tell him about the flower he had in the jar beside him on the floor. "Whoa!" Bill said as he touched Cooney's shoulder to stop himself from going down. Cooney noticed the look on Bill's face when he saw what he was touching there hunkered on the floor. He had seen the look before, startled, struggling to remain casual. Bill pulled his hand away as Cooney expected, but then a flicker of recognition came into the eyes. "Oh," Bill said. "I know you."

He didn't really know Cooney. He only remembered seeing him around town when he was growing up. He knew him about as much as Cooney knew Bill—hardly at all. But they recognized each other and both saw immediately that the other had changed. Cooney was a man now and Bill saw that he had been neglected. He was dirty and couldn't stand Bill's eyes on him. He only glanced up briefly, but in that instant Cooney saw that Bill had changed, too. He was thinner. His smile did not come easily the way Cooney remembered it from the year they had been in the same grade. In fact, Bill looked severe and Cooney was sure he would go on without another word. But he didn't. He fumbled for something to say and came up with Cooney's name. He didn't back away like many people did. "Bobby Jenkins," he said. "Sorry I bumped into you."

"It's Cooney now," Cooney stammered. "They call me Cooney."

Bill tried a thin smile and his eyes began to search for something other than Cooney's face to rest on. They found the jar on the floor. "What's that?" Bill spoke mostly as a defense against Cooney's stare.

"A flower," Cooney said. He saw a spark of curiosity in Bill's face.

"What kind?" Bill held his hand out toward the jar.

"Don't know. That's what I come for." Cooney handed him the jar. "Maybe a book."

Bill held the jar for a long time. He rotated it slowly in his hand and looked at the flower from every angle. Then he looked at the bookshelf in front of them. "You won't find a flower book here," he said. "This is literature. You need to be in the five hundreds."

That was the first time anyone had told Cooney that the books were in a precise order. Now he laughed to think back on himself, searching randomly for a book that would tell him the name of the flower in the jar. It turned out that the flower was a yellow lady's slipper, his first orchid—Cypripedium calceolus. The book they found that day was Wildflowers, Grasses and Other Plants of the Northern Plains and Black Hills written by Theodore Van Brogan. Its call number turned out to be just what Bill said it would be, 581.97. Cooney had memorized all that information. It was important knowledge to him then.

Bill helped him read the small paragraph about the yellow lady's slipper. He checked the book out in his name and told Cooney it was his for two weeks. But even though it was a short book, less than a hundred pages, he had only finished a quarter of it when the time was up. He labored long hours over each paragraph and the frustration of not knowing words could nearly make him cry. But he loved having that book in his cabin and waiting for the due date was like waiting for a death sentence to be carried out.

He shivered when he thought of the pain he suffered. But it made him smile, too. A lot had changed in fourteen years. Reading was still a major effort, but he could do it. He could do a lot of things now that he never thought he could, and Bill was the reason.

They were drawn together because they were both alone and both maimed. They had nearly four months together and although the Cooney Jenkins that sat on the braided rug of Bill Malone's first house in Spearfish was not the same Cooney Jenkins whom people knew fourteen years later, it was a start. Already he had become more sure of himself and began to gain weight. He was bathing more and wore clean clothes. But he would take years to evolve into the gentle hermit that now lived proudly in the cabin that his grandparents built in Spearfish Canyon. On the day Allison came, and ever after, Cooney believed that Bill had healed him. Though there was something mutual about the healing, Cooney knew that he was, and always would be, deeply in Bill's debt.

Allison had gobbled the ice cream and played with Bugs until they both fell asleep on the floor between Cooney and Bill. She had slept with the cat ever since. And Cooney had watched her change in ways that would make a butterfly envious.

Cooney had made a friend that first December night and had gone on, in the years that followed, to develop a special relationship with Allison. He'd helped see her through a lot of growing up and they had become so close that sometimes it felt like he could read her thoughts. Like now, something was troubling Allison. She was keeping up a brave front but something was wrong. Cooney could hear it in her voice.

He knew it had to do with her father. He had struggled over whether or not to engineer Bill and Margaret having the night alone, but when he mentioned it to Allison on the phone her voice had brightened. Not the fake brightness that she'd been presenting lately. The idea of Bill and Margaret together met with her approval.

Cooney was overjoyed to be such good friends with Allison. Next to Bill, she was the most important person in his life. But their relationship frightened him, too. There was responsibility in it because he was sure he knew her better than anyone.

The relationship began with Bugs and that night fourteen

years before. That first humble night had been important for both of them and Cooney still connected Allison's company with the taste of ice cream. That's why, when he called her from the pay phone at the Standard station on Main Street with his owl-calling scheme, he suggested they meet at Lena's ice cream parlor. He hoped the night would tell him more about what was bothering her.

THE TWO small pickups bounced into Lena's parking lot from opposite directions but at the same time. The sun had set and Allison's red pickup with running lights along the cab was hard to miss. It was several layers of dust cleaner than Cooney's gray, rusted Datsun. They pulled into parking spaces side by side, and Cooney smiled at Allison the way he always did. It took her a second to return the smile and Cooney noticed the hesitation.

Cooney came around the back of the pickups and waited while Allison gathered up her backpack. It was a warm evening for the end of September and she wore shorts that showed off her legs. Cooney couldn't help thinking how nice those legs had turned out when you considered the skinny things they had been just a few years before. "You got a sweater in there?" Cooney asked.

"Yep."

"Good. So who's buying?" Cooney asked.

"You are. You invited me out. I wouldn't be seen with you unless there was free food involved." Cooney tried to look hurt. "And besides," Allison went on, "you're the one with the job."

"You call tying flies a job?" They were moving toward the door of Lena's. "Eight dollars a dozen and the season is about done."

Allison opened the door for Cooney and waved him through. "I'll settle for a small cone." She tapped her flat stomach. "Have to watch my weight."

"A small cone?" Cooney was already looking over the day's selection of ice cream. He tapped his own ample stomach. "Watch my weight."

Lena's was a great home-owned ice cream joint. They made the ice cream in the back and it was always fresh and delicious. Allison chose maple nut and Cooney took a triple fudge royal. Allison paid.

Then without a word, they took their ice cream and went out to the picnic table at the side of the building. Cooney knew that Allison was not herself, that she was trying to keep things too light. So on the way out Cooney tried to let her know that the light mood was all right. "Did you ever smell that stuff?" He pointed to the cone in Allison's hand. It was an old trick that he'd played on her a hundred times. If she wasn't thinking she'd raise the ice cream to her nose and he'd bump her hand, leaving a nose print in the ice cream. But tonight she was on to him. She only smiled and moved the cone even farther from her face.

They sat down on the same side of the picnic table under the mercury vapor light where the last moths were circling in erratic flight. They watched the moths and licked at the ice cream but neither spoke until Cooney finally asked how her dad and Margaret were doing.

Allison nodded and smiled. "Good," she said. "He's training that merlin you brought over. I'm helping."

"Training him for what?"

"You know, falconry. Like he used to do." Allison's voice was steady but Cooney could tell that she was excited about the falcon, or Margaret, or both.

"He hasn't done that since I've known him."

"He used to be very good."

"I know," Cooney said. He was thinking back to the nights he and Bill had spent in front of his fireplace over the years. Bill had talked a lot about falcons and birds of every kind. Cooney had known, even then, that he lived for birds like some men live for money or women. Bill had been unfortunate. He had been injured by all three. It was wonderful news that he was finding his way back.

"Has he said anything about Andy Arnold?" It was a bold, abrupt way to begin, but Cooney knew no other approach. He didn't look at Allison when he spoke but from the corner of his eye he could see her left hand. It lay on the table near him and by turning his head ever so slightly he confirmed that it was trembling. So, he thought, the subject doesn't surprise her.

"You mean the Mountain Air guy?" she asked.

Cooney turned sideways and saw that she was chewing the inside of her lower lip. "Yeah, the Mountain Air guy. They got to wonder if he didn't have something to do with it."

Allison's head turned and her eyes snapped up to meet Cooney's. She wanted her eyes to blaze, but there was more smoke than fire and that was not the Allison that Cooney had known since she was six. "For Christ's sake, Cooney. Dad didn't do anything to Andy Arnold."

Cooney nodded but it wasn't an affirmation of anything. That afternoon Margaret Adamson had frightened him. He probably wanted to be consoled, told that everything would be all right the way Bill Malone had consoled him fourteen years before. But the look on Allison's face and the frailness of the voice told him that neither Bill Malone nor his daughter could console him on this one. What he saw frightened him even more, but he couldn't let it show. At that instant he realized that he had finally come of age and it could well be up to him, that he might have to find a way to make the consolation flow in the other direction.

He thought that Allison was going to cry. He'd seen her cry as a child but never as an adult. He knew a different Allison Malone than most people and he knew she seldom cried. The prospect that she might now was terrifying. She looked down at the picnic table and pursed her lips and swallowed. Here was the most precious person in his only friend's life. She struggled for control. Cooney thought he was frozen in place but, as if it belonged to someone else, his hand moved to her shoulder. He touched the shoulder tentatively and when her eyes closed he moved his hand to the back of her neck and began to massage. He had rubbed her back many times since she was a child and it had always calmed them both.

Cooney rubbed her neck until her strength returned. Her eyes came open and with her right hand she reached up and patted Cooney's hand in thanks. She took a single deep breath and forced a smile. When she looked at Cooney the fudge royal ice cream was melting over his hand. She pointed and forced a laugh. "What a mess," she said. "And God, that stuff smells awful when it melts."

Without a thought Cooney brought the cone to his nose. He knew he had made a mistake when the ice cream was an inch from his nose, but it was too late. He looked up in surprise but she didn't bump it into his face. She only smiled and shook her head. "I could have had you," she said. Then she stood up. "Let's go call some owls."

15

AFTER ALLISON left them alone, Bill and Margaret moved to the deck with their iced teas and watched the last of the autumn light drain from the sky. The few stars that shown weren't strong enough to hold Bill's or Margaret's attention.

They sat across the picnic table from each other and their eyes continued to drift across the other's face. Margaret's hands were folded in front of her, the fingers loosely intertwined. Bill still held the falcon on his left hand and he let his forearm rest on the edge of the picnic table, keeping the fist upright so the bird's tail hung down the back of his hand and off the end of the table. In deference to the bird, that side of Bill's body did not move. The result was his posture looked one-sided, rigid on the left and relaxed on the right.

Margaret watched the right hand. It was the right hand that had been so close to hers on Cooney's couch. She remembered how she wanted to reach out and touch it that night. Tonight, she did. She took Bill's hand in both of hers and held it firmly. She did not look up to meet his eyes even though she could feel them. She squeezed the hand, felt the knuckles, found the sinewy strength.

They sat like that for a long time and Margaret concentrated on the hand. She flexed the fingers, rolled the hand onto its back. Then she leaned forward and kissed the palm. She was aware of her breasts pushed against the picnic table and ran her tongue across Bill's palm and in between each finger. When she raised her head, her eyes were closed. "Yum," she said. Then she opened her eyes. "I've missed you."

Bill was leaning over the table, too. They stretched and only their lips met—gently, barely touching—but warm in the cooling September air. Then a bell, piercing the night. And their heads snapped to the falcon. It held its foot up, ready to scratch its beak. The bell sounded again and Bill and Margaret laughed.

"Is that the end of the round?" Margaret asked.

Bill was standing now. He moved around the table and put his hand behind Margaret's neck. He ran his fingers up into her hair and brought her slowly to her feet. "No," he said. "I think it's just begun." They kissed again and then, without either giving the cue, began to move into the house. They moved through the kitchen and down the hall, toward Bill's room.

IT WAS A slow time of year for Deadwood, even the new Deadwood. The summer tourists had gone and the winter sports season hadn't begun, so the traffic downtown was relatively light. More and more, with the gambling, the tourist seasons had begun to merge into one, but still it took Larson only ten minutes to drive home from his office. The antique streetlights came on as he drove and the surprise of it made him smile.

His house was in the city limits but built on a hillside with a great view of the gulch. He'd lived in the same house for over twenty years. His son had been raised there and now was in graduate school at Iowa State. Larson had paid for four years of undergraduate school, tuition, books, room and board, spending money—the whole shebang. He was proud of that, both the boy's education and his part in it. It hadn't been easy. He'd had to save his money and was never able to take a vacation to the ocean. Now it looked like he was going to get his chance.

The boy's name was John, and he was a good student. His area of study had something to do with computers. Sometimes Larson daydreamed about John coming around, maybe bringing the girl he'd been seeing for a couple years to introduce to his dad. Maybe someday they could fish in the ocean together. Yes, that would be great, wading into that surf with nothing on but a pair of shorts, casting that big rod with both hands and waiting for some damned huge ocean-going fish to grab on.

Larson was in his kitchen now, making a pot of coffee. With difficulty he managed to stop thinking about fishing with his son. He tried to force himself to think about Andy Arnold's death but he couldn't do it.

The coffee was still perking but Larson pulled the pot out and replaced it with his cup. As the coffee dribbled into the cup he poured more into the cup from the pot. He spilled some and it sizzled on the heating element. He spilled more when he took the cup away and replaced the pot. But he had his coffee and took it with him as he moved through the house to the back porch.

There was no view from the back of Larson's house. The steep hillside that formed the north wall of Deadwood Gulch was thirty feet from his backdoor. There was just room for a storage shed and Larson's Royal Coachman recreational vehicle. It was dark in the backyard because the house and the hill blocked all the light from the neighbor's house and the town below. Larson sipped his coffee and reached out to flip on the yard lights.

They were extra bright lights he had installed when he first got the Coachman. He'd bought it cheap from a dealer in town who had salvaged it from an accident on Interstate 90. It belonged to an older couple from Mississippi who swerved to miss a deer. They'd taken the ditch instead of the deer and ended up with a totaled seventy-thousand-dollar recreational vehicle. The couple wasn't hurt, and Larson supposed the insurance company had to buy them a new RV. The dealer in Deadwood, who had since sold his property and moved to Spearfish, bought the wreck for a few thousand dollars. Larson got it from him for a few dollars more and had a friend who owned a wrecker maneuver it into his backyard. Larson installed the yard lights so he could work on it after he came home from his office.

That was almost six years ago. The engine and transmission survived the crash, but everything else was bent and wrenched. All the glass was broken, none of the kitchen appliances worked, and the back axle was broken. Larson fixed it all himself.

It started out as just a crazy project, something to keep him occupied. He had more time back then. Deadwood was still a pretty sleepy place, no gambling, no new construction, no plans for a multimillion-dollar development. It had been over forty years since he'd done any bodywork, and even then it was just a part-time job after high school. But it came back to him quicker than he thought it would. He bought some old tools and went to straightening all the metal panels. The boys at the body shop laughed. Nobody straightened sheet metal anymore, they replaced it. But Larson was looking for something to do—he wasn't in a hurry.

Now he gazed out at the rebuilt Coachman and smiled with pride. She was a beauty. He'd painted it beige with brown striping—subtle, classy. His only concession to flamboyance were the moon hubcaps he'd ordered from a catalogue specializing in car accessories from the fifties. He'd had a Chevy with moon hubcaps back then and had promised himself he'd buy a set if he ever again had a vehicle they looked good on. Well, they looked great on the Coachman.

It must have been during the restoration process that he began thinking seriously about warm places, beaches, surf fishing, and getting himself a real tan. He'd always liked the sun, of course, but the truth was he'd never even been within smelling distance of an ocean. Living in the northern tier of states at an altitude of five-thousand feet was about as far as a person could get from the ocean. But something about all that water and sunshine fascinated him. His little obsession came into focus on the day he straightened the back bumper of the Coachman. Apparently it had hooked something in the crash because one end was bent at nearly a ninety-degree angle. Larson had to unbolt it from the frame and lay it on his temporary workbench to heat it with an acetylene torch. He hadn't paid any attention to the stickers on the bumper until the cherry heat started to move through the metal and the stickers began to burn. The first few were already gone when he noticed what was happening. The only sticker he saw well was the very last one. That was the one that he believed affected him. It was a human figure made out of oranges and wearing a tropical hat. The figure was in a boat filled with fishing tackle and it wore sunglasses. The words below the figure said: "Sunshine's good for you. Go for it."

There was just time to read the last words before the heat consumed them. But they remained lodged in Larson's mind. So that was what he printed below the driver's window of his restored RV: "Go for it." He could read the letters from his back porch and they made him smile. Everyone should have a secret, Larson thought, and this was his—nestled here in his own private canyon between the house and hillside. Very few people even knew it was there. Some nights he'd work on the Coachman until four in the morning. And no neighbor had ever mentioned it.

He got the urge to go out and look at the fishing gear he had accumulated and stored in the Coachman. The night was getting cold. He could feel winter just around the corner and he thought of snow. Some years it fell to a depth of four feet in his backyard. The amphitheater between his house and the Coachman could fill like a bowl of whipped cream.

Carl Larson came off the porch with a chill at the back of his neck like he could not recall having before. He walked across the lighted grass to the door of the Coachman and went inside. He was gone for ten minutes and when he reappeared he was dressed in baggy yellow shorts and a orange tank top T-shirt. He was barefoot and carried one of the three surf casting rods he had ordered from a catalogue. There was no line on the reel yet, but he moved to the middle of his backyard and practiced the motion of casting anyway.

GRAY MORNING light had been building inside Bill's bedroom for twenty minutes. He lay on his bed and watched the light bring Margaret's sleeping face to life. She lay on her side, facing him. The sheet ran over Bill's rib cage and diagonally down to cover part of Margaret's hip. Bill let his eyes glide along the curve of her body—the breasts covered demurely by Margaret's left arm, the tight waist, the rise of her round hip. It had been a very long time since Bill had awakened with a woman in his bed. Even longer since he had woken with this woman in his bed.

Their lovemaking had been different than it had once been.

It was better. What they had lost in muscle tone, energy, and smoothness of skin they had more than made up for in tenderness and consideration. There had been a new hunger, something much stronger than the desire of their youth, and Bill shivered when he realized the hunger was still there. He reached out and touched Margaret's face gently and she smiled and turned her head to take a finger in her mouth. As Bill slid closer, the fragile silver sound of the merlin's bell filled the room. It was the sound of the falcon waking for the day and even though Margaret's eyes stayed closed, her smile broadened. Bill was already looking at the falcon, hooded and perched on the back of a chair at the foot of the bed. "Duty calls," Margaret said with the finger still in her mouth.

"Sorry," Bill said.

Margaret let go of the finger. "I love it," she said without opening her eyes.

Then Bill was up and dressed. He took the falcon onto his fist and slipped out of the bedroom leaving Margaret, still on her side, still with her eyes closed, still smiling.

He set about building a one-handed breakfast. Bacon in the skillet, toast in the toaster, eggs cracked into a bowl, all with one hand. It was a bigger breakfast than he had eaten in years. He hummed to himself and before the bacon began to sizzle he heard the sound of Margaret in the shower.

By the time Margaret appeared, the table was set and the eggs were done. She stood smiling in the doorway with her freshly scrubbed face and wet hair. "Pretty good service," she said.

"We aim to please. Have a chair."

They sat grinning and eating while the kitchen filled with bright autumn light. The glass doors that opened onto the deck transformed the light to warmth and for a few minutes the kitchen felt as good and safe as an incubator. But then the doorbell rang and Bill slumped. "Crap," he said.

As he moved into the hall that led to the front door Margaret felt uneasy. It was her sixth sense for trouble, and involuntarily she rose and followed Bill so that she was standing behind him in the hallway when he opened the door to find Hemmingford and Lonzo.

"Mr. Malone? We'd like to speak with you." Hemmingford had not noticed the falcon on Bill's fist. "My name is Barry Hemmingford. This is Danny Lonzo. We're with the state division of criminal investigation. We'd like to ask you some questions."

"What do you want?" Bill asked.

"May we come in?"

Margaret moved to Bill's side. "No," she said. "They don't need to come in."

"Why, Miss Adamson, the lady cop. You're here early."

"What do you want," Bill said.

"Danny?" Hemmingford said without looking at his assistant. Lonzo stepped closer. "We were wondering where you were on the night before Arnold was killed."

"You know I was at the public hearing."

"We were wondering what you did after that," Lonzo said.

"I got drunk. I figured I needed it. Figured I deserved it."

"And just what did you do that made you feel you deserved a drink?" Hemmingford asked. "Maybe an overwhelming feeling of a job well done?"

Margaret moved to get between the men but Bill caught her arm. There was an instant of silence before Hemmingford went on. "And where did you spend the night?"

"You don't have to answer any of his questions," Margaret said.

"It's okay," Bill said. "I slept on a friend's couch."

"But your car was downtown for part of the night." Lonzo had a notebook out and pretended to refer to it.

"That's not true."

"You got some bad information," Margaret said nearly to herself. She felt Bill's eyes on her.

Hemmingford smiled. "I think our information is true," Hemmingford said. "I also think it's true that you told a friend . . ." He nodded toward Lonzo's notebook.

"All developers should be killed," Lonzo said.

"That's stupid," Margaret said.

"Not according to one of Mr. Malone's friends." Lonzo looked at the notebook again. "A Miss Anne Casey from Chicago."

"You don't have to say anything," Margaret said.

"You know the law, don't you?" Hemmingford turned to Bill. "She's right. You don't have to say anything. Not yet." He moved closer and his voice lowered. "We wanted you to know that we're on to you and that we're watching. Don't leave town because we'll want to talk to you again." His face was expressionless.

He moved off the porch and Lonzo followed. They were just getting into their car when Allison's pickup pulled into the driveway. The men stood at their car, with their hands on the door handles, and watched Allison get out of her pickup. They stared at her and she stared back. But finally Allison's eyes gave way. She turned her back on them and came across the yard toward Bill and Margaret. Her face was rigid and white but she moved with long, elegant strides.

16

THE OWL calling was a success. Allison and Cooney spent most of the night driving along the gravel roads of the Black Hills in Cooney's Datsun. He rigged a speaker from the old Chevy Impala in his backyard to the roof of the Datsun and ran the wires into the cab. He hooked the tape player to the speaker so he could broadcast owl noises without leaving his truck. It worked great.

They called up five great horned owls, four screech owls, two long ears, and a possible saw-whet owl. Their modus operandi was to find a lone dead tree just off the road where Cooney could park the pickup on an incline so the headlights would shine upward and illuminate most of the branches. Then they turned off the engine and the lights and cranked up the tape player. The tape had half a dozen different owl calls and Cooney found the one that seemed right for the habitat. He played it loudly for a few minutes, then began to turn the volume down. By the time the squeaks and hoots were low enough to whisper above, they usually began hearing squeaks and hoots from the blackness outside the pickup. Cooney continued to ease the volume down. They listened to the night to try to figure out where the visitor was perched. When they determined he was in the dead tree, Cooney switched on the headlights.

The owls swiveled their flat faces into the light and blinked their huge round eyes and Cooney and Allison inhaled with awe. The owls never seemed upset at being revealed in their nocturnalness. They usually did not fly away and sometimes continued to hoot and crane their necks at what they took to be a trespasser.

The evening let Cooney and Allison relax but there was still tension in the air. They only spoke about Bill once, obliquely, when they got back to Cooney's house just before sunrise and Allison was settled onto the couch for a couple hours' rest. They looked at each other and knew they were both thinking about Bill. "Don't worry," Cooney said. "Things will work out."

Allison was gone when Cooney woke up. It was still morning and the sun was just beginning to find its way to the bottom of Spearfish Canyon. Cooney walked out onto his porch and surveyed his domain. For a short time he imagined he was an owl caught in the headlights. He turned his head slowly and blinked his eyes. He hooted twice.

Cooney spent the next hour wandering around the backyard. He was looking over all his stuff. That's what he called it, his stuff. He never called his stuff belongings, possessions, or even things. He made a special point of using the word *stuff* because a sixth-grade teacher once told him it was a slang word, that it was ugly and illustrated the user was lazy. It had been over thirty years since Cooney was in the sixth grade and the teacher who had told him never to use the word *stuff* was probably dead by now. He knew it was silly to assert his independence by using a word forbidden by a dead person, but that teacher had never liked him and he couldn't help himself. It was like little kids and swearwords. Even after all those years, there was a sweetness to the word that he could not resist. He said the word out loud: "Stuff. Let me peruse my stuff."

Late September canyon light in the western mountains has a texture unlike any light on earth. It's the aspen, golden from the first high country frosts, that causes the light to thicken and go still and luxuriant. Before the floor of Spearfish Canyon gets direct sun the shadow of the east rim descends the west face. As the light creeps downward the only light coming to the dwellers along the river is reflected from shimmering aspen leaves higher up the canyon wall. A person standing on the rim, bathed in new sunshine sees only the black hole the river carved. But a person within the canyon breathes in heavy, reflected light and can't help feeling fortunate and complete.

That's the way Cooney felt as he viewed his stuff. My God, there was tons of it, he thought. At the very end of the lot, farthest from the river, was some kind of old farming equipment. His grandfather must have dragged it in from somewhere far away because there was no farm ground in Spearfish Canyon. Maybe someone had tried it once in a meadow the beavers had built, but never in Cooney's lifetime. If they did try farming the meadows, they couldn't have tried for long. A good spring storm would have wiped their work away overnight. Cooney chuckled at the thought; what was one wheat field more or less?

He spent a few minutes climbing over rusted machines. There was a disk and a plow, very old, maybe even built for horses to pull. They were tiny things laying overgrown with grass and didn't seem nearly as sinister as the big shiny machines used on the prairie now. It didn't look like these pieces of iron could turn the soil faster than the earth could heal itself. Cooney decided that he liked these little machines. They were good stuff.

He moved a few feet closer to the cabin, through the fuzzy light, to a pile of fifty-five gallon drums. There were twenty-six of them. He knew this because he had gotten them free from the oil distributor in Spearfish when they switched over to buying oil in bulk. He hauled them here in his Datsun pickup. He thought he might be able to make something out of them, maybe cattle feeders or planters. Three drums fit under the topper and two could be tied on top. He'd made five trips and on the last trip put one barrel beside him in the passenger's seat. That made twenty-six drums. He'd piled them where they were now and never did anything with them. They were beginning to rust around the bungs but still, they were good stuff, too.

Now he was close enough to the cabin to hear the river. It was the perfect sound to go with the light, a bit fragile but still substantial and steady. It was something to count on, more dependable than anything else in Cooney's life. More dependable, he thought, than anything in anyone's life. He laughed again and turned to an old wood-burning cook stove he'd rescued from a house in Deadwood that was being demolished. He'd always thought it would be nice to fix it up but when he'd taken the corroded chrome pieces into town he found it would cost two hundred dollars just to get them rechromed. The stove had remained where he'd unloaded it. That was maybe five years before. Cooney knelt down and looked inside the stove at the grates. They were good as new and he figured the stove was still worth saving. But something told him that job would be left up to someone else.

Just then he heard a vehicle on the road. He stood still, knowing that the car would turn into his driveway. But it was not a car, it was a small pickup truck. It was Allison and Cooney could see that the tension they felt the night before had boiled up and over. She drove fast but not recklessly. When she brought the pickup to a stop, in the exact place she had left only an hour and half before, she did not look to Cooney. She stared straight ahead. Cooney did not move from the old stove. He knew she was going to tell him that her father was in trouble. He'd been expecting it. There was no way a person like Bill Malone would be left alone.

Allison came to him and told him about the men who came to their house. She was more upset than Cooney had ever seen her, more upset than was good for her or her father. Cooney had to take her by the shoulders and make her look at him. "They're policemen." Cooney said. "They're doing their job. Don't make too much of it."

She stared at him. "Don't make too much of it?" she said. Then she seemed to change gears. She began to cry. To sob. She slumped and Cooney held her up. He felt her convulse, rocked her until she was drained. And as her fear came out it engulfed Cooney. By the time she had calmed, he had come to feel, if not everything, at least part of what was powering her.

Allison pulled herself together as quickly as she had fallen apart. "I just came to tell you," she said. "I thought you'd want to know." In ten minutes she was gone and Cooney was left where she had found him. He rubbed his hand over the porcelain corner of the stove and a tiny pang of conscience swept over him. There was the rough beginnings of rust under the porcelain. But it didn't matter. Cooney believed that all things were the same.

Rust, iron, flesh, manure, soil—even death and life. Everything was temporary, changing. It was silly to pick favorites. Still, there were those twinges of guilt. They were inexplicable and silly. No one had that kind of responsibility.

Then he turned and saw his face reflected in the glass side of the bird feeder Bill Malone had made for him that first fall they had known each other. He stared for a moment, not at his face but at the feeder and all that it meant to him. Finally he nodded. "Yeah, yeah," he said. "Yeah, yeah."

He went on around the cabin, looking at his chickens in their cages made from the dryers he'd salvaged from a Laundromat fire. They all looked happy and Cooney was tempted to take his favorite rooster out and hold him. But the sun was fully up now and the chickens were enjoying its warmth. He hated to bother them.

Before he went into the cabin to look at his inside stuff, he let his eyes swing around the yard. He had never been able to get a battery in the '52 Mercury to hold a charge. The '68 Impala was not only missing a speaker, it had a cracked block. It was a goner. Only the rusty gray Datsun pickup had the heart to keep going. Too tough to die, Cooney thought. Or was it too dumb? He turned and walked up the steps to the porch, then turned again to listen to the river. When the moon was bright he could see the river sparkle from his porch. But now, with the sun going high in the sky, the river lay flat and was hard to see. He knew it was there only by the music of the water. In the heat of the day it was sound that assured Cooney the river was still there.

Cooney looked around one more time. It was a poor place for his grandfather to homestead. All the old timers said his grandfather was an impractical man. There was no way to make a living here. No agriculture and the hillsides were too steep to log. It made no economic sense, but Cooney understood why his grandfather chose the place and he was glad he had been so impractical. The Jenkinses had owned this place since it was first considered a possession of a man. Cooney's father had not seen the good of the homestead and lived his whole life in town. But Cooney's grandfather must have understood the importance of a place like this, and Cooney certainly did. At least he did now. He'd had a wonderful tenure here since Bill had showed him what he had. Just now, he felt a terrible sadness, but still he was thankful for the years at peace in this place. He would miss it.

MARGARET WAS outraged by what had happened at Bill's house. She stopped by the hotel to change her clothes before going to find Larson and found it odd coming back to her room in the morning and seeing the bed still made. There had been a lot of hotel rooms but this was a first.

When she went to the closet, the first thing she saw was her uniform and she nearly put it on. But no. She decided on blue jeans and a crisp, brown shirt. It was the look she wanted for dealing with Larson. She was ready to leave when the phone rang. The second she heard Bass's voice she remembered she had promised to call. He spoke slowly and, as before, his sincerity came through.

"Sorry," she said. "I meant to call, but a lot has happened."

"I don't know what's going on. I haven't heard from anyone and I'm worried. My job, all the people I know. I don't know what to do."

"Relax," Margaret said. "You're off the hook. The sheriff said it himself."

Bass was silent for a beat. "But what's going to happen?"

Bass couldn't know how innocent he sounded. "I don't know, Troy. But you're all right. I think they've found someone else to focus on."

Margaret hung up the phone and didn't let herself hesitate. She drove directly to Sheriff Larson's office, but the door was locked. It was Sunday. She checked the phone book for Larson's home phone and address. No listing. But the second waitress she asked knew he lived on Mulberry Street. "It's the place with the giant RV in the backyard. You got to look close; but get the right angle. It's a behemoth of a thing."

Margaret missed the house on the first pass but the waitress was right. After she'd turned around and began driving the street from the opposite way, the RV jumped out at her. It was crammed into the narrow backyard and Margaret wondered how Larson got it in there.

No one answered the front doorbell and while Margaret waited the phone rang inside. When she heard the answering machine kick in she moved around the house to the backyard. Larson was just coming out of the RV and saw Margaret at the corner of the house. He looked pained, but when Margaret closed the distance between them she saw it was mostly the sag of Larson's brow that made him look that way. His mouth was trying a smile.

"What in the hell is going on around here?" Margaret said.

Larson shrugged. He could see that what he hoped wouldn't happen had happened. "Hemmingford and Lonzo went to see Malone."

"They sure did."

"They didn't accuse him of anything, did they?"

"Not directly, but the intent was clear. They're trying to scare Bill into saying he had something to with what happened out on that job site. I thought you were the sheriff of this county."

Larson nodded. Margaret Adamson was angry, that was clear, but there was something more. "You and Malone go back a ways don't you?"

Margaret softened. "We go back a ways," she said.

The change in Margaret's voice interested Larson. "Come on in the house," he said. "I'll tell you what I know." He mounted the back steps slowly.

The answering machine beeper was going off when they entered the kitchen but Larson ignored it. He went to the coffee pot and poured himself a cup. He held up the pot to ask if Margaret wanted one. She shook her head and Larson took his cup to a microwave and put it in to reheat. Without turning, Larson began. "I can see you got a lot of belief in Bill Malone but he wasn't where you think he was the night those machines got vandalized." The answering machine beeped.

"They said his car was seen around town. Big deal."

"Could be a big deal." Larson still faced the microwave. He was waiting.

"How do they know it was Bill's car?"

"Someone saw it, wrote down the license plate number." The microwave dinged, Larson removed the coffee, and came toward the table. The answering machine beeped again. It's red light blinked from the counter.

"Don't you listen to your messages?"

Larson nodded. "They never amount to much." He took the two steps to the counter and pressed a button. There was a lag, then, "This is Avery Murdoch. There's nobody in your office but I found your number. I want to report some trash dumped on my ranch . . ." Larson rewound the tape then came back to the table.

"Those are the kind of calls I get," Larson said. "Hemmingford and his buddy Lonzo are doing the heavy lifting."

"Like harassing Bill?"

Larson sat down. "Someone messed with that front-end loader," he said.

"I saw what they did."

"No. Not just the spray paint. The brake fluid was drained." Margaret sat back in her chair.

"You're putting the vandalism and the accident together."

"Not an unreasonable connection. Even for an old guy."

"No, not unreasonable. But it could have been just bad maintenance," Margaret said.

"Thought you were sure Bass had nothing to do with it."

"I said no one was more surprised than Bass. I meant that, if he or his men are responsible, it was pure accident. *Pure* accident."

"*Pure* accidents don't make names for DCI agents. Hemmingford isn't saying that whoever's responsible meant to kill Andy Arnold. But that really doesn't matter. The vandalism was a felony and in this state, when a death occurs as the result of a felony, the charge is murder. Hemmingford might be trying to build a career-making case. At worst he'll make it a whole lot bigger than any I've handled."

Margaret sat down at the kitchen table and Larson came and

sat down across from her. "What happened up there with the loader scared some people," Larson said. "There are a lot of people who want that development to go ahead and the money people will bail out unless they're pretty sure nothing like that is going to happen again."

Margaret crossed her arms over her chest and looked down at the table. She thought for a moment. "These people are a little nervous about what they're doing?"

"Could be," Larson said. "But whatever the reason, they'll be pushing Hemmingford on this. They couldn't sell the accident theory and now they got Malone's car in a place it wasn't supposed to be. They got some strong talk in that meeting you-all had, and some loose talk in a bar the next day."

"That's nothing."

Larson shook his head. "No. You know better than that. They may need someone in jail, so Mountain Air can go on. Malone could be the man. I look for them to take him into custody."

"They? Who are they? You're the sheriff."

"Technically, yes. Practically, no. And even if I was, I'd probably be doing the same thing."

"He didn't do it."

"Right now the evidence doesn't look that way."

They looked at each other over the table until the silence was torn by the telephone's ring. Larson didn't jump the way Margaret did. He continued to look at her until the second ring had faded. Then he stood up and went to the phone.

He drawled a hello then listened. The silence returned and gave Margaret a chance to try to think. Nothing much came. She knew there was a chance Larson was right. She knew Bill was capable of sabotaging machinery, maybe worse. She could hear Larson talking now, but she was too involved with picturing Bill, full of whiskey, moving through the night with spray cans of paint and tools to disable the machines. Disable, that was what he had in mind—nothing like what happened. It was an accident. He'd get off. It was just an accident. This time she'd stand by him. This time it would be different.

Margaret was deep in her own thoughts and only gradually felt Larson standing above her. She shook her head and raised her eyes slowly. She expected to see the same tired face but when Larson came into focus his face was taut and surprised. "That was Hemmingford," he said. "He wants me to come and make an arrest." Margaret came to her feet but Larson shook his head. "No," Larson said. "Cooney Jenkins is in Hemmingford's motel room right now. He admitted he sabotaged the machine. He's the one that killed Andy Arnold."

17

ALLISON NAMED the merlin Caesar. He stood on her fist unhooded as she walked slowly around the interior of the garage.
The light over the workbench was on but pointed downward so
it glowed against the bench. The light was defuse, so no shape in
the garage was crisp.

One of the fuzzy shapes was Bill Malone. He leaned motionless against the back wall as his daughter took her turn manning
the falcon. Caesar had spent the entire day on one of their fists,
walking hooded and unhooded in partial light until now he was
beginning to accept people as one of the parts of his world that
was not lethal. He would eat readily while on the fist and had
even made a few tentative hops from his perch to the glove. He
was progressing rapidly and, if it hadn't been for the news that
Cooney Jenkins was being held in the county jail, Bill would
have been celebrating.

Earlier that evening Bill was in the kitchen with Caesar on
his fist when Rob Martin, from the Silver Dollar Bar, called. Allison was in the kitchen too and the sound of the phone froze
them both. Allison looked at the phone and shook her head.
She wouldn't pick it up. She moved into the back of the house
and because Bill couldn't move fast without frightening Caesar,
he didn't get to the phone until the fifth ring. Rob heard the
news from an off-duty policeman, Cooney had confessed.

As soon as he got off the phone, Bill called the sheriff's department but got only the law enforcement dispatcher for the
whole northern hills. Bill asked some questions but if the dispatcher knew anything she wasn't saying. He tried Margaret at
her hotel room but got no answer. He thought of telling Allison

what had happened but he couldn't. Not yet. The only thing to do was to keep manning Caesar until Margaret showed up, keep manning him until morning if necessary. He walked the bird around the living room for an hour then sat down and tried to read. But he couldn't concentrate so he slipped the hood on Caesar and took him outside.

The air was brittle with cold and it occurred to Bill that this could be the night of the first frost. The hardwood leaves were dying and turning their autumn colors but they had not begun to fall. If he turned his head just right and exhaled from deep in his core he could make a white puff that drifted downwind and was gone. The cold was good for Caesar. He would burn more calories and be more interested in food. He would want to eat more often. The trick was to get him associating humans with pleasant experiences. High on a falcon's list of pleasant experiences is eating so the cold would accelerate the training process.

There was no moon. As soon as Bill got away from the streetlights, the stars bore through the city's electric aura and he could pick out the big dipper and the north star. He turned and found Orion peeking through the limbs of a cottonwood. Orion was his favorite. Seeing Orion rise in the east always reminded Bill of the proper perspective of human events, but still he felt crushed by uncertainty. He thought he was walking without a plan but after nearly a mile of skirting along the edge of town he came to Spearfish Creek and knew that it had been his destination from the beginning. He looked down at Caesar to see if the sound of the tumbling water would make him turn his head to listen, but the little bird showed no sign that he noticed the river noise. He was hooded and stood perfectly still on the gloved fist. He was asleep. The cold felt right to him and the sound of moving water was natural. It was good that he could sleep, it meant he was responding to Bill's presence the same way he responded to the crisp autumn air and mountain water on its way to the sea.

Bill found a rock outcropping to sit on and instantly realized he had been holding his emotions back until he found a place like this. He told himself that he had chosen to bring Caesar with him because to leave him at home on his perch would have interrupted his training. But, sitting on the rock beside the night river noises, he knew that Caesar was with him because he wanted him there. The night would have been too cold and dark without him.

It all reminded him of manning birds in years past, of sleeplessness that numbed both falcon and falconer into tameness and finally new understanding. He had chosen the rock beside the creek because it was Cooney's creek and, though the cabin was miles up the canyon, he felt connected by that unbroken band of water. He wanted to think about Cooney and Andy Arnold. There were some terrible mistake and he wanted to get it figured out in his mind so he could articulate it when the time came. But he couldn't concentrate, and ended up only sitting quietly on the rock beside the river with the falcon on his fist until the lights of the town began to flick out and the piney mountains that surrounded him became his focus. As the town darkened, he made his way back home where Allison was waiting to take her turn with Caesar.

He smelled coffee from the deck and took an instant to savor it against the chill of the first frost. More memories. He stroked Caesar without making him stir. Then he opened the backdoor, stepped inside, and felt the dry, choking heat of the furnace that had come on for the first time since last winter.

Allison's head poked around the corner that led to the kitchen. She smiled, but she was wary. "There you are. Maggie called." She tilted her head to read her father's reaction. "She sounded upset. She said she'll be in touch."

Bill came into the kitchen and saw that she was dressed in faded blue jeans and a flannel shirt. Her face was smiling as she spread peanut butter on a bagel but the smile seemed stiff. "Just a bite and I'll be ready to take over. How's he doing?"

She was forcing this cheerfulness, Bill thought. "Fine," he said. "He'll be flying free in a couple days." He took a cup down from a hook under the cupboard and filled it with rich steaming coffee. He'd managed one tentative slurp before the phone rang.

Allison was putting the bagels out on the table and turned in surprise to stare at the telephone. It was nearly ten-thirty and she felt intruded upon. Bill moved to pick up the phone before Allison.

It was Margaret. Bill turned away from Allison as if the call were private, which in a way it was. "I know what happened. I heard about it a few hours ago."

"I'm sorry," Margaret said.

Bill stammered. "I really don't know what to say. It's hard for me to believe."

"They say he confessed."

Bill shook his head and exhaled. He could feel Allison watching him. "Can a person get in to see him?"

"Yes," Margaret said. "Visiting hours start at eight in the morning."

"Who have you talked to?"

"Larson, the sheriff. He said we could get in to see him first thing."

"I want to see you." Bill had given up the idea of a private call. Now he was looking at Allison as if it was her he was talking to.

"Come to the Franklin, room 327," Margaret said.

When Bill hung up Allison continued to watch him until he told her what was happening. She was stunned and turned away to go stand at the back window. She stared out at the night for a long time before she gathered herself and returned to look at her father. "I have to see him," she said.

Bill waved her off. He didn't want her to go to the jail. "Margaret and I are going first thing in the morning. Maybe you can see him later." He told her she should go ahead and take her turn with Caesar, that he was nearly manned and if they kept it up all night they would have the job about done. This thing with Cooney was a mistake. It would be straightened out soon. If they left Caesar alone for very long it would only retard his progress. There was some truth to what he told his daughter, but he was also concerned for her. He wasn't sure what he'd be getting into at the jail. He was afraid things might be more complicated if Allison was there.

He ate one of the bagels with Caesar on his fist, then transferred him to Allison and went to take a shower. They agreed
that Caesar's hood should stay on unless he was in the dimly lit
garage and so, when Bill was ready to go, they went to the garage
and Bill watched Allison slip the hood off neatly as she walked
Caesar steadily around the interior of the garage. Bill stood in the
shadows and saw that they were doing fine. On about the tenth
tour of the garage he stepped outside into the year's first really
cold night.

Once he was outside the responsibility of the falcon shifted
to Allison. He felt strangely confident in her ability at this new
undertaking and he strode quickly to his car. But when he sat
down in the driver's seat anxiety washed over him. He slumped,
his hands draped over the steering wheel. He closed his eyes and
lowered his head slowly until his forehead touched the steering
wheel between his hands. He stayed like that until his desire to
see Margaret pushed everything else from his mind.

He drove by rote and tried to think what they would say.
Would they talk about Cooney or would they talk about themselves? He built possible scenarios. But even as he climbed the
stairs in the hotel and moved down the hall to room 327, the di-
alogues were weak and confused.

When he pushed open the door he had no idea of where to
start. But it didn't matter. Margaret came to him and gathered
him up in her arms. They said nothing for the entire night.

THEY BEGAN to talk again the next morning on their way to the
county jail. Neither could imagine that Cooney had done what
he said. The talk was confident but they were covering for a huge
hollow feeling in their guts. Before they pushed through the
doors of the county building they looked at each other and their
eyes held. Finally, Bill shrugged and Margaret shrugged back.
They entered the building shoulder to shoulder.

In the third office they looked into they found a pleasant
woman sitting behind a steel desk. There was a man in a suit
asleep on a chair along the wall. The woman wore a uniform top

and blue jeans and smiled up at them as they entered. "Excuse me," Bill said, "we're looking for the jail."

"You wanting to see a prisoner?" She continued to smile as she swiveled a logbook their way and found a pen on her desk. "You got to sign in here. The jail is down that hall but I got to buzz you through to the guard station. Who's it you're wanting to see?"

"He just came in last night," Bill said as he took the pen from her and leaned to sign the book. "Cooney Jenkins."

The woman's smile faded and she looked to the man who had been sleeping on the chair. The man was already on his feet and moving to Bill's side. "I'm afraid you'll have to talk to Mr. Lonzo," the woman said.

Bill had to look up slightly to see into Lonzo's sleepy eyes. "Mr. Jenkins is kind of a special prisoner," Lonzo said. "What's your business with him?"

"I'm his best friend."

Lonzo turned to Margaret. "And you want to see him, too?"

"I'm with Mr. Malone. As you know, I work for the Fish and Wildlife Service." Margaret surprised herself by flashing her badge.

"Now you're a swamp smokey."

"Special agent," Margaret said.

"I hope you don't think you have any jurisdiction in this matter."

"No. We just want to see the prisoner."

Lonzo turned away from Margaret and back to Bill. "Are you an attorney, Mr. Malone?"

"Are you?"

"No. But right now I'm kind of working for the state of South Dakota and the question was whether or not you are an attorney. More specifically, Mr. Jenkins's attorney."

"I'm not an attorney," Bill said.

"Then I can't let you see the prisoner."

The muscles in Bill's jaw rippled and he started to move closer to Lonzo. Margaret stepped between them just as Sheriff Larson came through the door.

Larson looked over the situation and nodded to the woman behind the desk. "Morning, Betty."

"Good morning, Carl." Her face went cheerful again. "Nice to see you."

"Nice to see you, too. You got these folks signed in?"

Betty looked confused. "You mean Mr. Malone and Mrs. . . . ."

"Adamson," Margaret said and swung the book so she could sign it.

"Yes," Larson said. "Malone and Adamson. They're with me," He looked at Lonzo. "I believe Jenkins is in the custody of the county."

FIVE MINUTES later they had been checked through two locked doors and were out in a twenty-foot-square exercise yard. The walls were concrete block twenty feet high with barbed wire on top. They had confined Cooney to a twenty-foot cube of air. He could see no trees, just a square of blue sky with white clouds whizzing past like buses in a hurry. A few questions had nagged at Larson all night and he was there to ask them. It might be his only chance. He figured Hemmingford would take charge of Jenkins soon. That would be the end of casual visits for Bill and Margaret. They had come to comfort Cooney and Larson knew that, at this point, comfort was important. So he stood off to the side and watched as the three sat at the iron picnic table and talked.

Larson was there to see Cooney Jenkins but his attention kept shifting to Bill Malone. He'd seen him before, of course. In fact, Larson had been at the Mountain Air Estates meeting when he blew his cool. He knew Malone had a bad leg, yet he was surprised at the limp. He hadn't seemed crippled the night of the meeting. Looking at him now, Larson could remember a lot of the words he'd said that night. Larson recalled that he'd spoken with what seemed like great knowledge of the value of Brendan Prairie. He had listed a dozen species of plants and animals that lived there, talked about how water was absorbed into the earth through low spots in the prairie, and how that absorption likely charged springs for a hundred miles. Larson hadn't known any of that before the meeting. He remembered tiny details from Malone's speech. But he had forgotten that Malone was crippled.

Knowing so little about Malone troubled Larson. He knew only the kinds of things a sheriff knew about people; he had had a minor scrape with the law, he taught biology at the university. So why was he suddenly so interested in the way Malone had embraced this misfit Cooney Jenkins? Why did he notice his hard bare arms and veiny hands laid flat on the picnic table? So what? The three of them were smiling now and Malone pointed upward. A group of small black and brown birds darted in and out of the exercise yard. They fluttered under a small ledge made by a course of blocks and into what must have been their nests. The three at the table nodded and Margaret leaned toward Malone until they touched.

Larson found himself noticing Margaret's shoulder against Malone's. All their hands were on the table. Larson turned his attention to the hands. Three pairs on the table and not a finger twitched. Margaret's finger was nearly in contact with Malone's. Then Malone's left rolled over and took Jenkins's wrist. Larson could see that the grip was firm but gentle and, though he knew instantly that a big part of Malone's attraction was in that touch, he dismissed it as affected. It was almost effeminate, he thought, then felt a twinge of guilt for thinking that.

Now they were all standing and Larson moved to join them. He was surprised at how big Cooney Jenkins was. "I've got a couple questions for you, Mr. Jenkins," he said.

Cooney nodded but didn't say anything. Larson gave Margaret and Bill a look that told them he wanted to talk to Cooney alone and they moved away. Larson was wearing his light green jacket and pushed his hands deep into the pockets. He looked up and saw the birds again. There were a dozen of them flying back and forth to the nests under the ledge. "What kind of birds are those?" he asked.

Cooney's eyes came up and Larson saw they were a pale blue. They looked harmless but Larson tried not to be deceived. "I thought they were some sort of swift," Cooney said. His voice was much brighter than Larson would have expected. "But Bill says they're barn swallows."

"And Bill knows, right?" Larson looked to the nest. They were mud cups stuck to the wall just under the ledge and long, thin, black strings hung down from them. "What's that stuff hanging from the nests?"

Cooney seemed pleased by the question. "They build their nests of mud and fiber they carry in—sometimes from a long way. Those guys are using a lot of horsehair. But it's unusual for this time of year. That's what threw me off. They should be heading south by now."

Larson cleared his throat. "You told Miss Adamson that Malone spent the night the vandalism took place at your house. If you work for his alibi why wouldn't he work for yours?"

Cooney didn't hesitate. "He'd been drinking. He couldn't tell you if I was there or not." Cooney grinned.

"The master brake cylinder on that loader was drained. Is that what you meant to do?"

"Yes."

"Why sabotage the brakes? Why not drain the transfer case? Plugs were just the same, only a foot apart under that machine. Do more damage by burning up a transmission. Bad luck, huh?"

"I already talked to Mr. Hemmingford."

Larson looked back at the birds. "Well," he said, "Hemmingford's the big cheese in this case." The birds were flying in and out of the exercise yard. "What kind of birds did you say those were?"

"Barn swallows."

"I'll be darned," Larson said. "I've run this jail for thirty-five years and this is the first time I've seen barn swallows."

Hemmingford was waiting for them when they came out. He was mad but trying not to show it. Lonzo stood behind him, expressionless as always. Hemmingford nodded to Bill and Margaret. "Larson, I'd like a word with you. Could we use your office?"

"Looks like you just got out of bed," Larson said.

"As a matter of fact," Hemmingford said, "I did. May we?" He moved toward the hall.

* * *

BECAUSE WORK on Mountain Air Estates had come to a halt, Bill and Margaret walked Brendan Prairie. It was the first time Bill had been there since before the hearing. The line of yellow earth movers was still there but he ignored them. Maybe they'd never be let loose on Brendan Prairie. It felt good to be walking the trails of his favorite place again and, though he knew it was dangerous thinking, he couldn't help wondering if this place hadn't gotten a reprieve.

The last time he was here, all he could see in his mind was the rolling pine country being pushed into shapes that would accept foundations for condominiums and swimming pools. He'd imagined the earth-rattling noise of the big machines. But today the noises were subtle, a pine siskin's *tit-i-tit*, the canary song of a goldfinch, the light northwesterly breeze swirling in the scattered pine tops. It was a great day to be on Brendan Prairie, and being with Margaret made it perfect.

They walked the trail that led from the road to the top of the main basin and on the way Bill turned to watch Margaret coming up behind him. He wondered if she really could outwalk him now. Sure, he had the stiff leg, but she had been confined behind a desk for all those years. He smiled at himself. She could probably outwalk him with ease. But it was silly to even think about it. Who could walk faster and farther had never been a issue between them. What had always been important was to be out and engaged with what they were doing and what was going on around them. That was what had attracted Bill to Margaret all those years ago. He recalled the way she smiled for seemingly no reason on the first hike they ever took together. Now, twenty-some years later, Bill paused and looked back to see that she was smiling the same way. The grade was gradual but she had to watch her step because of the yucca plants. She planted her feet with the same sort of joy that some people reserve for opening Christmas presents. Despite what was on her mind she bounced up the slope of yucca and came to rest beside him.

"Have a look," he said and swung his arm over the prairie.

They were at the edge of Brendan Prairie, near the black trees, and could see the whole nine-hundred-acre island of grass. It was a high mountain meadow that had never been farmed or grazed too hard, a totally unique place. At its edges the golden aspen followed the water courses up into the pines like veins of precious metal between jade green stones. They didn't speak and both assumed correctly that the other was thinking of nothing. They stared for a long time at the grass that pulsed in waves before the hard thoughts began.

They thought of Cooney but there was no conclusion within easy reach. Margaret looked out over the expanse and worried about the life she would have to face when she went back to Denver. How had it become so dull and woody? She wondered what would become of her and whether or not she would ever do anything important again. She knew what was important and had the courage, at that moment, to face her real possibilities.

Bill watched those thoughts wriggle beneath the surface of Margaret's profile. She looked out over this patch of grassland hidden in the center of the Black Hills, and he was sent spinning back in time. He couldn't resist the similarity of this scene and one that he thought had been laid to rest in his memory.

In the last years they were together Ellen would turn pensive at times like this. She used to look out over a piece of land that was vital to Bill and begin thinking about something he couldn't fathom. After Allison was born she had changed. Before, she was always ready to go with Bill, always ready to spend the night camped in some canyon where peregrine falcons might be nesting or on a section of grassland where sharp-tailed grouse sliced the cool, evening sky. But those things ceased pleasing her, and by the time she began talking about her discontent, Bill sensed what was coming. She stared out over a deserted sage flat like Margaret was staring now and asked him if this was what he intended to do for the rest of his life. He knew her interest in him had waned, but he was taken off-guard with the thrust of her question. The words drove deep into him because they revealed that her attraction for him had been mostly infatuation. She must have thought his passion for the birds was temporary and that he would tire of days in the wind. She never realized that what she saw was what she got.

The answer to her question had been yes, this was his life. But he didn't say it because he loved her and was hurt. He knew the minute she asked that question she would eventually leave him. He knew what her question meant. It was part of what had attracted him.

Now it was Bill's turn to be observed. When he shook himself back from the past he found Margaret watching him. They looked at each other for an instant and Margaret squinted with recognition. "It's Ellen, isn't it? You're thinking of Ellen."

Bill's face didn't change. He nodded. "Yeah."

Margaret let her eyes fall away from Bill's. "I've been really stupid," she said. "I thought you and Ellen were solid. I thought you went to New Mexico together. I didn't know she went there to be with Jamie. I had no idea you went there to get her back."

Bill nodded and looked out over Brendan Prairie. Then he touched Margaret's arm. "There is a lot you don't know. Let's walk."

The trail rose another ten feet then leveled off along the rim of a shallow, grassy draw. They walked in silence until they reached a cluster of four ponderosa pines that grew defiantly, a hundred yards from the nearest other trees. Bill stopped and turned back to Margaret. "She would have come back on her own. At least for a while. I had Allison." Bill let that soak in. "I didn't go to New Mexico to get Ellen."

"You didn't go to bring her back?"

"No." Bill went completely earnest. "You don't know, do you?"

Margaret shook her head. "Know what?"

"The gyrfalcon that was confiscated from me in Montana."

"I'm sorry." Margaret said. "I should have told you this before." She couldn't face Bill. "It could have been me that tipped off Mathews. He asked and I told him."

Bill laughed and raised Margaret's chin. "Of course you did," he said. "You're only fault is your honesty. But you didn't know where or when. No. It wasn't you. I figured it out long ago."

"Figured what out?"

"Ellen told them what I was doing. She told Jamie. Jamie told Mathews. Ellen was the only one that knew the details. I'm sure they kept you in the dark. Probably your superiors were in on it. Maybe it went even higher."

Margaret was befuddled. She shook her head. "What are you talking about?"

"I didn't go to New Mexico to bring Ellen back. I went to bring the gyr back. But it was too far gone. I killed it because it would never fly again. I didn't want it to suffer and die in the desert of another continent."

"The bird they confiscated?"

"The gyr was a gift from our government to Jamie's boss—a little sign of appreciation for allowing someone to drill an oil well somewhere." Bill looked out over Brendan Prairie. He spoke almost to himself. "But the sheik didn't get the gyr and Jamie didn't get Ellen. Turns out he didn't really want her. She was just another thing for him and when he told her as much and she saw what he did to me, she took his car and drove it off the road at ninety miles an hour."

Margaret found a large rock and slumped to a sitting position. She rubbed her face with both hands, then looked up and opened her eyes wide. She inhaled. "What did he do to you?"

"After they caught me and saw that I'd given the gyr an injection they dragged me out to where they had been planting some shrubs. There were two Pakistanis who did all the work around the place and I didn't bother to struggle. I'd done what I came to do. But just as we got out into the sun, Jamie and Ellen pulled up in the Mercedes. You should have seen the shock on their faces." Bill sat down beside Margaret and patted her leg gently. "The Pakistanis held me tighter as they came close. It was the coldest thing I'd ever seen, and the only time I'd ever seen Jamie pick up a shovel without being threatened. He surprised me. He was really a gentle guy but when they told him what I did, he picked up the shovel and swung it with all his might." Bill paused. His eyes were open wide and something like a smile played at their corners. "It broke my kneecap and tore most of the ligaments."

Then Bill was finished talking. They sat quiet for a long time. The clouds had time to rearrange themselves over Brendan Prairie. A red-tailed hawk flapped out of the trees above, caught a thermal, spread its wings, and soared into the fluffiness of the prairie sky. After a time, Bill put his arm around Margaret and held her firm. Bill's arm felt good and for an instant Margaret hated herself. But the feeling passed and in its place came a resolve to try for something important again. She knew it would do no good to apologize or go over old ground. She put her hand on Bill's bad knee and let it rest there. Then a flutter in the brush caught her eye. They sat still as a robin-size bird with a long graceful tail bounced in the undergrowth. "Is it a brown thrasher?" Margaret whispered.

Bill hesitated before he spoke. "No," he said. "It's a beige dolorosa."

Margaret squinted at him. "Are you sure?"

Bill's eyes were smiling. "Come on. Let's move." He stood up and the bird darted away.

"Let's walk down that way," Margaret said. She pointed to a group of aspen near the creek that wound through the middle of the prairie.

Bill nodded. "Good choice."

They cut through the tallest bluestem and in five minutes came into the aspen. The branches were half bare and the golden leaves lay ten inches thick on the ground. They were as big as a man's hand and rolled away from their feet like huge gold coins. It was impossible not to play in them and soon both Bill and Margaret were tossing the leaves up and letting them shower down on their heads. They danced through the grove until they came to a line of grade stakes. The stakes were twenty feet apart and an orange Day-Glo flag was tied to the top of each. Without hesitation, Bill pulled the first one and tossed it deep into the shadows of the aspen grove.

Margaret stopped her play and when Bill saw the horror on her face he laughed. "Hell, Margaret, break out." He took the next stake in line and sent it after the first. "Today Brendan Prairie belongs to us."

Margaret followed behind him and the gold coin leaves continued to billow away from their feet. Bill pulled another stake and let it sail into the trees. She laughed and kicked some leaves at him. Then she raced ahead.

She beat him to the next stake and jerked it loose on the run. When she threw it it turned slowly, its orange flag rotating neatly through the aspen leaves that still clung to the trees. When the stake reached its zenith they both stopped to listen. It swished the air on its way toward the shadows, but they never heard it hit.

18

AFTER THE walk on Brendan Prairie, Bill went to the office of an attorney he knew and asked him to go talk to Cooney. "I don't think he did it," Bill said.

"What makes you think that?" The attorney was all silver— silver suit, silver hair, gray eyes. He made Bill feel inferior sitting there in his mud-splattered jeans and messed-up hair. All he could do in response to the attorney's question was shrug.

"You'll see him, won't you?"

"Yes, I think so," the attorney said. "You'll be taking care of the fees. Is that right?"

Bill shrugged again. "Sure."

He felt silly and slipped out as soon as he could. All he wanted was to get home. And when he got there he found Allison carrying Caesar around the backyard. She didn't hear him pull up and didn't notice him leaning against the garage. It was wonderful to see her with a bird on her fist. She might look like her mother but he couldn't help thinking that she had inherited his love for the birds. That could be good or bad, he thought, as he watched her neatly loosen the braces of the hood with the fingers of her right hand and her teeth. She was smooth with the hood. A chip off the old block, he thought, and a sad smile came over his face.

Then Caesar was unhooded and Bill wondered if he'd get excited, try to fly, and have to be restrained by the leash. But the bird sat calmly and Allison leaned down to pick up the end of a braided nylon string that Bill had not noticed. She tied the string to Caesar's swivel and removed the leash. My God, Bill thought. She's going to call him to the lure, she's going to let him fly. This was unscheduled and, though he would be secured by the string, Bill thought it was too early. He almost moved to stop her but held back. Let her try.

Allison moved to a perch she had staked in the yard and held Caesar next to it. She rolled her hand away the way she had been taught and Caesar stepped onto the perch. This is where he'll lose it, Bill thought. But Allison moved so slowly that Caesar couldn't feel threatened. She backed away, keeping her eye on the bird but not staring, not intimidating him at all. When she was ten feet away she pulled the lure from her hawking bag and tossed it onto the lawn.

Caesar bobbed his head once and came like a rocket. Bill's eyes went wide with surprise but he didn't make a sound. This was a critical time. The little falcon latched onto the dead sparrow tied to the lure and looked around suspiciously. Bill found himself whispering directions that Allison couldn't hear. "Easy." Then, "Easy, let him start eating. Use the corners of your eyes. Use the edges. Don't stare."

And that's exactly what Allison did. She stood still until Caesar's head went down for a pull of food. Once he got the taste, he went at it with enthusiasm. "Now," Bill whispered. "Move slowly, at right angles. Cut the distance gradually. Get a tidbit ready. A piece of something good. A heart or liver."

In a few moments Allison was on her knees in front of Caesar. She still didn't look directly at him but put the piece of heart on the glove and eased toward the feeding falcon. Now the suspicion was gone and Caesar plucked the heart from the glove between pulls from the lure. Allison eased the glove back and reloaded it with a larger piece of meat. When she held it out, Caesar reached over and clutched the glove with the talons of one foot. He pulled at the meat. But Allison didn't let him have it. He pulled again and realized he'd have to bring the other foot up and step onto the glove to eat. He did it with only a furtive glance at the lure he was leaving.

Allison remained kneeling in the grass until Caesar was nearly done eating, then rose to her feet. When he finished the last bite, she slid the hood over his head and gently pulled the braces tight. She turned to find her father watching her and smiled. Bill smiled, too. It was only consideration for Caesar's wildness that kept them from whooping with delight. Consideration for Caesar and the fact that Cooney was still in jail.

LARSON HAD hoped to simply put in his time until he could drive his Royal Coachman south. But the evening after Cooney Jenkins's confession, Margaret Adamson turned up at his house and asked the exact question that had been bothering him. "What about this car business?" Her eyes were steady on him and he could tell that she really didn't want to ask the question.

"Malone's car was downtown when he says he was supposed to be at Jenkins. It was a big deal to Hemmingford until Jenkins confessed. Now he must have decided it isn't important."

Margaret swallowed and nodded. "I hope he's right. How can we check it?"

Larson took a moment to consider what Margaret said. Before he spoke he rubbed his face with his right hand. "You sure you want to check it?"

"I don't know if I want to or not. But what if Cooney didn't do it?"

"Someone else did," Larson said.

"We don't really have a choice, do we?"

Larson was looking down at his kitchen floor as if he had forgotten Margaret was there. It looked like he was done talking. But then his head began to nod. "Okay," he said, "I've got an idea."

Since he had been sheriff, and probably before, there had been a fanatical group of Christians who watched the comings and going of cars on Deadwood's late-night streets. The group's mission was to identify the patrons of Aphrodite's, the local house of ill repute and, in so doing, close down the place. They had been after Larson to move against the establishment since he first took office. In the early years, the group's leader had barged into his office a couple times with the list of license plates they had recorded as being parked downtown after hours and demanded that something be done. Larson had been younger then and basically threw the man out.

Even though Larson had received calls from the group's leader for years, when he needed it he couldn't recall the man's name. He had to call a friend at the *Deadwood Daily Call* who heard from the man on a weekly basis. Harlan Williams was a reporter and laughed into the phone when he heard what Larson wanted. "You mean old Holier-Than-Thou Rowe? Reverend Benny Rowe of the Lost Lambs Baptist Church? Tries every week to get me to publish the license plates of everyone parked on Main Street. He might have had a point before gambling, when there was only one place of business open at that hour."

"Little different now," Larson said.

"I'll say," Williams said. "Aphrodite's is the least of our problems now."

LARSON AND Margaret drove to Rowe's church and walked into the reverend's office unannounced. Rowe looked about like what Margaret imagined; bifocals, a pallid face, and long hair parted to cover a bald spot. By the time they got into the church it was getting dark and for some reason Rowe had not turned on the light in his office. He sat behind a large wooden desk and flared his nostrils when Larson mentioned his campaign to identify all customers of Aphrodite's. "It wouldn't be necessary to expose the patrons of that—" Rowe's anxiety rose as he searched for the right word, "—that *place*, if people like you would do your job. You're supposed to defend family values."

They were getting off on the wrong foot so Margaret tried to slide to Rowe's side. "You're probably right about that, Reverend," she said. "I'm sure the sheriff has tried to tell the states attorney's office. But I'm afraid they don't share our traditional point of view." Margaret's eyes caught Larson's and she saw him smile.

"I won't be around much longer," Larson said. Margaret thought he would stop there but Larson was warming to his part. "You'll find my replacement very, how can I say it? Worldly? Harder to deal with than me. In a word, liberal."

"Good Lord," Rowe said, "the entire area is being inundated by secular humanists. Now the sheriff's department!" He spoke this like a pronouncement from the pulpit. Then he smiled and leaned across the desk toward the two of them. It was so dark in the office that Margaret had to squint to meet his eyes. "What can I do for you?" Rowe said.

Margaret looked to Larson. He exhaled. "Would it be possible to get the list of people parked near Aphrodite's on September ninth?"

"Certainly. You plan to expose them? We long for exposure."

Larson was slow to answer. Margaret watched him from the corner of her eye and could see that he was thinking. "Yes," he said, "That's the plan." His old eyes sparkled at Margaret. "Why not?"

Rowe stood up and walked to a filing cabinet. "We'd like to have names attached to those license plates, then have the whole list published." He leafed through a file and came out with a three-ring notebook. "Let's see, September . . ."

"Ninth," Margaret said. Larson stood up and moved to Rowe's side. The room was very dark.

"Do you have some lights?" Larson asked.

Rowe looked at him suspiciously. "Of course we have lights," he said. But he didn't turn them on. He flipped through the notebook to the September ninth page. "Oh yes, Helen Evert was in charge that night. She's dedicated, very dedicated. Here you go." He handed the book to Larson who took it and moved to the window so he and Margaret could read. The sun was nearly down and Larson had to hold the notebook up to make anything out.

It was very well organized. From the handwriting, Helen Evert had to be a little old lady. Probably wears tennis shoes, Margaret thought. Larson ran his finger down the column and there it was; Bill's license plate number. The car had been parked right in front of Aphrodite's in the early morning hours of the ninth of September from one-thirty to three forty-five.

Larson closed the notebook and looked up to meet Margaret's eyes. She was already wondering how far it was from Aphrodite's to Brendan Prairie. Would there be time to get out there and back before or after the car was known to be on the street? "Is that all you wanted?" Rowe said. Both Margaret and Larson ignored him. The fact that the car was on the street didn't really mean much. They knew they would have to do more checking, poke around, investigate.

"You're going to do something?" Rowe stood close in the darkened office.

"Lonzo should be doing this," Larson said.

"He won't," Margaret said. "They have the case solved. They're happy."

Larson handed the notebook back to Rowe. He moved too abruptly and the notebook hit Rowe in the chest with a bit of a slap. But Larson didn't notice. Margaret was already moving toward the door.

When they were back in the car and headed toward Deadwood, Larson said, "He might not have been driving his car. Maybe he parked behind Jenkins, blocked him, and Jenkins took Malone's car."

Margaret didn't respond until they had traveled another mile. "I guess we'll find out," she said.

The lights of Deadwood were illuminating the canyon walls ahead. "We can stop right now," Larson said.

"I wish we could," Margaret said.

Larson didn't take his eyes off the road ahead. "And you tried to tell me you weren't a cop."

They started at the Gilded Edge Casino. Its nickname was the Gelded Edge, or sometimes the Guilt Edge. It was run by two homosexuals named Ed and Larry and was right next door to Aphrodite's, which was upstairs above a fancy pizza joint. Larson liked the owners of the Gilded Edge. They moved in from Key West when gambling started up again and as far as Larson was concerned they were the best casino operators in town. They were always joking and seemed to at least enjoy their work. That was more than he could say for most casino owners who seemed to spend a lot of their time rushing around in bad suits, complaining about one thing or the other. Ed and Larry still wore their Key West clothes; sandals, flowered shirts, and baggy pants. It was amazing that they didn't freeze to death in the winter. Of course, the casino furnace was always blowing hot air from above the blackjack tables. Ed liked to stand facing the hot air, close his eyes, spread his legs and arms and, with great emotion, say, "Oh God, I miss the beach."

It was the only casino Larson went into on a regular basis. He didn't gamble, but he got a kick out of the Gilded Edge and listening to Ed and Larry talk about their lives in Key West. That was the reason they started there. "Oh my God," Larry shouted when he saw Larson. Then he turned to the kitchen. "Burn the hell out of a cup of espresso. Sheriff Larson's here."

They talked with Larry and found out that Hemmingford and Lonzo had done the rounds the day before. Neither Larson nor Margaret had a picture of Bill and they felt silly trying to describe him.

"Oh Carl," Larry said, "you're so intent."

Larson waved Larry quiet and tried again to describe Malone. Margaret was surprised by the details he could recall. Larry listened closely.

"Good-looking. With a limp?" Larry shook his head. "I was here that night. I'm sure I would have remembered someone like that." He shrugged. "*No se*," he said.

"A real sheriff would have remembered a picture," Larson said as they left the Gilded Edge. "Maybe cases of trash thrown into ditches is more my speed."

The man at the pizza joint hadn't seen Bill either. The cocktail waitresses in the three closest bars could not recall anyone that fit Bill's description. By then it was ten o'clock. They stood on the street not knowing what to do next. "Maybe there was a mistake," Larson said. "Maybe Malone really was sound asleep on Jenkins's couch."

"I'm sure he was," Margaret said. But she wasn't sure. She had a bad feeling about all this. "You want to be back home with your Royal Coachman. I don't blame you. Why don't you go on. I can walk back to the hotel."

Larson nodded but he stayed where he was. He let the

stream of sidewalk people split to get around him. "Look," he said. "Even if he was down here between one-thirty and three forty-five, all it would prove is that he wasn't at the Mountain Air site. It's a good drive out there. I don't think a person could do both."

"That's what I'm thinking," Margaret said. "If I could establish that Bill was here and that a person wouldn't have time to drive to Mountain Air, Bill would be . . . how do you say it? Off the hook."

"Bill's not on the hook," Larson said. "Jenkins is."

"So I wouldn't prove anything."

"That's not exactly true," Larson said. "You'd prove that Malone lied about where he was." Larson pulled his cap down tighter. "You'll be all right?" he asked.

"Sure."

"Good night then," Larson said. "Be careful."

Margaret leaned on the lamppost on the street near where Bill's car had been parked and watched Larson disappear into the crowd moving along the sidewalk. It was late for Margaret to be out on the street and she felt out of place, like she was somehow a different species than the people passing. She felt foreign and conspicuous but no one seemed alarmed to see her loitering there. She knew she should go back to the hotel but she wanted to know what had happened the night of the ninth. She leaned against the post until her eyes wandered to the windows above the pizza joint. Aphrodite's was dimly lit and the lace curtains tied up at the sides made them appear to be winking.

The stairs were rickety and she felt disreputable standing on the landing after ringing the bell. Margaret sensed an eye behind the peephole in the center of the door. She was both relieved and tense when she heard the dead bolt click open.

"I think you're lost." It was a small, thin woman with tightly curled blond hair. She wore a pink negligee but, on her feet, instead of the high heels Margaret expected, she wore huge woolly slippers with ears and a tail. She looked like she had dogs for feet. She was amused to find a woman at the door.

"I'd like to ask a couple questions," Margaret said.

The woman's expression chilled. "We don't answer questions." She started to close the door.

Margaret stopped the door with her left hand. "Hold on," she said. She pulled her badge with her right hand and that stopped the woman. The United States Fish and Wildlife Service couldn't mean anything to the woman but she knew a badge when she saw one. She pushed hard on the door but Margaret held it. They battled each other with the door until Margaret put all her strength behind her push. The door came open eighteen inches.

"Get the hell out of here!" The woman screamed. "We're not doing nothing in here!"

"Stop it!" Margaret shouted. The woman went silent. "I'm not here to do anything to you. Just ask some questions."

"I ain't answering any goddamned questions."

"Look, I'm not here about you. I don't care what your business is. But, unless you want me to start caring, you better start being cooperative." The woman was going to say something nasty, but Margaret got right down in her face and said, "I mean it. I'll have you busted bigger than hell."

That took the woman out of gear. Margaret pushed the door all the way open and came into a hallway. Beyond was a room with red velvet wallpaper. Two other women peered around the corner. "It's okay," Margaret told them. "It's okay." She turned to the small blond woman. "What's your name?"

"Daiquiri."

"Daiquiri?"

"Yeah, Daiquiri."

"All right, Daiquiri. Were you working the night of the ninth? A week ago Tuesday?"

"Yeah, I work every night." Daiquiri pulled a pack of Winstons from a pocket.

"You know a guy named Bill Malone?"

Daiquiri shrugged. "Maybe. We don't use names much up here. Is he local?"

"Spearfish. He might have been here on the ninth. He's got a limp. He's a nature nut. Loves birds."

Daiquiri's face broke into a smile. "You'd have to talk to Cary. She's our naturalist. She likes the earthy types."

"Cary?"

"Yeah."

"Was she working last Tuesday?"

"Yeah, I think so. She can probably help you," Daiquiri laughed. She was glad to pass Margaret along, glad to be off the hot seat.

They walked down the hall and into the room with the velvet wallpaper. Margaret was having a difficult time believing it, but this place was just like she had imagined it. The two women who had looked out to see about the commotion sat on separate couches smoking cigarettes. One had a romance novel laid open on the cushion beside her. Their eyes followed Margaret.

"Cary?" The woman with the novel nodded. "This lady wants to talk to you about nature."

Cary stood up with no expression on her face. She was a little overweight with short black hair. She took a drag on her cigarette before she butted it in the ashtray balanced on the arm of the couch. "I don't do girls," she said.

Margaret shook her head. "Neither do I. I just want to talk."

Cary shrugged. "So talk."

The other women were watching with interest. "You know Bill Malone?" Margaret saw something change in Cary's eyes but Cary didn't answer. "Is there a private place?" Margaret asked.

Cary looked to Daiquiri for permission. Daiquiri shrugged.

"Follow me," Cary said.

They moved down the hall and into a room. Cary breezed into the dimly lit room and sat on the bed. "Shut the door," she said.

The room was small and neat. A miniature lamp with a red shade burned on a table by the bed. Margaret leaned against the door frame and noticed that Cary's name was printed on a sign that hung on the door from two brass hooks. She moved into the room and closed the door behind her.

Cary took off her bracelet and rubbed her wrist. She chewed her gum like a nervous teenager. But she didn't look like a girl.

Margaret guessed her at mid-thirties, just about gone by for this kind of work. She stopped fiddling with the bracelet. "So talk," she said. She pulled her legs up onto the bed, leaned against the headboard.

"You know Bill Malone, don't you?"

This time Cary was ready and her eyes revealed nothing. She grinned and shrugged. "Maybe."

Margaret focused on her teeth. They were nice. She wondered if Bill had been attracted to them. "Look," she said. "This is very important. You have to talk to me."

"Why?"

"There could be an innocent life in danger."

"Nobody's innocent," she said. But her tone had softened. "Look," she said, "Officially, I don't know anyone. Nothing like that leaves this room."

There was a chair in the corner of the room and Margaret pulled it toward the bed and sat down. She waited a moment before she spoke. The tension rose in her chest. "Was Bill Malone here last Tuesday?"

Cary looked at her and understood that Margaret expected her to say yes. But she told the truth. "No," she said. "I've never met Bill Malone." Margaret slumped in the chair. Then Cary went on. "But his friend was."

For an instant Margaret was confused. Then it came to her. "Cooney?"

Cary nodded. "He's kind of a customer." She shrugged. "Hell, Cooney's a friend."

Margaret couldn't believe this. "Cooney Jenkins comes here?"

"Not often," Cary said. "He doesn't have much money."

Margaret was still stunned. She couldn't imagine Cooney Jenkins and this woman—any woman. "Cooney comes here?" she said again. "Comes here and . . ." she pointed to the bed.

Cary laughed. "Maybe," she said. "I'd never talk about anything like that." She laughed again. "But mostly he comes to talk. Like you."

Margaret crossed her arms then uncrossed them. She was

having trouble understanding what she was hearing. "And that's how you know Bill?"

"I only know of him because Cooney talks about him all the time." She moved her legs to the edge of the bed and stood up.

Margaret felt drained. She wasn't sure yet what any of this meant. But still, she had the feeling that something had changed. Cary switched on the overhead light and the room became bright. It hurt Margaret's eyes and she squinted as Cary moved to the window. She pulled back the curtains. "He brought me this," she said.

In the new light the room looked more ordinary. Cary held the curtain back. At first Margaret thought she looked younger, but no. Just more normal. "Cooney built it for me," she said. "He came to put it up last Tuesday." It was hard to see what she was talking about from the chair beside the bed so Margaret rose and went to the window.

The window glass reflected the room and Margaret had to hold her hands up to the glass to see. She looked out onto an iron fire escape. It looked like the bones of a dinosaur in the alley light. Then she saw what Cary was talking about. It was a bird feeder, made of old barn planks and a couple pieces of Plexiglas. "They're really starting to come in," Cary said. "Mostly juncos right now, but other kinds, too. I got a book, I'm committed." She laughed at herself and Margaret continued to stare out the window and into the night. How long would it take to drive from here to Brendan Prairie, she thought. Would Cooney have had time to vandalize the earth movers before one-thirty? After three forty-five? If he didn't, who did?

19

MARGARET AND Allison met at seven o'clock in the morning on a gravel road halfway between Spearfish and Deadwood. Margaret had not slept well. Her thoughts had tumbled over one another all night and even now her mind was somewhere else. She had something she should be doing but she had made plans to run with Allison. She dreaded the task ahead of her that day and welcomed the chance to put it off for a couple hours while they ran.

Margaret left her car parked along the side of the road and got in with Allison. They drove Allison's pickup up Spearfish Canyon a couple miles then to the west for a quarter mile. They parked the truck just off a gravel road and began their run on a gradual uphill that took them along a tributary to Spearfish creek.

Before they left the pickup, Margaret put her wallet in the glove box. The neatness of maps and papers reminded her again how much Allison was like her mother. As they ran, Margaret shook her head to recall how she accidentally dumped half the contents of the glove box out on the ground at Cooney's, how she never found one of the wrenches. The old juxtaposition of perfect Ellen and klutzy Margaret was being relived except that Ellen was gone. Allison had taken her place.

They followed the little stream for a mile and a half then took a trail to the south, over a hogback and into the next drainage. Everything had been uphill to that point. It took a lot of effort so they didn't say much until the trail flattened out and they began to descend along another watercourse. Allison spoke calmly and evenly between breaths as they wound their way down the south watershed in a loop back toward the pickup. The way she kept a half smile on her face as she ran again reminded Margaret of Ellen. At first she only answered Margaret's small talk: How was school? What did she plan to do afterward? But on the last leg of their run, about mile five, Allison began to ask her own questions.

"Cooney," she said. "What is he actually charged with?"

The question was a nonsequitur. Cooney had not been mentioned. They hadn't spoken of Brendan Prairie but suddenly Margaret understood that those were the things Allison had been thinking about. A déjà vu swept over her. Allison had just performed the same leap her mother had performed in a conversation about falcons the day after she slept with Bill for the first time. Of course, Margaret hadn't known Bill's soul had already been stolen so she answered the question without guile. "Bill's last day of work is October tenth," she told Ellen. They moved in together on the fifteenth.

"They've charged Cooney with felony murder," Margaret said.

Allison nodded. "Murder," she said. They jogged on another fifty yards. Then, "He'd go to prison?"

"Yes. If he did it he might have to go for a long time."

The trail came out onto the gravel road where the pickup was parked. They slowed to a cool-down walk for the last quarter mile. Allison took long slow strides to stretch her legs. She stared at the gravel road. "How long?" she asked.

"It's hard to say."

"How long?"

"At least fifteen years."

Allison stared at the ground. "Life," she whispered.

They talked very little on the way back to Margaret's car. After they said goodbye, Margaret headed for Deadwood and the task she was dreading. Allison went home. She had promised to take over with Caesar because she knew her dad would want to go for a walk.

Bill was waiting with the hooded falcon on his fist. He transferred it to Allison's and drove away without saying much. Allison walked slowly into the house and down the hall to her bedroom. She put Caesar on the back of a chair and lay down on her bed. She looked up at the ceiling and began to cry. The door was closed and she was alone, still she didn't make any noise. The tears simply slid from her eyes and meandered slowly down over her temples and into her blond hair. She told herself she needed to rest. But as soon as she closed her eyes she didn't feel tired. Her eyes came open again. She felt no need to even blink.

In fact, she hadn't slept much for a week and only poorly for a month before that. She should have been exhausted but something in her was keeping her going, like caffeine in her veins. She lay on the bed with her hands beside her and the palms opened upward. She moved them to her solar plexus and intertwined her fingers. But her thumbs grazed the underside of her breasts and she had to slide her hands lower before she felt comfortable.

Even then she didn't feel really comfortable. She'd been avoiding thinking of it but now she admitted that she would have to see Cooney. What did the inside of a jail look like? Was it cold and sterile and gray? Did noises ricochet metallically forever without finding something soft to absorb them? Poor Cooney. She wondered what had possessed him to confess to killing Arnold? It would be straightened out. It had to be. Cooney would not do well in a jail.

The tears had dried at her temples, but she could still feel some wetness in the fine hair just in front of her ears. She had resolved to lay there until that sticky feel was gone. She hated to move with dampness against her skin, but she also hated the feel of the tears drying, and finally her hands came up fast and rubbed the wetness away violently. She was left with her hands over her ears as if there was something terrible being said to her.

She left her hands over her ears and forced her eyes closed. She would have to go to the jail. The thought of it frightened her. She squeezed her eyes shut even harder and let her fingers dig into her hair while her palms held out the hollow noises she imagined bouncing around inside Cooney's cell.

* * *

MARGARET DROVE to the exact place where Bill's car had been parked the night before Andy Arnold was killed. She checked her watch. Eight-thirty. She drove out of town toward Brendan Prairie, being careful to drive at the speed limit. But she turned on the logging road north of the prairie. She stopped the car where she had come out of the forest the day she had walked from the site of Andy Arnold's death. The drive took her nearly an hour. At night, with a bag of spray cans and some tools, it would take at least forty minutes to walk to Brendan Prairie. Forty minutes back. Say another half hour doing the deed.

Margaret drove the logging road loop and came into Brendan Prairie from the opposite direction. She drove near where Andy Arnold had died. She was computing the possibility of Cooney driving out from town, walking through the forest, sabotaging the machine, and returning before one-thirty or after three forty-five.

She was not expecting to see a car parked on the shoulder of the road ahead. But even before she could see it well she knew that it was Bill's. The area was open and the trees did not get thick until the ground rose on the edges of the prairie a couple hundred yards away. Before she had fallen asleep the night before, she planned to wake up and go immediately to the county jail to talk to Cooney. But she'd slept fitfully and the first thought of the morning was that after her run she should go to Brendan Prairie.

Sitting in her car, squinting down across the rolling grass of the prairie, the dreams of the night before came back to her. She hadn't let herself remember the dreams until that moment. The dreams were wild and disjointed, the kind Margaret seldom had. The images embarrassed her, but here they came, wafting through the car window from Brendan Prairie.

An auditorium filled with people sitting quietly in sections. Sheriff Larson was in one section, Hemmingford in another, Lonzo in another. Every section with a different person and everyone in that section looking like the person whose section it was. Hundreds of Larsons, Hemmingfords, Lonzos. Thousands and thousands of people—hundreds of thousands perhaps—and there she was in her own section and there was Bill and Cooney in theirs. Only Bill was by himself. Just sitting there with no real expression on his face. But when Margaret saw herself, she was smiling and the woman beside her, who was also Margaret, looked cool and distant. The next woman, Margaret again, was stern. And the next was laughing and the next angry. In her sleep she had searched from face to face until she was frantic. Sitting in the car, she shook her head. She didn't want to talk to Bill. But she wanted to see him. She wanted to look carefully at him.

She fumbled in the glove box for the binoculars. There were few chances to use them anymore but it was like riding a bicycle. She twisted the knob under the middle finger of her right hand and the prairie tightened into focus. She scanned the rolling landscape in front of her and immediately found two white-tailed deer lying just off a trail a quarter mile to the east. One was a big buck with three points on one side and four on the other. The deer pulled Margaret's attention away from what she was doing and she had to fight to get herself to continue searching the prairie. The binoculars had just begun to move again when a raven drew her attention upward. The giant black bird circled far out and was quite clear in the binoculars. She brought her focus back down to earth and began to follow the trails and open drainages of the prairie. She'd passed over Bill twice before she realized what she was seeing.

When she refocused the binoculars, Margaret could see Bill was sitting on a gray outcropping of rock with his arms wrapped around one knee and the other leg out straight in front. In the morning mountain light, she was surprised at how handsome he really was. Bill moved slightly. He pulled his fingers through his longish hair and looked into the underbrush. He began eating something small and purple from his hand and when Margaret noticed the same color in the bushes, she realized that it was probably wild fruit. Bill had walked to the center of the prairie and was simply sitting on a rock eating wild plums. How could he be so at ease?

Margaret checked the time again. She refigured everything in her head. No matter how much leeway she allowed, there was no possible way Cooney could have sabotaged the machine that killed Andy Arnold. He would have had to be two places at once. He was lying. Margaret raised the binoculars one more time. The wind moved in Bill's hair and he raised another wild plum to his mouth.

20

JUST BEFORE five o'clock Allison walked into the courthouse and asked Betty Swindel if she could see Cooney. Betty called Sheriff Larson at home. Everyone knew the county was about to lose control of the prisoner but nothing had happened yet. "Sure," Larson said. "Let her in. Why not?" After she hung up, Betty smiled and punched the intercom button. She told the guard a woman was coming back to see the guy that confessed.

The guard stood behind a barred door as Allison walked slowly down the stark white hallway. The polished tile floor sounded hollow under her clogs and she wished she had worn tennis shoes. He was an older man and nodded as he waved her through the barred door. They walked down another hall and into the courtyard where Cooney, dressed in green coveralls, sat at a metal table in the gray light that filtered over the walls and down into the exercise yard. He stood up when he saw her but waited until she was through the last door before he moved to meet her. She had been searched by Betty Swindel but the guard still watched them closely from where he leaned against the wall.

They did not touch but they came very close, stopping less than a foot apart, and looking at each other for a long time. When a tight smile came across Cooney's face they sat down but most of a minute passed before Cooney spoke.

"You shouldn't have come here," he said. He was glad to see her but he had to look away. The barn swallows swooped in and out of the exercise yard. He pointed at them.

"Barn swallows," Allison said. "What are they doing here so late in the year?"

"I don't know. They should be heading south. If they stick around until the snow, they could die."

They watched the birds coming and going for a moment more. "You shouldn't have come," Cooney said again.

"I had to come."

"There isn't anything you can do."

"Yes there is. You know there is."

Cooney squinted at her, thinking back. "I'm not Bugs," Cooney said. Allison knew what Cooney was talking about. It was a secret between them, something that happened a long time ago and only Cooney knew about. He watched her, trying to see if the memory affected her. She stared straight into Cooney's eyes the same way she had stared at him that day ten years before.

Bill was gone and Cooney was watching Allison, when a dog came into the yard and found Bugs beneath the deck. It was not the first time the dog had come for the cat but this time Bugs was not paying attention. If Allison and Cooney had not been there, and a two-by-four left from construction of the deck had not been handy, the dog surely would have killed Bugs. But Cooney got to the two-by-four and drove the dog off before there was serious damage. There was a broken leg and a flap of skin torn away. They had to take Bugs to the vet where he spent the night.

When Cooney brought the little girl home he anticipated an afternoon of tears. But there were no tears after Bugs was safe at the vet's. They sat on the deck and talked until Cooney was satisfied that Allison was all right. Then he went into the house to make something for them to eat. But when he came back onto the deck, Allison was gone. He put the plate of sandwiches on the picnic table and called for her. But there was no answer and he began to search the backyards and alleys of the neighborhood.

It was a half hour later that he found her, by following the yelps and growls. She had cornered the dog in a garage and was beating it with the two-by-four. The dog was backed into a tangle of empty cardboard boxes and stood its ground, growling and barking. But when the two-by-four came down the dog screamed and lunged at Allison. She had closed the door behind her and was standing firm against the dog's snarls and attacks. Like she was driving railroad spikes, she swung the two-by-four with all her might and Cooney could not get to her until it had landed twice more.

He gathered the little girl and the two-by-four in his arms and it felt as if he was embracing a calf at branding time. He held firm and she bucked and quivered to get at the dog as it scurried behind them out the door. It took several minutes of gentle talk but finally the steely little muscles relaxed. When he could, Cooney pulled back from her and looked into her dark eyes. They were still dancing but as he watched they went oddly calm.

"I'm not Bugs," Cooney said again.

"No one is going to believe you did what you say you did," Allison said.

"It's important that they do," Cooney said. "If they don't, it will come down on your father."

"But he didn't do it."

"I know that," Cooney said. The gentleness was gone from his eyes. "I'm going through with this, Allison. No matter what I have to do."

They stared at each other, trying to read the other's mind, trying to understand what would happen. Finally Cooney saw something beginning in Allison's face. He was afraid she was going to say something he did not want to hear. He stood up and motioned for the guard to take her away.

MARGARET SAT in her car at the curb in front of Larson's house. She had to tell him what she'd found out, but she'd been putting it off as long as she could. The few hours at Bill's house were oddly pleasant once she decided not to tell Bill or Allison what she knew. It was best to leave it in Larson's hands, then go on to Denver.

She'd only gone to Bill's house to say good-bye. She thought visiting Bill and Allison would be difficult and would last only a few minutes. But except for a nagging, gloomy intuition it was not difficult. Margaret was touched by what she found at Bill's house. She experienced that sweetness of memory that can take people by surprise. Bill sat at the kitchen table with a falcon on his gloved fist and Allison hovered over a steaming pot on the stove. The huge old cat was curled on a chair. There was an undercurrent of doom about Cooney in the house, but Bill and Allison were doing their best to carry on. Bill smiled and, with his falcon-free hand, indicated a chair. Allison was glad to see Margaret and came and sat down at the table. But she did not stay long. After fifteen minutes she stood up and excused herself.

When she was gone, Bill told Margaret that Allison had gone to see Cooney and when she came back she seemed more relaxed. She planned to see Cooney again that night, during visiting hours. Margaret nodded. She imagined Larson would be there by then. Cooney would be set free when she told them what she knew. They didn't speak of Cooney anymore. They sat in silence like friends of twenty years can do. Margaret tried not to think what might happen. She tried to be happy to be near Bill. It was good to see him with a bird again and Margaret couldn't help studying the small movements. Bill smoothed the feathers of the bird's left wing, he adjusted its talons on the glove. The falcon preened the pantaloon feathers on its right leg.

"Maybe I'll come down to Denver," Bill said.

Margaret did not look up from where she concentrated on the blackness of the falcon's talons. All she could think to say was, "Maybe I won't stay there."

"You're ready for a move?"

"I'm ready for something."

Bill mocked the tight frown on Margaret's face and it melted into a self-conscious smile. She felt remorse for what had happened to them. "I'm sorry," she said.

"Nothing is your fault," Bill said. "Nothing is anyone's fault."

"I'm always messing things up."

"You? How about me?" At first Margaret honestly didn't know what he was talking about. "I walked away from you," Bill said. "Shouldn't you be angry that I went a little crazy?"

"People go crazy when they're in love. You were in love."

"And you?"

"It's different," Margaret said.

"Why?"

"Because you're different . . ." Margaret hesitated.

"And?"

"And you're not really that tough," Margaret smiled but she meant it. "People strike out at you because they admire you. But that doesn't mean you can take it."

Bill nodded. "And is that why some people are so good to me?" He motioned toward Margaret.

"We can't help it," Margaret said. Bill smiled at that, but Margaret was being sincere. Like everyone, she had been drawn to him. The fact that he didn't realize that he had that power made him more attractive. They fell silent again but after a moment Bill snapped his fingers.

"I found something I wanted you to have." He went to the counter and returned with a falcon hood.

They stared at the hood in his hand. It was the size of a tennis ball and made of three pieces of leather. The dark mahogany-colored center piece shown like a piano top and the two curved eye pieces were a dark green, polished into pools as deep as the falcon eyes they were intended to cover. The plume was made of covert feathers from a sharp-tailed grouse and the braces that slid to tighten the hood were waxed and stiff as quills. "It's the last hood I ever made," Bill said. "For a gyrfalcon I never flew. Take it. I want you to have it."

"I couldn't," Margaret said. "It's too beautiful."

"It's yours," Bill said. "But maybe you should read what's written inside first. I added it when I came back from New Mexico. I was not in good shape."

Margaret picked up the hood. It was impossibly light. She rolled it in her hand and looked carefully inside at the tiny stitches that held the three pieces of leather light-tight together. There was a circular piece of leather, no larger than a dime, sewn to the inside top. She had to squint to read it: " 'I dreamed I heard a coyote call and I was glad I didn't work for the government.' "

"It's a quote from a book. Famous author." Bill said. "I guess I was angry, I don't feel like that anymore." He was smiling. "I want you to have it."

"You may need it."

"It would only fit a gyrfalcon."

"Who knows?" Margaret said.

In the end she took the hood and now, as she sat in the car outside Larson's house, she again rotated this exotic artifact in her hand. It was exquisitely made and she wanted to show it to Larson. But she knew he would not appreciate it, so when she went to the house, she left it on the dash of her car, facing forward into the wind, the way it would face if it were on the head of a giant silver falcon.

A HALF HOUR before the sun set Cooney Jenkins was herded from the exercise yard and into his cell; concrete block walls, a toilet with no seat, a stainless-steel sink, bars on the front, and a door that slid and locked automatically. There were two bunks, but because his charge was so serious Cooney had no cellmate. The top bunk didn't even have a mattress.

When the door clanged shut behind him, Cooney looked around the cell. It was much neater than his cabin and in his mind he constructed an argument for a messy, lived-in home. But it was futile. No one would ever hear the argument. Though he'd lived most of his life alone, this was the first time he could remember feeling lonely. He moved to his bunk and looked around to be sure no guard was watching. Then, from the waist band of his pants, he slipped a ball of horsehair he'd taken from the barn swallow nests in the exercise yard. He slid the hair under his pillow where he already had a stash from his morning exercise period. He planned to do a little braiding when things quieted down in the jail.

Had he been at his cabin he would have tied a few flies. He thought of his fly-tying bench and again felt a jab of loneliness. His *Oncidium tigrenium* would be blooming soon and he hated to miss it. But he'd have to forget about orchids and mayfly imitations. He'd have to forget about braiding horsehair, too. For an instant he doubted his course. But Allison had frightened him. He didn't know for sure what she had done and had no idea what she would do now, but she was forcing him to another level of commitment. The whole thing made him sad and made him think about his cabin even more.

But he knew that was stupid. The cabin was just a place to keep stuff and it was all right that he'd never see it again. He wasn't interested in monuments and had always believed it would be best to pass from his world without leaving a trace. He sat down on the bed. The evening meal would be coming soon. He'd eat and do his braiding before the evening visiting hour. The man from the state capital would be there again, along with his tall, pale sidekick. They'd come the last two nights to ask the same questions and Cooney was tired of them. The attorney that came to see him earlier said he shouldn't talk to them without a lawyer present. Cooney thought that was a good idea and told the man so. The attorney was nice to him because Bill Malone had sent him. But when he got up to leave after twenty minutes of talk, Cooney told him not to come back. It was a waste of time. Now Cooney sat on his bunk waiting for his meal and told himself, over and over, that it was all a waste of time.

MARGARET DIDN'T want it, but she got the tour of the Royal Coachman. Larson showed her the compact stove, the tiny bathroom, the table that folds down into a bed. He explained about the years of restoration. She listened but her mind was somewhere else. Larson's chatter was slightly manic and Margaret let him go. The longer he talked the longer she could keep from saying what she'd come to say.

Larson disappeared into the Royal Coachman and reappeared with two bottles of beer. He twisted the caps off and handed Margaret a bottle. He started to sit down at the picnic table, then changed his mind.

"She's ready to roll," he said, picking up his monologue about the Royal Coachman. "Really haven't decided what I'm going to do. Could pull out of here sooner than some people think. I'll be done in November. I thought I might stick around, but lately I'm thinking I won't. Maybe I'll just take off. Drive right down to the Gulf of Mexico. If I do, I'm going to hang out on Padre Island for a while. Maybe a couple months. Maybe I'll go on down into Mexico."

"That would be great," Margaret said. She could see Larson in Mexico. The old gringo.

"But not inland. I'll be sticking to the coast. I want to fish, you know."

"I know. You're a big saltwater fisherman."

Larson frowned. "Not really," he said. "Truth is, I've never even seen the ocean."

"I know," Margaret said, "You're in for a treat. They got lots of ocean in Mexico. You can fish forever."

"You been there?"

"Yes. A couple times for work. Migratory bird treaty stuff. Even got so I could speak a little Spanish."

"Really?"

"Not that much. I can ask where the bathroom is. I can order beer." She held up her beer. "*Dos cervesas.*"

Larson laughed. "What's that mean?"

"Two beers."

"You ready?"

Margaret looked at her beer. It was still half full. "No. I have to drive tonight, but go ahead."

Larson looked at his own beer. It was half full, too. He shook his head. "Fishing," he said. "It's always fascinated me. Think of all those critters that live down there. I mean, hell. There's no way of knowing what might grab a hold of your bait."

"You like that, huh? Not knowing what might grab your bait."

Larson thought for a second, then began to nod. "Yes. I guess the idea appeals to me. But besides that, it would just be different, you know. If you were fishing in the ocean, it wouldn't matter if anything grabbed your bait or not."

The backyard was lit only by the lights from the Coachman.

Beyond their small circle of light was deep darkness. There was no way to tell that they were parked in Larson's backyard in the Black Hills of South Dakota. "And what about you?" Larson said. "You must have a dream. You must think about retiring, or vacation, or something."

For an instant, Margaret sat paralyzed by the thought. She searched through her memory and found no dream, no fantastic plan, nothing but fifteen more years of work. The inscription inside the gyrfalcon hood was affecting her. "No," she said. "No great dream retirement for me." And as soon as she said it, she was certain she couldn't go on doing what she was doing. She didn't know what she would do, but she wasn't going to spend her whole life in the service of the bureaucracy that stole Bill Malone's gyrfalcon and planned to send it ten thousand miles away to die. For an instant she was transported with the gyr and she cringed to think of Bill sliding the lethal needle into its muscle. She cringed again at the image of Bill's knee shattering under a blow from a shovel.

When she turned and looked into Larson's eyes she saw that he guessed what she was thinking about. "Look," she said, "we both know I've been avoiding the subject of Bill and Cooney." Margaret shook her head. "If I could, I'd just leave it."

Larson turned his back and walked a few steps away. "Don't say anything you don't want to say."

"I've got to tell you what I found out last night," Margaret said. She hunched her shoulders. It was her instinct for trouble again. Bill Malone was in danger and the danger was very close.

Margaret sat at the table with her back to the Coachman and her hands flat in front of her. She stared at Larson for an instant, then bowed her head for a moment.

When she looked up, Larson held his breath and bit the inside of his cheek. He didn't want to hear whatever Margaret was going to say. She was ready to speak, but then her expression went wary. At first Larson thought she was looking at him. But her gaze went past him. She squinted into the darkness behind him, then her eyes grew round with surprise. Larson spun around just as a wiry old man stepped into the light. "Excuse me," the man said. "I'm looking for Sheriff Larson."

The man was short and thin and wore faded jeans and boots. His white hair stuck out from under a beat-up gray stockman's hat and he held a cardboard box with both hands. Larson stood up with a jerk. "I've called several times," the man said. "My name's Avery Murdoch and I want someone to do something about this trash."

The tension should have slipped from Margaret's heart. But it didn't. Avery set the box down on the ground in front of Larson. "Used-up spray cans of paint," Avery said. "They tried to bury them in my pasture. You ought to catch these people and punish them. Throw their asses in jail." Avery pointed a finger at Larson as if he was at fault. "I'm turning it over to you. I expect you to do something."

Larson sunk to one knee, reached into the box and gingerly moved the cans around. He came up with a short steel bolt. He brought it into the light. "That, too," Murdoch said. "Got to be the plug off of some machine. Oily as hell." Larson touched the plug with the index finger of his left hand. It came away slick with fluid. "There's a wrench in there, too." Murdoch pointed to the box but Larson took another instant to study the plug. He felt Margaret move to his shoulder and without looking at her laid the plug gently back in the box. When his hand came up again a wrench dangled from his little finger. He held it in the light. The chill came back hard to Margaret. She recalled the night in Cooney's front yard. She recalled the coolness, the stars, the wrenches rattling out into the starlight. "Craftsman," Larson read. "Three-quarter inch."

Margaret brought her hand to her mouth. Her instincts had been right. Bill was threatened. But not with loss of his freedom. Worse. The loss of his daughter.

21

LARSON AND Avery Murdoch disappeared around the corner of the house and left Margaret sitting at the picnic table. She looked after them, then let her gaze go to the sky. All the air went out of her lungs and she left them empty for as long as she could. When she breathed again, the air felt cool as February.

Larson came back to the patio and stood with the light from the Coachman spilling over him. He watched Margaret for a moment before he sat down. The night felt especially close and there were the noises of the city and unnameable animals in the trees.

"You all right?" Larson said.

"Sure. I was just surprised to see that stuff."

"Lot of times that kind of trash turns up."

Margaret wanted to tell him everything she knew but she felt limp and they sat in silence while images of that night after the Mountain Air Estates meeting flashed through her head. Allison must have believed she was standing up for her father. She would have slipped out to Brendan Prairie while Bill was drinking. Cooney guessed what happened and was protecting her. Protecting Bill, too. Margaret rubbed her face. Would Allison let Cooney do this?

She looked up and found Larson studying her. His face was questioning but he didn't speak until she looked away. "It's just a box of trash," he said.

Margaret nodded. "Yeah," she said. "Just a box of trash."

They sat at the picnic table in the yellow light for several minutes before Larson spoke again. "I suppose you're worried about Jenkins."

Margaret shook her head and Larson squinted, trying to understand. "Malone, then."

"Kind of."

"He'll be all right. You shouldn't worry about him."

That brought a smile to Margaret's face and she shrugged as if there was simply nothing that could be done. "But I do."

"You're in love with him."

"Sure. But it's even more than that. He stands for something that is almost gone." Margaret looked to Larson and found his face blank. "You just hate to see him swallowed up by the same thing that's swallowing the rest of us."

Larson was not following her. "What is it that's swallowing the rest of us?"

"Our jobs, our ambitions." She shrugged again. "Our whole culture maybe. Everything that separates us and insulates us from all the real stuff." She swung her hand in an arch to indicate the backyard, the trees, the night, and the stars beyond. "We're being swallowed by everything that's been keeping you from the fish in the Gulf of Mexico."

They sat in the quiet another minute and the sound of branches rubbing together above them seemed to fill the night. Larson had never noticed the sound before but for that minute it was all he heard. "I'm not a big thinker," Larson said. "I'd be more concerned about Jenkins, he must be the one that tried to bury that box of junk. But you got Malone on the brain." He thought for a moment. "Is it because of the things he said?"

From the way Margaret looked at him he knew she didn't know what he was talking about. "Those things he said at the meeting about the grass and the water and all the animals that live up there on Brendan Prairie?"

Margaret shook her head. "No, it's not what he says. It's what he is. It's what he does."

She didn't avoid Larson's gaze. Her eyes took it on and Larson became uncomfortable. He looked away, but when he turned back she was still staring at him. "I need to go to the jail." Margaret said. "I need to see Hemmingford and I need to talk to Bill." She stood up and left Larson with his head down.

His hands lay on the wooden table and for the first time Margaret noticed how old they were. He pushed himself to his feet. "I'd never be able to enjoy my fishing if I let you go alone. I don't know what you're thinking and I don't want to know. But I'm with you."

LARSON ASKED Margaret to ride with him to the jail but Margaret wanted to be ready to leave town. She drove her own car. Maybe she had stayed too long already. There was a feeling that the situation was sliding into something she didn't want. It was as if she was fated to be a catalyst for Bill's pain. She didn't care when she got back to Denver but she needed to be able to get into her car and go when this thing was over. She was already numbed by what she was doing and longed to be alone on the highway. The taillights of Larson's car blurred in front of her. She watched them and followed without taking note of anything they passed.

Her eyes only strayed from the two red lights long enough to focus on the falcon hood still riding on the dashboard of her car. The hood was a splendid, compact piece of work. It was like a tiny, finely wrought sculpture with a purpose. She imagined the polished leather slipping neatly over the perfect feathers of a gyrfalcon's head. She imagined the calmed, unseeing eyes, enormous and jet black. Then the taillights of Larson's car flashed and turned into a parking place. Margaret was forced to look up and check her surroundings. There was a large parking place fifty feet ahead and she pulled into it nose first.

It wasn't until she had stepped out and started back toward the jail where Larson waited that she realized Allison's pickup was parked just behind her. She did not stop but slowed and looked into the pickup through the side window. It was just the way it had been the night she had dumped the contents of the glove box, neat and orderly. A map and a case for sunglasses rested on the dash.

When Margaret got to Larson she took his arm. "They're in there," she said. And when Larson questioned her with a look

she went on. "That's Allison's pickup. She's in there with her
father. They've come to see Cooney." Larson looked at the
pickup as if to memorize it. He said nothing, but he nodded and
Margaret felt the stringy biceps of his right arm tighten.

By the time they pushed through the double glass doors and
into the lobby of the courthouse, they had separated and Margaret led the way. The first thing to greet them was the pallid
face of Danny Lonzo. His lips parted in a flat smile. "Old home
week," he said.

Margaret came face-to-face with him. "I need to talk to Bill
Malone," she said. "Then Hemmingford." Lonzo's eyes were
glassy gray and Margaret felt her confidence flagging. She nearly
looked away. But Larson stepped up beside her.

"Let her through," Larson said.

Lonzo laughed.

"I'm still the sheriff," Larson said. Lonzo kept grinning but
he stepped aside.

"I need to get this over with," Margaret said.

The door to the sheriff's office was open and Larson and
Margaret came through to find themselves in the middle of a discussion. Betty Swindel was not there. The guard stood with his
arms folded over his chest. He was only listening. The discussion
was between Bill Malone and Barry Hemmingford. Everything
stopped when they entered and all eyes turned. Hemmingford
was behind the desk where the guard should have been. Bill was
leaning over the desk but looked over his shoulder at them.
There was an unnatural silence and Margaret felt the pressure in
it. She looked around the room and found Allison, standing behind them, near the door. When Allison felt them looking she
raised her head and thrust her chin out. A few strands of hair fell
across one dark eye.

"I suppose you want to see him, too," Hemmingford said.

Margaret didn't speak. She looked at Bill and saw that he
didn't know about Allison. Then she looked at Allison and her
breath caught in her throat. Allison's eyes were steady. She
seemed determined. She's going to tell, Margaret thought. She's
going to come clean.

Margaret moved to Larson. "They need to see Cooney," she said. She reached out and touched his arm. "This is important."

Larson looked at Margaret's hand on his arm. He hesitated for only a instant before he turned to the guard. "Open up, John."

The guard shrugged and looked to Hemmingford. "That's what I've been trying to explain to Mr. Malone," Hemmingford said. "Jenkins is being transferred out of here. Danny and I will be doing the transferring. He's our prisoner as of an hour ago."

"Don't do this," Margaret said. "You don't understand."

"Oh? Is that so?"

"Let these people see him," Margaret said. She turned to Larson and the old man's head began to nod.

"He's still in my jail," Larson said. "He's still my prisoner."

"There's no good reason why we can't see him," Bill said. "My daughter wants to see him." Everyone looked to Allison.

Her expression did not change but she held everyone's eyes for an extra heartbeat. "I have to talk to him," she said. When she released them, Margaret's eyes went to Larson's.

"She has to see him," Margaret said. She stared at Larson, willing him to understand. Allison was going to do this herself. It was her last chance to salvage something for her father. Margaret bit her lip—please, let her do this herself.

Larson stood frozen, thinking. He squinted and studied Margaret's face. Finally there was a nearly imperceptible nod. He looked away from Margaret, then took the two strides to Hemmingford. "Get out from behind the desk, Barry. You're in my chair."

Hemmingford stood up but didn't move. He stared at Larson until Bill moved to the sheriff's side. Their shoulders were an inch apart.

"For God's sake," Bill was saying.

Larson moved forward and Hemmingford retreated. "Let them in, John." Larson sat down in the chair and Margaret moved between Hemmingford and Bill.

"You got a couple things to learn," she said to Hemmingford. "Maybe we all do."

Hemmingford raised his hands. "Okay," he said, "it's the lady cop's call. You want these people to see their friend, fine." He gestured toward the door. "Have at it."

He turned away and Margaret nodded.

"Take them in," Larson said.

Margaret allowed herself to relax. She let her eyes travel from face to face. The last face in line was Allison's. She expected Allison to look hard and dark but she was smooth, flawless. She looked directly into Margaret's eyes. She whispered. "Thank you."

"Go on," Margaret said. "Go with your dad."

The room cleared and Margaret and Larson were left staring at Hemmingford's tight smile. Margaret leaned against the back wall as the guard's keys rattled in the lock. Hemmingford patronized them with a smirk. "You two are cute," he said. Lonzo was expressionless.

Margaret fought against the anger rising in her throat but finally couldn't hold it back. She stepped forward and pointed a finger at Hemmingford. "You're an ass," she said. "You came here looking for a way to keep a crummy business deal alive and you never gave a thought to truth, or honesty, or what was right." She was spitting the words. "Well, you're nothing. You've got no idea who really killed Mr. Andy Arnold."

"Jenkins killed Arnold," Hemmingford said. "We've got it in writing."

"There are things you don't know," Margaret said.

Hemmingford laughed. "Why would a man admit to something with such dire consequences, if it wasn't true?"

Margaret hesitated for only a second. "Maybe he thinks he's doing the right thing."

Hemmingford laughed even louder. So loud, in fact, that the laugh mingled with Allison's scream and left them all momentarily confused. But in an instant they were running, through the door, down the hall, and along the row of jail cells. They found Allison backed against a wall with her eyes wide and her hands covering her mouth.

When they followed her stare, they pulled up short. Bill and the guard were trying to get Cooney Jenkins down from where he hung by the neck. His eyes bulged out and his tongue protruded from his slack mouth. A neatly braided horsehair rope was tight around his neck.

Hemmingford remained frozen, but Larson and Lonzo rushed ahead—Larson pulling a penknife from his pocket. Margaret went to Allison and folded her into her arms. She held Allison's head to her shoulder while the men cut Cooney down. They strained to keep him from hitting the floor hard. Hemmingford moved in and was shouting about CPR as they hovered over the body. But it was clearly too late, and after a few moments the excitement drained out of the voices.

The guard was the first to stand up straight and move away. Then Hemmingford stood back. And finally Lonzo and Larson. They left Bill Malone, sitting on the jail floor with his stiff leg out straight and Cooney's body cradled in his arms. He held the distorted face against his chest and rocked gently back and forth. The hard room was silent. Allison trembled in Margaret's arms but turned her head back to find her father. They all watched a moment longer as Bill took a deep breath and closed his eyes. He continued to rock Cooney's body.

The sight of her father on the floor was too much for Allison. She inhaled deeply and Margaret knew she wanted to speak. But Margaret pulled her in tight. She held her hand firm on the back on Allison's neck. "Be still," she whispered. "You can't set it right, be still."

"Shit," Hemmingford hissed. His face was red and the veins in his neck stood out. He was beside himself with rage and moved to within inches of Margaret as she continued to hold Allison. "I suppose you think this is the act of an innocent man?" Margaret's eyes met the fiery little man's. "Now what, miss lady cop? You still think Jenkins was innocent?" He paused, trying to get himself under control. "Don't you think this proves I was right?" He took a breath and bore down on Margaret. "Doesn't this prove I was right?"

Margaret held Allison's head tightly against her shoulder. She glanced around the cell. The guard and Lonzo were watching her. Larson, too. Then Bill looked up from the floor. Their eyes caught and Bill stopped rocking Cooney. At first they looked only pitiful there on the floor, but Margaret took an instant to look more closely and found Bill's chin was up and his eyes were clear, the way she remembered them.

"Isn't that so," Hemmingford was saying. "Doesn't this prove I was right? Doesn't it prove Cooney Jenkins killed Andy Arnold?" Margaret was still watching Bill. Even with the crippled leg and the body of his friend in his lap he looked the same. Margaret's head began to nod.

She had been holding her breath. Now she let her eyes move back to Hemmingford and she exhaled. "Yes," she said. "Pretty well proves you were right all along." She drew Allison that much closer. "You were right all along," she said.

LONZO AND Hemmingford left the courthouse as soon as Cooney's body was loaded into the hearse. Bill had taken Allison home but promised to return as soon as he was sure she was all right. It was nearly midnight when Margaret and Larson came out onto the street. The antique streetlights shown yellow in the heavy night air. Two blocks away the traffic on Main Street was still lively but only an occasional car passed in front of the courthouse. Margaret looked up at the sky, but the streetlights dulled the impact of the stars. There was no moon and there was little to say. They stood leaning against Margaret's car for several minutes.

"You could come back over to my house," Larson said. "We could sit in the Coachman and talk."

Margaret smiled. "Maybe have a cup of coffee?"

Larson smiled back. "Sure, maybe a whole pot."

A car came around the corner and slowed. It was Bill. He pulled up against the curb a hundred feet down the street. Larson smiled. "There's your boy."

"Right."

Larson pushed himself away from the car. "Guess I'll head on home." He started to move away but Margaret stopped him with a hand.

"Thanks," she said.

"Don't know what I did."

"You did the right thing."

Larson nodded. His lips were pursed. He shrugged and grinned. "I'm going fishing," he said. Then he moved down the street.

As he passed Bill, he nodded, but neither man spoke. Bill turned to watch him slide into his car and Margaret came up to Bill's side and took his arm. There was no tension in the muscles. Together they watched Larson's car pull away from the curb.

Bill was nodding. "I know what you did."

"Do you?"

Larson's car had disappeared around the corner and Bill's eyes slid to Margaret. "I wasn't sure until Allison told me. Just a few minutes ago." There was anguish in Bill's eyes. "She was going to tell."

"I know she was," Margaret said. "But there's no need now." Bill started to speak but Margaret reached out and touched his lips. He closed his eyes and she moved her fingers lightly over the creases of his face. She touched the eyelids. "I always wanted to be able to do that." She let her hand fall away.

"I want you to stay," Bill said.

Margaret's arm was wrapped in his and she guided him down the sidewalk to her car. "Thanks. It's nice to hear you say it." She let her arm slip away from Bill's. "But Allison is going to need your undivided attention for awhile. And I'm going to need to be alone. I'm looking forward to being out on the road. Sometimes I can think very clearly when I drive in the dark. Maybe tonight will be one of those nights."

She put both hands up and touched Bill's face again. Her fingertips moved lightly over the cheeks and the jawline. She shook her head. "Nice," she said. Then she reached into her car and took the gyrfalcon hood from the dashboard. She felt the texture of the leather in her hands. She longed to take it home with her, to hide it away where she could go and hold it when she needed the smell of it. "Take it," she said. "It's wasted on me.

Maybe you'll use it someday. Maybe you'll need it." She slid into the car and started the engine.

Bill held the hood in the light from the street lamp and hefted it as if it had weight. "Think I'll ever use something like this again?"

"You might."

"Then you keep it," Bill said. He laid the hood back on the dash of her car. "If I need it, I'll come and get it."

"I don't think I'll be in Denver long."

"I'll find you," Bill said. Then he leaned close and kissed Margaret's forehead. "I'll find you."

Margaret nodded. She took her foot off the brake and touched the accelerator. The car eased from the parking place and onto the street. She drove slowly at first, watching in her rearview mirror. Bill Malone stood in the middle of the street with his hands in his jacket pockets. A streetlight shone down on him and the bill of his cap cast a shadow at an angle across his face. She took her eyes away from the mirror and her gaze fell on the falcon hood. She took an instant to admire it, then she made the turn onto Highway 85.

FOUR HOURS later Margaret was in Torrington, Wyoming. When she gassed up at an all-night station, the eastern horizon was just beginning to lighten. The Colorado line was another two hours. She could be in Denver in time to go to work.

The road south was flat and straight. Sagebrush was beginning to stand out along the ditch in the new light. There were no cars. This was the time Margaret thought she would be able to think about what she had done. It was not in her nature to let the truth go unspoken and she thought it would bother her. But when she tried to think of the words to express the truth, nothing came to mind. She drove and concentrated on the feeling of flying down the road.

The image of morning light sifting diagonally through the pines and grass of Brendan Prairie came to her and she wondered how long it would be before the surveyors came back. She imagined a man dressed in a orange vest, maybe Troy Bass, walking up into the aspen, carrying a surveyor's rod. Bass was a good man but he would go to where she had pulled out the grade stakes and plant the rod and look back at the surveyor. The sun would be hot out there where there was no shade, and the surveyor would sweat and sight down his instrument and wave for Bass to move left or right.

It would be as quiet as the gray prairie that Margaret was streaking through in her car and Bass would feel a chill at his back. The surveyor would direct him with hand signals, deeper into the aspen, deeper. Margaret could feel what Bass would feel as he planted the rod and heard the first swooshing sound. From the corner of his eye he might see a blur. But he'd concentrate on holding the rod still. Because he is a good man, he wouldn't let his eyes follow the bird. Then the surveyor would wave for him to move to the next aspen draw and a second, larger bird would swoop by. This time Bass would spin with the bird and watch it race after the first bird, through the aspen, and disappear at the dark edge of the pines. He would remember only a crisp, silvery sound mixed with the slice of wings.

Driving slower now, Margaret remembered how the forest surrounding Brendan Prairie opened slightly at the edge of the understory. Bass would be drawn into the forest and he would find Bill Malone in that opening, bent on one knee, the other leg straight out to the side. Bill would be concentrating on something in the pine needles, and when Bass looked closely, he would not believe his eyes. Caesar would be tame and docile by then and Bill would be able to reach out and touch the bird as he dipped down for another bite of bloody meat.

Margaret could almost feel Bill stroking Caesar's breast, she could see how gently Caesar would take the tidbits from Bill's fingertips. Bass might think of moving forward to talk to Bill. But he would be unable to move because Allison would be standing in the pine shadows. Margaret shook her head to think of Bass's face when he saw how wild she is, how calm, and strong. The electricity in her gaze would freeze Bass in his tracks.

A car coming from the other direction brought Margaret back. She was fifty miles closer to Denver. Traffic was beginning to pick up. She had to be more careful. The sun was above the horizon now and a trace of heat came through the window glass but warmed only her face. She frowned to think she'd make Denver in time to go to work. Maybe she'd call in sick. Maybe she'd go up in the mountains, find a trail along a creek, and walk until late afternoon. If she got tired, she might soak her feet in the creek and lay back somewhere out of the wind. It would be good to close her eyes and give the sunshine a chance to warm her to the core.